Judy Astley was born in Blackburn, Lancashire and educated at Twickenham County School for girls. After taking a degree in English, she worked at the BBC for a while and then became a dressmaker and designer for Liberty's, followed by several years as a painter and illustrator.

Judy Astley's previous novels, *Just For The Summer*, *Pleasant Vices*, *Seven for a Secret*, *Muddy Waters*, *Every Good Girl* and *The Right Thing*, are also published by Black Swan. She lives in Twickenham and Cornwall with her husband and two daughters.

EXCESS BAGGAGE

Judy Astley

BLACK SWAN

EXCESS BAGGAGE
A BLACK SWAN BOOK : 0 552 99842 7

First publication in Great Britain

PRINTING HISTORY
Black Swan edition published 2000

1 3 5 7 9 10 8 6 4 2

Set in 11-on-13½pt Melior by
County Typesetters, Margate, Kent.

Black Swan Books are published by Transworld Publishers,
61–63 Uxbridge Road, London W5 5SA,
a division of The Random House Group Ltd,
in Australia by Random House Australia (Pty) Ltd,
20 Alfred Street, Milsons Point, NSW 2061, Australia,
in New Zealand by Random House New Zealand Ltd,
18 Poland Road, Glenfield, Auckland 10, New Zealand
and in South Africa by Random House (Pty) Ltd,
Endulini, 5a Jubilee Road, Parktown 2193, South Africa.

Reproduced, printed and bound in Great Britain by
Clays Ltd, St Ives plc.

The island of St George, the Blue Reef Hotel and all characters in this book are fictitious (apart from Sr Pavarotti). But – this comes with love and thanks to staff and fellow guests at the Hawksbill Beach, Antigua, where we spent the night of 20 September 1998 cowering in bathrooms and closets from the devastation of Hurricane Georges.

One

The clock radio woke Lucy Morgan with 'Here Comes the Sun'. It was too blearily early in the morning for her to sing along with the Beatles but she let the lyrics dip into her mind a few times over the next hour, like pebbles skimmed pleasingly over a smooth whispering sea. She was ready for the sun after a long soggy summer in which radio DJs had played 'It might as well rain until September' until the joke wore as thin as the flimsy strappy holiday frocks that disappointed women had shivered in all around the British coast.

Lucy's holdall (hideous puce nylon, part of a three-for-two bargain) was crammed with swimwear and sarongs and loose light clothes for a reliably un-English climate, with no space allowed for the usual cautious cover-up for evenings. You didn't fly three thousand miles (in economy, on a charter) and turn down two lucrative weeks' work (repainting Aline Charter-Todd's kitchen yet again, Ocean Blue being so *last year*) just to have to cater for a chill breeze and the possibility of showers. In her hand were keys, two passports and a Sainsbury's bag full of cat food to leave outside Sandy's basement flat. Sandy was also custodian of her ladders and brushes, which were locked safely away in her garage.

Lucy's daughter Colette was impatient by the door, giggly and overexcited. Just now she looked a lot younger than twelve, much more like a very small child who doesn't yet doubt the existence of Santa Claus and good fairies. Lucy smiled at her, hoping a hint of her own disappointment didn't show in her eyes. Ross wasn't coming with them.

'Passport's expired, sweetie. Sorry, should've checked,' he'd drawled, with not even the pretence of real regret, down the phone the night before. She'd heard him slurp some wine, heard the clink of glass and the unmistakable click-clicking of high heels across his pale new Augusta oak floor in the background as he spoke. The clicking had been Lucy's replacement, presumably, checking out the lie of the land and the route to Ross's bedroom. With luck those spiny heels would have gouged ugly pitted holes in the immaculate wood and ever after remind him that for this he'd dumped a woman whose idea of a perfect shoe was something innocently flat with a harmless soft sole.

'We've got to go! It's nearly seven!' Colette's fingers were clumsy as she hurriedly unfastened the safety chain, then bent to wrestle with the stiff bolt at the bottom. 'I must oil that, when we get back,' Lucy muttered as she picked up her bag and followed Colette out into the shabby communal hallway that no-one felt driven to clean.

'Why? We'll only be here till Christmas. Then we'll be living somewhere new.'

More enviable youthful innocence, Lucy thought as she slammed the main front door behind them and sent Colette down the basement steps with the fortnight's worth of cat food for Sandy to feed to the cat. 'Somewhere new' at the right rent, in the right

8

area, and the right size had yet to turn up and the expiry date of her current lease wasn't negotiable. She'd do serious flat-searching after this holiday. For now, all she had to think about was getting the two of them to Gatwick and praying her rusting resentful heap of a van wouldn't choose this drizzly early morning to spring a leak from its radiator or split a vital hose.

'Why have we got this?' Colette's bag was on the pavement next to the van and she was pointing at the big square of paper stuck to the windscreen. 'Mum, it's been clamped! But we're residents!'

Lucy read the notice. 'Residents without road tax,' she said, her heart thumping as she frantically thought out a potential plan B for getting to Gatwick.

'Sod it, bugger it. We'll have to get the train. Is that bag too heavy for you to carry as far as the station?' Without a word, or even a glance, Colette hauled it over her shoulder and started marching ahead of Lucy, her rigid back and over-fast walk proclaiming 'blame' with every step. Lucy kicked the van's nearside back tyre as she passed and was surprised when it didn't cave in and deflate miserably. She thought hard as she walked. Mortlake to Clapham, trains every what, twenty or thirty minutes? Clapham to Gatwick, every couple of seconds if you believed the adverts. They'd have plenty of time to spare, it was just a pain, that was all. In her head she could hear her older, hyper-organized sister Theresa tutting and muttering 'typical', and she hoped Colette would forget to mention the van and its lack of tax.

Ahead of her, Colette's stroppy pace slowed and she swung the bag awkwardly onto her other shoulder. Lucy caught up and gently pulled it off her. 'We'll take a handle each, it'll be easier for you,' she coaxed.

Colette smiled, her pink face clearly showing a threat of anxious tears.

'We've got hours,' Lucy assured her. 'And just think, two weeks of wonderful Caribbean sun, palm trees and turquoise sea, your cousins and aunts and uncles, Gran and Grandad and no school when you should be at school. The Government wouldn't approve.'

'And no Ross.' There was deep satisfaction in the girl's voice and if Lucy had chosen that moment to look at her closely she'd have seen a face smug with secret worldly wisdom. Colette knew well enough that a man who worked for an airline and spent half his life travelling didn't carelessly let his passport lapse. He was another enemy vanquished, another suitor seen off.

It was very satisfactory having exactly the right car for once. Theresa Bosworth was more used to feeling acutely the lack of a gleaming Mercedes. The Honda Previa was perfectly suitable for the daytime use of a largish family, but she would have liked something less functional for evening events. Swishing up the gravelled Surrey driveways in the huge Previa (which Mark unamusingly referred to as the van, as if it was a clapped-out rotting old heap like Lucy's), out for supper or drinks, reminded her of when she was little and her mother had made her put her old school mac over her pink organdie party dress. That coat had crushed her spirits along with her frills and she'd craved a velvet sapphire-blue cape, tied at the neck with silk tasselled cord, preferably scarlet. Not much had changed about Theresa since then. Just now, though, watching the au pair shepherding the three children into the Previa, while she adjusted the seats to accommodate their mountain of luggage, she felt the rare satisfaction of form corresponding with function.

'Marisa, don't put Sebbie in the middle, just in case,' she reminded her. The dough-skinned Swiss girl gazed back at her blankly. 'You know, *just in case*,' Theresa repeated, hissing out the hint of appalling consequences. Still nothing. '*Quoi?* Say in French maybe?' Marisa pouted, not terribly prettily.

'Jesus. *Malade, mal de voyage*,' Theresa explained. 'But just don't say anyth—'

'Ah! I understand!' Marisa interrupted. She hugged the stocky-four-year-old and cooed at him, ''S'OK, Sebbie, *petit*, you won't get sick, will you? Not today?' Each side of him, his six-year-old sisters giggled and wriggled and made retching noises across him to each other.

'Oh bugger,' Theresa muttered, 'exactly what I didn't want. Just the mention of it and he'll be off.'

She strode back into the house for some just-in-case plastic bags and caught Mark sitting on the stairs reading the *Times* financial pages. He was ready to go, expensively casual in his navy linen jacket and beige chinos, his puppy-soft leather bag showing the outline of a tennis racquet. *He* was ready, that was all that mattered to him: the preparation of the rest of them was simply not his job, for this was a holiday with his wife's entire family; it was their show, at their expense and he had bagged for himself the conveniently unproductive role of being merely along for the ride.

'Sorry, darling, did you want me for something? I was just checking shares.'

'That's yesterday's. I cancelled the papers,' Theresa snapped. He should be more useful. He should be like Daddy back in the Devon days, packing luggage into the car as meticulously as a well-stocked picnic hamper.

11

'You could turn off the gas,' Theresa suggested, still recalling her father's long-ago duties.

'Lord, could I? Do we usually?'

Theresa sighed, a long-drawn-out, hard-done-by sound. 'No I suppose not. The Aga would go out.'

'Right, and then your Mrs Thing would phone all the way to St George and report the disaster.'

Teresa picked up the nearest suitcase and glared at him. 'She's not just *my* Mrs Thing. She cleans *our* house and she's called Gwen.' She'd have swept out with justified haughtiness if the bag hadn't been so heavy.

'Here, let me.' Mark took the case from her, just in time to stop her bursting into overwrought tears. If only he knew, had even the smallest clue, how much organization it took to sort and pack clothes for herself and three small children. And most of theirs were new, because they'd so thoughtlessly grown since their last kitting-out. Summer clothes had had to be tracked down like rare relics at ridiculous expense now the shops were full of winter and back-to-school, and of course they wouldn't fit again by next year so it was all an exorbitant waste. At last sensing tension, he put the case down, leaned across and kissed her cheek and then stroked her hair, his hand encountering the inevitable black velvet Alice band, an item he loathed.

'You're not wearing that hair-thing, are you? To the Caribbean? Awfully hot I'd have thought.' And suburban and matronly and dull. Her fine honey-coloured hair had a permanent dent across it like a rabbit track worn through a wheat field.

'Well, what else can I . . .' Theresa looked at herself in the hall mirror, seeing a tall angular streak of pent-up worry. She ripped the band out of her hair and shook her head hard, fluffing out the layers and taking years off. Now she looked more like her wacky free-spirit sister Lucy and less like her uptight edgy brother Simon.

'That's better. Sexy.' Mark smiled, the sideways sort he always did when he was thinking about bed. Theresa allowed him a small grin in return, left the hairband on the hall table and carried the children's three small rucksacks full of journey-entertainment out to the car. Mark, before he set the burglar alarm and shut the door, dashed through to the kitchen and shoved the hated velvet item in the bin. It could be Mrs Thing's (OK, *Gwen's*) fault.

'Right. Me in front, Ma and Pa and Plum just behind, I think, then Becky and Luke in the far back well out of harm's way.' Simon Morgan, the luggage safely stowed, chuckled and gave the driver a grin that invited amused response but got none. The driver shrugged and opened two of the big Volvo's doors at the same time, then looked at his watch and waited for Simon's children to arrange themselves in the car. Becky and Luke glared and scowled, their eyes hooded in the usual way of teenagers hauled out of bed long before their preferred twelve hours were up.

'Those seats face backwards. I mean when you said it was gonna be a *limo* . . .' Luke grumbled.

'Yeah, backwards like li'le school-run kids,' Becky agreed.

'*Little* – the word's got a "t" in it, Becks.' Simon had promised himself that on this holiday he would limit himself to one telling-off per day about their speech. It wasn't even eight o'clock yet, on day one, and he knew he'd never last.

'Lit-tle. And there's two "ts", actually Dad,' Becky mocked. Simon sighed and just managed to stop himself running his fingers through his hair. Strands of it came out, these days, when he did that. It might be a sign of something, some disease, or just age. Either way, he didn't want to be standing there on the pavement wafting hairs off his hands and everyone seeing.

'Look, you can't expect Gran and Grandad to climb in the back and face the wrong way, now can you? After all, this holiday is their treat for us, they're the ones forking out a fortune.'

'You keep saying that,' Luke pointed out. 'They never say it, it's just you. You keep going on about us being so *lucky* and about how we've got to *behave* and be *good* 'cos they're *paying*. *They* don't go on all the time, and if they didn't like us the way we are they wouldn't have asked us to come, would they? They'd have said, "Everyone's really welcome but not Becky and Luke because we hate them." But they didn't, did they?'

Speech over, and shattered by his own early-morning verbosity, he slumped into the car and settled himself with his feet on his bag. He fastened his seat belt and clamped his headphones to his ears, isolating himself from further contact. Simon sighed again and wondered about his blood pressure. One teenager in, one to go, then the rest of them could get in the car. If the whole fortnight was going to be like this . . .

Simon's wife Penelope looked at the Volvo and wondered, as her son had, what had happened to the pram-like Daimlers so beloved of small-town mayors and senior royalty. She hoped Simon's parents weren't disappointed, seeing as this was the only aspect of the trip they'd allowed her and Simon to pay for. It was always hard to tell what they thought, priding themselves as they did on having the good manners to keep

14

trivial carping and criticism to themselves. It wouldn't surprise her if during these two weeks they tried to teach Luke and Becky a thing or two about that. They'd find it uphill work: all teenagers were self-obsessed and growly – it went with the territory and the rest of the world was just supposed to lump it for the duration. Theresa, who'd forgotten she was ever under thirty, tended to assume teenagehood was something nastily infectious and gathered her children to her like a litter of threatened pups whenever they were in range of *youf*-contamination. Plum took a last loving look at her tall, reassuring Edwardian house, hoped the dog would forgive them for putting it in kennels and that Simon's patients would forgive him for all the last-minute cancellations and not take their orthodontic problems elsewhere. She started jollying her in-laws towards the car. 'In you get, Shirley. And Perry, do you want to go round to the other side?' She took hold of her mother-in-law's arm and steered her across the pavement.

'No need to fuss, Plum. We may be old but we haven't got to the stage of requiring heavy engineering just to get into a vehicle.' Shirley Morgan, full of lady-of-Cheshire independence and enough breakfast to sustain her for a journey far longer than this one, pulled her arm free from Penelope and slid herself along the seat next to Perry. She inhaled the scent of clean leather and felt pleased with life. You had to have done well to be able to afford to take your three grown-up children, their spouses and six grand-children off to a Caribbean island for a fortnight, even if it was September and about the cheapest season you could get. Christmas would have started to be in the shops when they got back, with winter in the air and nights well drawn in. This holiday would set them all up. The driver of the Volvo had a Christmas-tree-shaped air-freshener hanging from his rear-view mirror. Shirley assumed he hadn't bought it recently, that it was left over from the year before. She sniffed discreetly, but couldn't smell pine or cinnamon, just the delicious, expensive leather.

'You all right, Ma? Not getting a cold, are you?' Simon turned round at the sound of the sniff and looked anxious.

'No, Simon, I'm not. Nor, before you ask, do I have any chest pain or tingling in my arms or a cold feeling in my leg or anything else. So please don't worry. We're all going to have a lovely time!'

Penelope laughed. 'He likes worrying, it's his hobby; leave him alone.'

Perry tapped the back of Simon's seat. 'It's all covered by insurance anyway. I took out the Platinum Scheme. For that price they'll fly the bodies back in hand-carved marble coffins on a chartered bloody Concorde. And you'll know where to go for the cars, you could get a good few in this for the funeral.'

Simon could feel his left eye twitching. They might laugh now, but what *was* this sudden, short-notice, no-expense-spared trip all about? He and Theresa and Lucy hadn't been on holiday with their parents since the last Devon visit, and those used to be carefully arranged a good six months in advance, not rushed into at three weeks' irresponsible notice. He must have been in his mid-teens for that last Torquay fortnight, at the age when you just prayed you'd be swallowed into the sand rather than have a bunch of giggling girls on the beach twig that you were with your mum and dad. They'd gone on taking Lucy away long after that of course, seeing as she was ten years younger than him. He vaguely remembered his mother showing holiday

16

photos and saying things like, 'This is the little friend Perry found for Lucy on the beach.' He could imagine his dad accosting small girls of the right age and luring them to the immaculate sand castle he'd have constructed for Lucy. Parents now would be narrow-eyed with suspicion but Perry had simply been buying time off for Shirley with every ice-cream offered to a stranger.

'North Terminal, sir?' The driver interrupted Simon's thoughts.

'Oh, er . . . Gatwick already. Yes, North Terminal, thanks.'

'Oh and look, there's Lucy and Colette by the luggage trolleys.' Plum leaned forward and shoved her arm past Simon, pointing through the windscreen.

'She looks as if she's arguing with someone,' Perry commented.

'No change there, then,' Shirley muttered, watching, as their Volvo pulled up, her younger daughter furiously crashing her bag onto a luggage trolley that was being tugged at by a stout young man in an orange tracksuit. Colette was a few yards away, staring at the sky.

'God, is that Ross? Her new bloke? He doesn't look her type. Or anyone's come to think of it.' Becky sat staring while around her Simon and Penelope unloaded the bags.

'What new bloke? She's not bringing a . . .' Simon craned past the throng of holidaymakers.

'A what? An outsider?' Plum murmured to him. 'If she has, that's her choice and her business. Just because she hasn't had the marital luck you and Theresa have had. Please don't you start picking fights too.'

*   *   *

17

'You only picked on me because I'm female,' Lucy hissed at the man as she wrenched the trolley away from him.

'I only picked on you because you nicked my fucking trolley. I'd bagged that. I've got a family of six over there.'

'Oh, that gives you priority, does it? The nuclear family, the nation's pride and joy. Me, I'm just a lone parent, bottom of the social heap,' she sneered.

'Take it, lady. You deserve it for being a nutter.' He gave way, hands up in surrender, let go of the trolley and walked off.

'We didn't need it, Mum.' Colette was looking embarrassed. 'We've hardly brought any stuff. We could have just carried it.'

'No way. I got there first, it's mine. You have to learn to stand up for yourself when there's no big fix-it super-hero taking care of you.' She giggled suddenly. 'But it's got a wonky wheel.'

'Lucy! Don't rush off, we're all here!' Simon caught up with her and Colette. He looked, she thought, flustered and already exhausted.

'You OK, Si? You look knackered.'

'Tricky journey. Moody kids and I'm sure Mum's coming down with something.'

Lucy leaned on her trolley, conscious that they were obstructing the busy corridor. 'How tricky can a twenty-mile trip in a chauffeured limo be? You should try the Gatwick Express, matey. Clapham Junction is a delight in the rush hour.'

'I thought you were bringing your van.' Simon's brow wrinkled. 'Dad booked you into long-term parking. And paid for it.'

'Change of plan. Not mine, the local clamping mafia. They'll tow it away and scrap it while we're sunning

18

ourselves and I'll never have to see the sodding thing again. The only bit that was any use was the roof rack and that's stashed in Sandy's shed with my ladders.'

'Lucy! Well done, pet, you got here nice and early!' Shirley emerged from the stream of travellers and hugged Lucy.

'Did you think I wouldn't, Ma?' Lucy grinned at her and then reached across to kiss her father.

'Punctuality was never your strong point,' Perry said as they walked towards the check-in desks.

'When I was twelve. But I'm all grown-up now, Dad, I can do VAT returns, tile a bathroom and check tyre pressures all by myself.'

Shirley looked Lucy up and down. 'I suppose that old sweatshirt's all right, for the back of the plane. And what have you done to your hair? It's all short and spiky.' She lowered her voice, 'It makes you look as if you're *fishing from the other pond*.'

Lucy counted to ten and plastered on a smile. 'Well, you won't have to look at me, Ma, lording it up front in club class.'

It was important to be patient. She'd promised herself she wouldn't rise to the slightest crumb of bait, wouldn't revert to the third-child, baby-of-the-family petulance that seemed to overtake her whenever she spent more than a few hours in the company of her parents. As they scanned the departure screens to find out where to check in, she wondered if the same thing happened to other people who'd assumed, wrongly, that by their mid-thirties their relationship with their parents would have stopped being so ludicrously immature. At what point did parents realize it was not their place to worry about whether you'd renewed your TV licence? When did they start pouring you more than a token half-glass of wine when you came

19

for Sunday lunch? Perhaps it was simply because Lucy hadn't actually married anyone and therefore had not been handed over to be someone else's responsibility. Or perhaps it was something to do with being what her mother so coyly used to call the 'little afterthought' of the family, meaning, Lucy only realized as she'd entered her teens, the little mistake, little contraceptive failure, or, as she'd squeamishly recognized as she in her turn discovered sex, the little night of passion that was just too hot for considering consequences.

'It says that desk over there in Area B, but that can't be right because there's the most ghastly queue.' Theresa appeared at Lucy's side. 'We're all there by that pillar, waiting to see where we're really supposed to go.' Lucy looked at where she pointed and saw Theresa's children, swinging energetically from Marisa's hands and looking ready to make trouble. They were bouncing up and down and laughing and making grabs at the doughnuts Becky and Luke and Colette were munching. Mark was observing them rather uncertainly from a little apart, as if wondering whether he was supposed either to join in and play with them and risk being blamed for getting them overwrought, or do nothing and be accused of copping out.

The queue that so distressed Theresa was a long snake of overburdened baggage trolleys and vividly dressed people, many already kitted out in holiday garb with shorts and flip-flops, sleeveless vest-tops and straw sunhats that were too awkward to pack. Fractious, shrieking children were scrambling up and over the mountains of luggage and women in cotton floral dresses and pale bare legs were handing out sweets and crisps in an attempt to keep them still. Theresa looked deeply puzzled, as if the process of the holiday exodus of her fellow humans was one that had

20

passed her by till now. This was, Lucy recalled with a quiet smile, the woman who'd once confessed that the best day in her life was the one when Sainsbury's started doing home deliveries and she no longer had to queue at a check-out with ordinary mortals. She was wearing a knee-length black linen skirt, white shirt and a long cream knitted jacket (Joseph, she was sure), a choice that Lucy suspected had been made with the fervent hope that she might be (surely *would* be?) selected for an upgrade to club class. It certainly wouldn't stand up to nine cramped hours with three small children.

'This is the right place, Theresa. We just have to join the riff-raff, you see. It'll be an experience for you.'

'One I could well do without.' Theresa stood awkwardly, her hands resting warily on her trolley rail, the set of matching leather bags gleaming expensively among the cartloads of sports bags and chainstore suit-cases. 'And so many people are *eating*. Why?' She moved backwards a little, avoiding the sticky hands of a small boy with a bag of lurid-orange crisps.

'They're hungry?' Colette suggested pertly.

'Surely they could wait for some proper food in a proper place. I'd never let mine scoff on the hoof like this. Even Becky and Luke are chewing disgusting doughnuts, full of additives and sugar and God knows what rubbish.'

Colette tugged at Lucy's sleeve, pulling her a couple of steps back. 'Is she going to be all snobby like this all the time?' she whispered.

Lucy grinned at her. 'Yes she is. By the end of the flight she'll have mentioned at least six times that we should all have gone to Tuscany and complained that the airline food isn't organic. We're going to have a wonderful time.'

21

*   *   *

'A cocktail party! That's the last thing I feel like!'
Theresa sat on the edge of the bed, prodding the mat-
tress to check it wasn't too soft. She rather liked the
room, which was large and light and furnished with
bleached wood and blond cane fittings. The bathroom
had no suspicious stains, leaks or creeping wildlife
either, which was more than could be said for the last
holiday they'd taken, where all the creepy-crawlies in
the Dordogne seemed to have homed in on their particular *gîte*.

'It's just the management handing out a welcoming
drink.' Mark propped the invitation up by the television set and opened a couple of cupboards, looking
for the minibar. 'You've got time for a bath.'

'So I should hope. Though I don't know what I'll
wear, everything will be creased.'

'I expect you could have a drink, Becky, but make it
just the one, OK, otherwise your dad will blame me.'
Lucy watched as Becky selected the largest glass of
rum punch from the waiter's tray. With any luck she
wouldn't actually like it and wouldn't sneak several
more when she thought Simon wasn't looking. In fact
Simon *shouldn't* look. If he could try to avoid catching
her out for the whole two weeks, they would all have
more fun and less hassle.

It was sunset, still steamingly hot and the terrace
was crowded with slightly subdued holidaymakers,
many of whom Lucy recognized from hanging around
the airport's baggage carousel. The new arrivals were
easily identifiable by a pallor that made them look ill
and by their air of exhaustion. An exception was a
woman she'd seen alone with a young son, buying
hectically covered paperbacks in the bookshop at

22

Gatwick, who was now dressed in full-scale cocktail rig of chiffon-layered yellow dress and enough gold bracelets to melt down into a doorstop-sized ingot. Talking to the hotel entertainments manager was an arm-in-arm young couple who might well be on their honeymoon. Lucy could see the back of them. The man was fondling the girl's bottom, shoving at it gently like a tentative cook kneading dough. The girl's hand was pushed just inside the top of his trousers, as if she couldn't bear to have fabric between her fingers and his flesh. There were several of these couples: pretty young pairs who looked as if the only sights they intended to gaze on were those in each other's eyes. Lucy thought of Ross and worked out that now, at almost England's midnight, he was probably mid-coitus with her successor. She smiled at the thought: the girl might well be at the stage of gritting her teeth as he got up to full speed, anticipating the supremely irritating (laughable, actually) habit he had of barking like a starving sea lion at the climactical moment. What a prat – whyever had she stayed with him all those months? She went and looked down at the darkening beach from the terrace, conscious that she was being watched by half a dozen of what appeared to be an outing from a computer company's middle management, standing around in a group close to the source of the drink. They looked uncomfortable, fingering the chestfront area of their polo shirts where their ties would normally be.

'Steve,' a voice announced in her ear. She turned. The bravest had peeled off from the others and was standing beside her with his smile ready and his hand out.

'I'm Lucy,' she said, shaking his hand.

He looked nervous. Behind him, still at the bar, she

could see his companions nudging each other, possibly even taking bets. They weren't Lucy's type. Too clean, too neat-haired, too executive. She couldn't imagine she was their type either, too spiky-haired, too skinny, and, in her fringed skirt, too much of a hippy. But this was holiday territory and the pulling rules, she assumed, in the pursuit of uncomplicated leg-over, were probably more flexible.

'You on holiday?' he ventured at last.

'Well yes, isn't everyone here? Or are you here for some kind of conference?'

'Er, well, we're on a corporate sales jolly, reward for ongoing achievement. We're the six who most actively processed Phonetech's mission statement over the last sales period.' So a Caribbean freebie was what you got if you sold a vast number of mobile phones. It was almost worth considering selling her ladders and brushes. He shuffled a bit closer. 'You here on your own?' She smiled past him, indicating Colette running up the steps from the beach. 'Not exactly. There are fourteen of us altogether. And this is my daughter, Colette.' His grin wavered but he persevered. 'And your husband?'

'I don't have one,' she said, adding, in case he got the wrong idea, 'but I keep looking.' That should see him off.

Two

Someone was singing beyond Lucy's window, out on the beach. She rolled over in bed and squinted at the hands of her watch glowing in the dark. Nearly six o'clock. An hour till the hotel started serving breakfast on the semicircular open-sided verandah above the beach. She was starving already and glad she'd done as Simon had suggested and kept the little packet of custard creams that had been handed out on the plane with tea just before they'd started the descent. It was the sort of thing he would think of – small practical solutions to problems no-one else would waste time anticipating. If he was a woman he'd be the sort who sent in handy domestic tips to the staider magazines and won the odd tenner for suggesting a wedge of lemon down the waste disposal kept the sink drain smelling sweet. She'd seen Mark smirking at him from across the aisle, read his mind as he condemned Simon as a fussy old hen. Mark's idea of a useful hint would be something like 'always drive at least fifty miles per hour over the speed limit: that way your attention really can't wander.'

At home it would be midmorning and the populace, apart from students and shift workers, would be starting to think about lunch. Lucy hadn't slept this late since before Colette was born, when she was living with Jack who had thought it intellectually sexy to sit propped up against the fraying cane bedhead smoking spliffs and talking very slow and muddled politics till the early hours. At the point where she'd allow herself to collapse properly into sleep he'd pounce and pull and shove at her flesh as if trying to bring her back from the dead. Sandy had once told her that some men's preferred idea of sex was for women to be completely unconscious so that they wouldn't have to please anyone but themselves, an observation that was certainly true in Jack's case. Still, for someone who was so slow to get revved up in bed, he'd certainly picked up speed the moment she'd told him she was pregnant. She'd never seen anyone pack and run so fast.

The song outside wasn't particularly melodious. It sounded like a leisured and contented soul crooning to himself in a bath, snatches of something half-remembered and only half-consciously voiced. It was still dark. In the other bed Colette was sprawled out under the sheet like a starfish, with one pale tender foot hanging out at the side. Lucy climbed out of bed, pulled back the curtain and unlatched the window. She'd never liked living on the ground floor, being nervous of making life too easy for passing crazed murderers and opportunist burglars, but here it was bliss just to be able to slide the window aside and step out onto a terrace surrounded by fronds of bougainvillea, pink papery flowers tickling against the glass. The sky had a yellow-grey tinge to it as the sun began pushing its way up on the east side of the island, and the air was softly warm and humid. She could hear the sea washing lazily over the sand, and the singing was coming from somewhere in one of the low-growing trees along the beach. Lucy peered in the darkness but couldn't see anyone. Suddenly the song stopped and there was a sharp blast of what sounded like a hunting horn.

'Hey, early-up there!' The singer was calling from the branches of the closest tree. Lucy stepped over the balcony rail and padded across the fat-bladed, spiky grass to where the sand started, wondering if the horn-blower gave any kind of toss that he was probably waking the whole hotel. It was possible he was drunk, winding down after a long rowdy night. In London, Lucy never gave unexpected pre-dawn sounds close investigation; she left that to naive fools or other drunks seeking trouble. Here she felt the invulnerability of an outsider.

'Jet lag, huh?' a cheery voice called down to her. The man was sprawled comfortably in the tree as if it was a snug sofa, reclining backwards on a forked branch. 'Where're you from?'

'London,' Lucy said to the figure. There was a scuffle and a clatter and the singer landed on the sand next to her clutching a giant conch shell, the source, she assumed, of the peace-shattering noise. He was younger than she'd expected, close to her own age. Somehow she'd assumed only the generations way beyond hers liked to sing to themselves – her own tended to hum tunelessly along with their personal stereos. He had streaky short dreadlocks, a mixture of black and fairish, that reminded her of Ruud Gullit in his Chelsea-playing days, and skin the colour of cappuccino, rippling over sinewy well-muscled limbs. His shoulders were as broad as a gangster's jacket. He beamed back at her. His teeth were so perfectly even that Lucy almost wished Simon was there to admire such an example of either nature's generosity or a rival orthodontist's skill. He didn't seem to be drunk, just happy. Perhaps being up a tree, singing, was how he started every day. Perhaps it was a local custom.

'London, huh? My pa was an islander but my mother, Glenda, she's from Chiswick, but not since way back. She sent me back over there to her family for schooling. I didn't stay long, hated the cold, and I learned a lot more back here too.' He chuckled, deep and throaty, and Lucy felt suddenly conscious that all she was wearing was a T-shirt and pink lacy knickers. She shoved her fingers through her hair, forgetting she'd had it cut so short and wispy and could no longer hide in it. The man was inspecting her, looking her up and down with interest. She wrapped her arms across her body.

'You into diving? Scuba?' he asked.

'I haven't tried it. I like snorkelling, I thought I'd do some of that.'

'You come to see me at the dive shop later on the morning, down right along the beach there. I run all the water sports for the hotel,' he said, and then held out a hand. 'And welcome to St George.' He bowed slightly as she shook his hand. 'Come to the shop, ask for me, I'm Henry.'

'Lucy,' she told him. He grinned again and then strolled off, barefoot and whistling, along the sand.

'And you went out and *spoke* to him?' Over breakfast at the big table Theresa was wide-eyed with outraged incredulity. 'But anything could have . . . he might have . . .' She seemed at a loss to select the direst possible fate for Lucy that could result from talking to a dark stranger on a pre-dawn beach.

'He was fine, really friendly.' Lucy shrugged. She picked up a slice of pawpaw and sucked the flesh away from its skin. Juice dripped down her chin and she scooped it away with her fist then licked it. Theresa frowned, cutting up her own fruit (grapefruit, mango and melon) neatly with a knife and fork. Lucy smiled: Theresa looked so exactly as if she was at a dinner party, doing her very best etiquette-eating with scrupulously correct cutlery. She'd been the same the day before on the plane, carefully inspecting the plastic knives and forks and lining them up in size order between the hot foil carton containing the surprisingly tasty turkey and rice in mushroom sauce and the miniature starter of prawn and tomato salad.

'Right. What are we all doing today? Everyone sleep OK?' Simon bustled into the dining area and stood by the table rubbing his hands like a jolly scoutmaster. 'Terrific arrangement this,' he said, approving of the way the hotel had put together a table large enough to accommodate all fourteen of them. Theresa gave him a dubious look. 'I didn't think communal eating was going to be compulsory,' she commented. She glanced across to where Marisa was coaxing bits of banana and croissant into the twins. The girls were pulling the bread into tiny pieces to share with the bold greedy black birds that swooped in from the trees below the balcony. Sebastian was eating Rice Crispies with the kind of pondering expression that Theresa could tell would soon result in the conclusion that the milk wasn't exactly the same as he got at home, after which it would be judged untouchable. A separate table, possibly even a room, for small messy children and their minders would have been a bonus.

'Nice for Mum and Dad though, Tess.'

'Well, I'm sure it would be, Simon, but they're poshing it up having breakfast in that natty little villa along the beach that they've got all to themselves, and besides, half of us don't seem to have actually got up yet.'

'Colette's had hers, she's out on the sand.' Lucy hoped Theresa wasn't going to keep her waspish tone going for the entire fortnight – how hard could it be to enjoy herself in such a beautiful place? Mark's absence from the table might have something to do with it, she thought, wondering which of them had had to get up at three a.m. and entertain the jet-lagged infants.

'Plum's swimming before the pool fills with kids. And Becky and Luke, well, they'll be along when they're hungry. Talking of which . . .' Simon wandered off to help himself to food from the vast buffet area in the centre of the room. Long tables held huge steel dishes of bacon, hash browns, grilled tomatoes and sausages as well as selections of hams and cheeses. Staff were cooking eggs to order and there were trays of grapefruit, pawpaw, pineapple, watermelon, figs, bananas and dried fruits – everything a far bigger and more lush version of the puny, underripe average greengrocery produce back home. He joined a line for fried eggs and wondered if it would be pushing his luck, cholesterol-wise, to have two. He also wondered what Shirley and Perry were having, across at the end of the little bay, tucked away in one of the hotel's five top-of-the-range villas. As his own eggs fizzled and spat in the pan, he imagined his father indulging in a full-scale fry-up, complete with brown sauce and an array of ulcer pills, indigestion potions and any other medication he might keep out of sight of anyone who was still suspicious about the reason for this sudden holiday.

'It's not like Mum and Dad, admit it, Lucy, splashing out on this trip. They've always been pretty careful with their cash,' Simon said as he sat down. Theresa had finished her food and gone and he was glad. She'd say he was imagining things. She'd always said that, as if the possession of imagination was a nasty, undesirable complaint best got rid of as quickly as possible, like acne or a streaming cold. Plum, in a rare moment of cattiness, had once said that explained why Theresa managed to be happy with Mark – only a woman who simply couldn't imagine meeting anyone more interesting would have settled for him.

Lucy considered what Simon was saying. 'But that's why they *can* splash out, isn't it? Because they saved all their lives, always had the money waiting for the insurance man every Friday, ran their own business and sold it for megabucks. You know, Simon, if one of them was ill or something, I'm sure they'd have said something before now. I mean, if it was anything . . .'

'Terminal?' Simon supplied through a mouthful of toast.

'Yes I suppose so, well they'd have known for a while. It wouldn't be this sudden. Dad said it was finally offloading the last of the car dealerships that really brought in the cash and if he didn't spend it it would all end up as tax. He's always been pretty canny, making sure he owned the freeholds of the showrooms' land. All those odd midtown acres in the smart bits of Cheshire must have been worth a bomb by the time he offloaded them.'

'Yes, but even though he's been long retired he's enjoyed keeping his hand in. Why has he suddenly sold the last one now? Ask yourself that.'

'No, Simon, if you really want to know, *you* ask *him*.' Lucy got up, eager to get to the beach, and left Simon alone and thinking.

It sounded simple enough, but suppose he did ask and they told him the worst? Then he'd be anxious and miserable and Theresa would get him on his own and drag it out of him and then accuse him of spoiling things. She used to do that in Devon, just over small incidents. It was a holiday speciality of hers, when she wasn't at home with her friends or her schoolwork to keep her occupied and out of his way. She'd catch him trying to hide a sulk and then nag at him quietly and with a great big persuasive show of sympathy till he told her what was wrong. It would always be something that didn't matter (he could see that, now he was grown-up and rational) like wishing he'd chosen a strawberry ice cream like hers when he was halfway through a vanilla one. She'd ask him why he was being slow, ask him if there was something wrong with it and when, trusting her, he'd tell her the flavour was over-sweet and sickly, she'd turn on him and flare up about being ungrateful and tell Mum not to waste money on treats for *him* because he didn't appreciate them, he was spoilt and he *spoilt things*. He wouldn't ask either parent about being ill. He'd wait, but he'd watch – someone had to.

Becky stretched out on a sunlounger that she'd dragged into the shallow edge of the sea. On her flat bare tummy rested her breakfast – three croissants, a thick slab of pineapple and a banana. Further along the beach, beneath a palm-thatched sunshade, she could see a German couple setting up camp for a serious day's sun-worship. The woman (far too old and saggy to be topless, in Becky's opinion) unfolded a Union flag beach towel and laid it carefully on her sunbed and the man (far better condition, clearly the father of a tennis star) unfurled a gigantic Stars and Stripes. Becky could hardly wait to point out this pair to her dad: Simon so boringly believed in every possible stereotype when it came to Abroad, but here was clear evidence of a German sense of humour. They could play a version of I-Spy, looking for a Swede who was not tall, sexy and blond, an Italian woman who did not pamper her grown-up son and a family of quiet, modest Americans. Most of the hotel guests that she'd had a look at so far hadn't been of much interest – it was probably the wrong season for the marauding groups of sex-seeking younger people that she'd been hoping for. Everyone under thirty seemed to be in pairs, joined in unsplittable lovey-dovey coupledom that could only mean honeymoon or beachfront wedding very soon. There were some families, women who looked like Theresa, stylish but harassed, with piercing telling-off voices for use on their hyperactive pre-school children, and husbands who looked as if they were desperate to disappear and play golf. Lucy, over breakfast, had already christened these women the Putney Mothers.

Becky picked up the pineapple and bit it hard, letting the juice drip down her chin and into the shallow channel between her breasts. She thought she probably looked pretty sexy (though who for?) lying there in her scarlet bikini, covered in juice, stretched out with her fine taut teenage skin just crying out to be stroked. She lacked, she felt (apart from many adoring god-like males), only a silver navel stud, or a tattoo of a leaping dolphin, anything to make her dad go ape. Her mum wouldn't – it was a waste of time trying. She'd just smile in her isn't-life-wonderful way and say something like 'Oh that's so pretty, darling' and give her a big hug just like she had when she'd accidentally dyed her hair blue. Her body still had some colour from the trip to Majorca with ex-best friend Sybilla's family back in early August, and her long hair was no longer streaked with blue but with sun-blonding and a touch of help from L'Oreal. 'Because I'm *worrth* it,' Becky purred to herself through a mouthful of fruit.

'You're talking to yourself. If Theresa hears you she'll tell Dad you're nuts and he'll believe her because she's his big scary sister.' Luke came and plonked himself down beside her, sitting cross-legged in the sea. Small waves swooshed up and down his body and he swayed with them.

'She should mellow out. Do her good. She's got Marisa to take care of the brood and Mark to take care of the money so why can't she just let herself have a good time? She's got a face on her like she thinks she's about to be arrested.'

Luke shrugged and then lay down in the water, letting it wash over his face. He hadn't taken off his T-shirt and baggy blue surf shorts. Either he couldn't be bothered, or he'd gone funny about his body. He was fourteen; Becky hoped for his sake this wasn't the week he turned into the type of agonized boy she saw at school who walked round practically folded in half in the effort to disappear.

'She's probably still in shock from nine hours at the back end of a charter flight,' Becky went on. 'She's such a snob: I heard her telling Gran she thought the passengers were just the sort to clap when the plane landed.'

'More likely what's bugging her is a lack of sex,' was Luke's suggestion. He sat up and pushed his soaking hair back out of his eyes.

Becky laughed. 'Yeah, well you would say that, you're at that age. All wet dreams and wanking. Hey!' She screamed as Luke tipped the lounger over and she fell into the sea. She rolled over in the warm surf and shrieked, 'Sod you, I've lost my banana!'

Up on the pool terrace, Theresa was instructing Marisa on the proper way to anoint the children with factor 50 suntan lotion. She looked down at the beach and frowned. 'That's your two making that racket, Plum. Are they always this loud? I mean, this isn't Ibiza.'

Penelope, comfortable on a lounger with a pleasingly complex Ruth Rendell, smiled lazily. 'That's the sound of teenagers being happy. It's a rare noise, one to be savoured and ignored.'

'If you say so.' Theresa sniffed, rubbing the lotion hard into Amy's tender shoulders. 'Mumm*ee*!' the child wailed, protesting.

'Hush!' Theresa was sharp with her, pulling at her wrist to keep her still.

'Shall I do Ella for you?' Penelope offered, putting her book down.

'No she's done, it's OK. Marisa, the armbands are in the purple bag. No, that's the blue one, the *purple* one, over *there*.' Amy slithered out of her grasp and skipped away towards the pool steps where her twin, oiled and sun-hatted, sat kicking her non-slip Barbie-pink jelly shoes in the water. '*Hat*, Amy!' Theresa called after her. 'You must wear it *all the time!*' Penelope didn't know who to be more sorry for, the nagged children or their frantically cautious mother. She remembered what it was like, constantly keeping watch on small children. You couldn't relax, or at least back when Luke and Becky were little she couldn't, because she hadn't had anyone like Marisa to help. Surely the whole point of bringing the girl all this way was so that Theresa could put her feet up, close her eyes and trust that her offspring would be alive, present, well-fed and healthy when she opened them again. Around the children's paddling area, Plum could see that other parents were managing to combine relaxation with guard duty, rather in the way of birds that slept with an eye open.

None of them looked quite as fraught as poor Theresa.

'Where's Mark?' Penelope asked as Marisa finally hauled herself to her feet and ambled across to a seat in the sun from where she could keep an eye on her charges.

'Oh, he's gone for a lie-down on our balcony. He didn't get much sleep.'

'Children keep waking up?'

Theresa looked away and started sorting and folding the heap of clothes the children had flung off. 'No, not really. Seb was whacked out from the flight and the girls are in with Marisa so she's dealing with them. No, he's, well, he gets up in the night a lot, to pee.' She looked behind her swiftly, checking Mark wasn't creeping up to hear himself being discussed.

'Prostate, do you think?' Plum suggested.

'Doubt it. I'm pretty sure you have to be a lot older for that. He thought he might have a bit of cystitis so he got his golf friend Richie to prescribe some antibiotics. He said he didn't think there was any point queuing up at the surgery, just for that.'

Penelope pulled a corner of her pink sarong across a scorching bit of ankle. It wasn't even nine in the morning and already the sun was burning hot. Her skin would wither and flake before it got going with a tan. 'I didn't think men got cystitis,' she said.

'Well, of course they do!' Theresa gave her a scornful look. 'It's just they don't go on about it on the radio and in the *Guardian* all the time or go round setting up support groups the way women do.' She was frowning again, and Plum could tell she now regretted mentioning it. People always told her things, though, because she looked comfortable and solid and settled. A sitting Plum looked so Buddha-like and fixed that it seemed unlikely she would ever move from her chosen resting

36

spot. She made people feel secure, that they could take their time because she wasn't about to rush and bustle off to do something else. Skinny wiry people might run around being gossip-spreading traitors; round, sedentary people wouldn't waste the energy. She sighed and reached over to the table for her old blue linen hat, one she'd worn on every holiday for the past ten years. Even her hair was calm – cut in a neat safe bob, the dull brown colour of drearily wholesome lentils. When the hat came off again her hair would fall straight back into place as if it had never been disturbed. Plum suspected that part of looking restful was to do with being big and getting bigger. Six weeks regular weighing-in at Shape Sorters, with a diet that should have bored her taste buds into defeat, had given her only a confused and panicky metabolism which had her body clinging to every calorie consumed and packing it defensively away into flab to thwart the direst famine. Simon called her Plum – always had, in fact only her students now called her Penelope. But once, just once a few months ago, he'd squeezed her bum and called her Plump and been surprised she hadn't found it amusing. Well, who would? Why didn't he *think*?

'And of course he can't drink, which doesn't help,' Theresa went on.

'What? Oh, Mark. No alcohol? Why not?'

'Antibiotics. I told you.' Theresa was snappy now, impatiently cramming T-shirts and suntan-lotion bottles back into the children's bags.

Penelope picked up her book again, tactfully leaving Theresa to seethe silently to herself about her indiscretion. Down on the shore she could see Becky paddling with Colette, pointing out something in the water. On an English beach any number of horrors – syringes, sewage, sanitary towels – might wash their

37

way into the beach-surf for the curious to inspect. How completely wonderful it was that it would be fish they were looking at, stunning, multicoloured, exotic, pretty little fish.

'You'd think they'd be out and about by now.' Simon checked his watch as he and Lucy walked along the path above the beach. He looked anxious and was moving too fast, as if he was late for something. Lucy, who wanted to stroll and savour and smile at the blissful warmth of the day, had left her own watch in the drawer by her bed with her passport and ticket, and didn't intend to get it out again till she packed to go back to Gatwick.

'Chill, Simon. The day's only just started. Perhaps older people don't feel the jet-lag thing like we do. I can't imagine Mum and Dad pacing about at 4 a.m. and flicking through crappy TV channels till daylight the way kids do – or pigging out on all the Snickers bars from the minibar. They probably got their reading glasses out, read a couple of chapters and then went back to sleep like sensible souls.'

The beach ended in a raised headland which held five detached villas, each with its own fenced garden and a broad hibiscus-fronded terrace overlooking the sea. According to the brochure, beyond the headland and past a dense thicket of trees was a beach for nudists with a bar and barbecue.

'Smart up this end, isn't it?' Lucy commented.

'Very smart. And big – they could have parties up here,' Simon remarked as he opened the gate.

The door to the villa was open and Perry could be seen across the sitting room, out in the sun on the wall above the sea, drinking coffee. Lucy, who had been trying not to give Simon's anxieties any serious thinking-room, was relieved to see him looking so relaxed, summer-familiar in khaki shorts and a short-sleeved green checked shirt.

'Hi, Dad! We've come visiting!'

'Where's Mum?' Simon hissed at her. 'Perhaps she's not feeling—' Lucy nudged him hard to shut him up. Shirley's head could just be seen over the back of a sunlounger. She peered round as they walked across the cool tiled floor.

'Hello, you two! What do you think of our palace? Two bedrooms, two bathrooms *and* a kitchen! Far too big for just the pair of us but your dad insisted on treating us to the best. Have a look round. Our first house in Wythenshaw was only half the size of this.' Simon went outside and sat with his parents on the terrace but Lucy padded around the villa, admiring. There was the same pale golden cane-woven furniture as in the regular hotel rooms, and the curtain fabric was the same large patterned flowers the bold shades of a bowl of mixed citrus fruits. But here the ceilings were high and vaulted, lined with bleached wood slats, and instead of rather industrial air conditioning there were elegant brass ceiling fans whirring gently. It was a mock-colonial heaven. Lucy peeped into one of the bedrooms and saw mosquito nets draped from the ceiling round a four-poster bed. The bathroom was marble-lined and equipped with towels twice the size of those in the hotel's main rooms. Her parents were certainly getting a treat and a half.

'It's lovely,' she said, coming out to the terrace.

'You know, it's plenty big enough for you and Colette as well if you'd rather join us in here,' Perry suggested.

'Oh, well actually . . .'

'I expect she'd rather be over there in the main block with the others. And I'm sure Colette wouldn't want to be away from her cousins.' Shirley was giving her husband what Lucy and Simon used to call The Look. Lucy grinned, grateful for once that her mother had accidentally got it right. She'd always found it hard to say no to her father. He'd always looked so anxious offering her anything, even small things like extra potatoes at supper or a lift to school, as if by refusing she was turning down the offer of his soul.

'Mum's right,' she told him, 'the others would be none too pleased if I came and played Queen Bee up here with you two.' She gave Simon her own version of The Look before he could argue, and went to the edge of the terrace to survey the beach. A tall rangy man was hauling out yellow canoes from a wooden shack and arranging them on the sand below them, and further along by the water's edge she could see a couple climbing aboard a jet ski. 'That must be the dive shop the man I met was telling me about. I think I'll go and check it out, see how much snorkelling equipment is to hire. I could teach Colette.'

'Anything you want, Lucy love, just charge it to the bill,' Perry said quietly. She kissed his cheek. It felt dry, like warm cardboard, and she wondered for a second or two if Simon might be right to worry. And the attitude to money was new too: they'd been generous parents, but keen on value for money and being careful not to splash it around. Now they talked about not being able to take it with you. Only the year before, Perry had joked about being way past the threescore years and ten. 'Well into extra time now,' he'd said. They'd all laughed but Lucy had looked around for wood to touch.

Lucy ran down the steps to the shore and found Mark at the water-sports shop, pale, tired-looking and unmistakably English in beige linen shorts with a rigidly ironed crease down the front. She imagined Theresa back home in her cream and old-rose bedroom, packing as if she'd learned it, like her table manners, from a manual – tissue paper between each fold. Mark was inspecting a price list pinned to a wall of the ramshackle shop which was decorated with a flaking sea scene – badly in need of repainting – of vivid, cartoon-like pink and brown divers splashing in a turquoise fish-filled sea wearing scarlet flippers and outsize snorkels.

'Hey, it's the early one!' Henry greeted Lucy from a hammock under another low tree in front of the dive shop, shaded from the strengthening sun by lines of ropes from which hung souvenir sarongs and T-shirts for sale. Lucy wondered if there was any of his time that he didn't spend horizontal. He slid to the ground and stood with his hands on his hips, inspecting Mark. 'This your husband?' He put on an expression of brazen mock-disappointment. Lucy laughed. 'No, this is my sister's husband. Mark, this is Henry.' Solemnly Henry and Mark shook hands like a pair of new business associates.

'Come in the dive shop, let me do my job and talk you into parting with money. You got your PADI?' Henry asked Mark. Henry, Lucy noticed, had his hand on Mark's shoulder, guiding him into the cool shady shop like a spider trapping a big juicy fly. She followed, grinning at Mark who was looking at her with one inquisitive eyebrow raised.

'No, I've never done any diving, though I've often fancied the idea. Can I do it here?'

'Can he do it here! Bless!' A husky female voice came from the cool and gloomy back of the shop. 'This is the mother, the great Glenda-of-Chiswick,' Henry introduced her. Glenda was a tall woman, built for

41

strength, with long grey hair clinging to the last of blond streaks and with half a dozen brightly beaded braids on the left side, hanging and crashing around her perma-tanned face. She was wearing a purple and pink tie-dyed billowing smock which reminded Lucy of Colette's school production of *Hair*, for which she had persuaded Theresa to rummage in her attic and drag out the perfect hippyish outfit of multicoloured crochet tank top and flower-patched loon pants. She must have been at least sixty, Lucy reckoned, and with skin that seemed to have shown only contempt for moisturizer, but all the lines looked as if they were caused by laughter. Lucy speculated on how long she'd lived on the island: she could have come over at least thirty-five years before, perhaps brought back like a souvenir from England by Henry's father.

'We've got one of the world's most spectacular reefs, just a mile or two round the island,' Glenda said, waving an armful of silver bracelets in the direction of the south shore. 'You do the diving preliminaries in the hotel pool then it's out to sea. It's all supervised, all safe. Henry's a qualified dive master.'

'What do you think? Shall we?' Mark asked Lucy. He was looking eager, thumbing through a rail of wetsuits at the back of the shop. Lucy considered, wondered how much time it would take up. Colette wouldn't mind, she'd spend most of her time with Luke and Becky anyway. She thought of Simon and his worrying, of Theresa and her stress level and then she thought of the peace and calm of the below-sea world.

'OK, let's.'

Three

That young couple who'd been fondling each other at the cocktail party were in the pool. Wherever Simon went he seemed to come across various romantically inclined young pairs strolling, arms entwined, between the Sugar Mill bar, the Coconut spa and the small arcade of gift shops just beyond the hotel entrance. It was supposed to be the rainy season just now, which he assumed hadn't bothered them because they looked pretty pale, as if they'd been spending a lot of potential tanning time in bed. The hotel was big on weddings, going by the photos mounted on the board in the lobby. The favoured spot was clearly the elaborate white wrought-iron gazebo under the tamarind tree between the pool and the beach. Shirley said it reminded her of the bandstand on the seafront at Exmouth, but Perry thought it was more like a big version of the fancy kind of thing that smart gardeners bought to grow their runner beans up.

The pair in the pool had been larking about, splashing and diving and ducking each other and making the kind of shrieky squealy noises Simon usually heard from Becky when she'd got her mates round and they were holed up in her bedroom mucking around with make-up and gossip. It was hard to concentrate on his book, with piercing yells and splashes from those two punctuating every paragraph. Worse, when they went suddenly quiet and he happened to look up to check if they had gone, he saw them locked into a passionate clinch, snogging like kids at a late-night bus stop. The girl had opened an eye and caught him staring, which made him shift uncomfortably and feel an embarrassed extra warmth that was nothing to do with the hot sun. The only other pool occupant was a small boy floating on a lilo, and with the water barely churned up, Simon could see the girl's thighs wide apart, clenched tight around her husband's/boyfriend's body. It gave Simon a jolt of unwelcome sexual stimulation, like casually glancing at a magazine over someone's shoulder on the tube and finding himself reading scalding porn.

'Couldn't they go and do that in their room?' Simon muttered to Plum. She looked up from the Ruth Rendell and smiled. 'Oh, they're just happy and young. Don't you remember what it was like?' she teased. He didn't, or at least not like that, not in public. He remembered early sex with Plum (and an inadmissibly small assortment of girls before her) as a deeply furtive, back-of-the-car activity. There'd been her father's tool-shed (appropriate, he'd sniggered to himself at the time) one Christmas Eve, when he'd nearly knocked himself out standing on a rake and had a black eye till well into the new year. And there'd been the boat on the Norfolk Broads, holidaying with Plum's hearty out-door cousins who were so scrubbed-clean wholesome that Simon had been sure they thought babies were made by means of some strange practical handicraft as per instructions in a scout manual.

It had been almost disappointing to get married and realize that sex was not only permitted but compul-sory, and in a safe dull duveted bed. He'd much preferred the days when Plum's suggestion that they go for a walk in the woods would have him peering through the densest undergrowth in search of a good place to fuck. He rather envied the young couple in the pool, oblivious to everything but their own wants, much as he disapproved of their lack of discretion. In fact, really they were just showing off. He snapped his book shut and looked around. The rest of the family, apart from Lucy and Mark and the older children, was now assembled by the pool, sprawled out lazily on loungers, dozing away their lack of proper sleep or reading under the palm-thatched umbrellas. Even Theresa's brood were being quiet, all three placidly sitting in a double swingboat in the children's play area beyond the far side of the paddling pool, waiting with almost unnatural patience for Marisa to abandon her sun-worship and come and push them.

So much communal lethargy made Simon twitchy — he was surprised his mother wasn't geeing them up into more action. On the Devon holidays, sitting around lazing on a beach had been something that they were allowed to do only after the day's quota of sightseeing had been achieved, all those trips to gardens and castles and Paignton Zoo and Krazee Golf. Still, his mother was well past seventy now, surely more than happy not to have the role of family co-ordinator.

He stood up and stretched. 'Right, I'm off to find out about excursions and activities and such. Anyone coming with me?'

No-one replied, though his mother shook her head gently as she reached into her basket for more suntan lotion.

'We can't spend two whole weeks just sitting around here, you know,' he went on. 'Someone has to do the organizing.'

'Hmm. You do that if you want to, Simon,' Plum murmured. He felt cross immediately; she sounded as if she was indulging the whims of a small boy.

'Simon, we don't have to trek round everywhere all together like some big school trip, do we?' Theresa whispered as he strode past her lounger. He stopped and crouched next to her. 'Well, I rather thought that was the point, didn't you? For Ma and Pa to be with us all together. This is supposed to be a proper family holiday. Otherwise we might as well be on different continents.'

'God. I suppose so. But please, just not today, OK? We're all exhausted and it's enough just to sit around and get used to the heat. I'm not sure the brood are up to cultural visits either.' She closed her eyes and fanned her face with her hand, dismissing her troublesome younger brother.

Simon wandered into the blissful cool shade of the hotel lobby. A tall girl with sheeny skin the colour of the best bitter chocolate was watering a massive potted palm tree. He stood in front of the guests' noticeboard, turning a little to watch her. She had incredibly elaborate hair, braided into what looked like hundreds of tiny, shiny plaits and then woven into a pattern that must have taken hours to concoct. She wore the hotel's staff shirt, green with a pattern of white leaves and a slim navy blue pencil skirt that curved out over her high round bottom. White girls didn't have bums like that. Even slender girls who had any curves and substance at all sagged and wobbled lardily. Plum's globular bum, he thought with disloyal honesty, resembled an anaemic crème caramel that a child had prodded all over with a spoon and then abandoned. Even in the chill of the air conditioning, Simon found his hands were sweating and clammy with the effort of

46

not reaching across and taking hold of the girl's flesh. He was shocked at himself, appalled at the scene in his head: himself, drilled hard against her body, his hands roaming round to her breasts, his mouth nuzzling into the intricate hair. He could almost smell her, a mixture of jasmine and pineapple and a tiny thrilling hint of sweat. He never, well hardly ever, had thoughts like this at home. At home he only seemed to have contact with youngish attractive women as mothers-of-patients, discussing their children's overbites and whether the wisdom teeth would have to go. His receptionist only gave him cups of tea and rich tea biscuits, never a hard-on. Heart thumping, and terrified for his soaring blood pressure, he shoved his hands deep in his pockets where they were safe, turned back to the noticeboard and tried to focus on the lists of activities that the various tour operators had put together to tempt the guests out of their idleness.

'Hi, Simon, what are you doing?' Colette stood next to him munching on a rapidly thawing yellow ice lolly.

'I'm finding things for us all to go out and do.' A small traditional part of him baulked at her casual use of his name. Somewhere inside was still the small boy who, like Theresa, but not Lucy later, had to give all grown-ups some kind of courtesy title. Shirley and Perry still had several friends whom Simon had to stop himself prefixing with 'Uncle' or 'Auntie' whenever he met them. Early attempts to get Becky and Luke to do the same had had Plum ridiculing him for being antediluvian: 'What's wrong with their plain and simple names?' she'd asked. 'Showing respect isn't anything to do with silly false prefixes.' It was different for her though, teaching at the sixth-form college. Her pupils called her 'Penelope' whereas at eighteen he'd still been addressing schoolmasters as 'Sir' and secretly thought it wouldn't do Becky and Luke any harm to feel the same kind of mild terror about school that he had.

'So what are we going to do? Shall we go to this plantation and see how rum's made?' Colette ran her finger down the list. 'Or what about going into the rain forest in a Jeep and swimming in the waterfall?'

'Do you fancy that?' Simon asked, making mental notes. They'd need a fleet of Jeeps; he must check on car-hire rates.

'I do. And I want to do snorkelling. Mum and Mark are going to do proper diving though, real scuba diving with air tanks. They're going to do a course. She told me.'

'A course? What, lessons? Here?'

Colette shrugged. 'In the sea I suppose. I mean it's where you'd go, isn't it, for diving?' She gave him the kind of smile that told him she pitied his idiocy and ran off towards the pool. Simon borrowed a pen and some paper from the receptionist and copied out the list of events, wondering if he was wasting his time.

Becky could see Lucy a few hundred yards along the shore, walking back from the water-sports shop. She could see her holding up the edges of her sarong and wafting it to make a breeze as she walked in the shallow waves that broke so gently on the shore. Lucy had a very cool short fluffed-up haircut as well as good legs for an Old Person, Becky conceded, as she calculated how very few minutes she had before Lucy reached her and inevitably stopped to chat.

'Quick! My aunt's coming!' Becky hissed to the stocky boy rolling the fattest joint she'd ever seen in the shade of a low-growing tree. He sold jewellery and wind chimes as well as ganja, carrying a basket with a selection of shell necklaces, shark's-tooth bracelets and strings of tiny beads in the Rasta colours of yellow, red and green. She'd have to pretend to Lucy that she was choosing presents for all her poor friends flogging away in school back home.

'No problem,' he drawled, grinning at her and handing it over. 'Five dollars.'

Becky fumbled in her string bag for her purse and handed over the note. 'Thanks, that's great.'

'No problem!' the boy said again and sauntered away up the beach to offer his wares to sunbathers. Becky hid the joint in her make-up bag and prayed her eye shadow wouldn't melt over it and ruin it. Five Eastern Caribbean dollars wasn't a vast amount, but she didn't know yet how many of these five-dollars'-worth she could get through in a fortnight. Lots, she hoped, especially if she found someone to share them with, some gorgeous boy who would look impressive in the photos she'd be showing off at school. She'd have to make some serious effort to find one fast, otherwise the gruesomely embarrassing high point of her seventeenth birthday, less than two weeks from now, would be blowing out the candles on some hotel cake while her family sang 'happy birthday' and all the other guests watched and clapped as if she was only six. She pictured herself on the deserted night-time beach, nestled into the soft sand under a sky with an impossible number of too-close stars, curled up with an unknown someone, smoking, kissing, stroking, touching . . .

Lucy, thigh-deep in the warm shallows, watched as a cruise ship, about the size of an entire housing-estate's-worth of high-rise blocks, offloaded its passengers onto

49

a flotilla of smart little launches to take them into the island's capital for a day's sightseeing and shopping. The scuttling boats reminded her of the kind of wildlife programme where fat creamy larvae slither away from a bloated mother insect, the queen of the nest. The town, which looked dwarfed by the vast liner, was called Teignmouth, a fact which her mother admitted had influenced her choice of island when planning the holiday. Monserrat had Plymouth, Tobago had Scarborough and one of the Caicos islands had Whitby, but these had never been among childhood holiday destinations. Back then it had been Torquay or Dawlish, places accessible by train ('Your dad deals in cars for fifty weeks a year. He doesn't want to take one on holiday as well – we'll hire when we get there') and with just enough going on to keep children and adults entertained. Although they'd lived, then, just south of Manchester, their holidays had never been taken in the more usual northern resorts. It had seemed something of a matter of status to Shirley to make the long journey south, to have further-reaching holiday ambitions than her neighbours. (To venture overseas, other than to the Isle of Man, would have been ostentatious.) In the end the ambitions had backfired as one by one each of her children had gravitated towards London and its outskirts. Lucy didn't know, didn't risk asking, if pride in their independence, in being able to say, as Shirley could of Theresa, 'My daughter that's married to a banker, *lovely* house in Oxshott,' had been enough to compensate for being two hundred miles from her grandchildren rather than the round-the-corner, popping-in distance that her less adventurous neighbours and friends had.

As she walked on Lucy thought about the rented holiday flats they'd stayed in where the decor of each of them merged in her memory into a mess of dull sage green and old-mac beige. Those colours now starred on all the smartest paint charts, with names like 'Norfolk Herring' and 'Sphagnum'. Her heart sank, remembering those apartments that smelled of a thousand fry-ups, every time a client sought colour guidance and brought up the term 'historical shades'. Why didn't they travel to places like this, or even just look at photos, and choose clear bright tints that thrilled the heart like this ludicrously vivid sea, the colour of a bleached peacock? No wonder the British middle classes suffered from SAD, she thought, considering the dismal gloomy shades they thought it so tasteful to live with. Perhaps if they painted their surroundings with the translucent colours of life, rather than of the worst-weather skies, their winters would be a lot less miserable.

'Coming to get some lunch?' The slim shadow of Lucy fell between Becky and the sun. 'I know it's a bit early, but I feel like I've been up for days and now I'm starving.'

Becky thought for a second or two about the effort of moving off her lounger again. If Mark had been asking, or her mother, or Theresa, she'd probably have said no. But this was Lucy, the one she liked, the one who she instinctively felt knew what it was like to be always in the wrong inside the tender cage that's called a family. She scrambled to her feet and wrapped a tiny scarlet skirt round her hips. 'Yeah, I'll come with you. Where are we going?'

'There's a bar by the pool. They do lunch-type food like burgers and sandwiches and salads and stuff.'

'Oh good. Chips.' Becky giggled.

'Definitely chips. I can smell them from here. Just like home.'

Becky looked out at the sea. 'No, thank God, not a bit like home.'

Mark, walking under the trees, could see them all lying like pale pink sausages, grilling on loungers by the pool. Theresa was talking to someone, a straw-blonde deep-tanned woman with a gold swimsuit and a wrist-ful of bracelets that glinted in the light. She was lighting a cigarette, offering one to Theresa who shook her head. Shirley was fussing with Sebastian, pulling his blue gingham hat down firmly over his ears. Sebastian was fighting back, wrenching the hated thing off his head the moment his grandmother let him go.

Mark watched as Theresa stood up, stretched lazily and adjusted the bottom of her swimsuit. It was a sexy, artless little gesture. He'd have liked his fingers to be the ones brushing gently just inside the fabric, but there was a horrible problem getting in the way of sex. His penis was sore, aching with a flinty, constant pain. He couldn't even dull it with a drink, for the clinic nurse had been pretty emphatic that these particular antibiotics just didn't go with alcohol – the combi-nation would mean instant vomiting. He remembered her face as she told him, handing out this small piece of gleeful punishment. She'd had that careful look, the professionally indifferent, seen-it-all-before one that everyone in clap clinics (or 'sexual health' centres, as they were now called) had. Somehow, in the over-deft way she'd wielded the needle when she took a blood sample from his arm, there was a judgement, and a small not-quite-suppressed sigh that told him she was having to do this far too many times to too many men for her liking. She'd spent a long time washing her hands, vigorously sluicing away every trace of his tart-borne infection. Nice men don't pay for sex. Mark knew that. He was no longer a nice man. On five furtive and deliciously seedy occasions now he hadn't been a nice man at all and was about three hundred pounds and a nasty, persistent dose of NSU down on the deal. The nurse needn't have bothered; Mark's own remorse was punishment enough.

'Hey, Mark! Come and choose something for lunch!' Shirley was waving a menu at him, smiling. Mark grinned back and started walking towards the group which was now taking over several shaded tables close to the bar. Shirley's smile showed nothing but certainty that he was still the supremely Nice Man that her daughter had married. Once, years ago when he'd helped her choose the right savings account and explained some complicated banking pros and cons, she'd confided that he was just what she'd always wanted for Theresa, as if he was something she'd started trawling every shop in the land for since the moment Theresa was born: a safe, reliable, secure item that had been at the top of the christening wish-list. 'There's no silliness about you,' she'd said, but hadn't elaborated, leaving him to work out for himself what 'silliness' was. He'd decided it must be to do with deviousness, with what you see being what you get, a concept which Shirley's sensible Northern origins very much approved of. Now, as he took his place at the sun-bleached wooden table next to Theresa, he was pretty sure Shirley had also been approving his lack of adventurous spirit, a lack of imagination which would keep him faithful to Theresa and give none of them any trouble. He felt almost more guilty towards his trusting mother-in-law than towards his wife.

'Right, everybody here? Ready to order?' Simon was ready with a pen and notebook, bustling like a waiter.

'What all of us, all at once?' Lucy looked across to

53

the circular bar area where one lone barman was concocting fruit punches, taking food orders and directing waiters all at the same time. He seemed to be the only person moving fast.

'Of course all of us. The hotel accommodates over two hundred people, they should be able to cope with a lunch order for fourteen,' Simon told her.

'Now Simon,' Shirley warned, 'we don't want unpleasantness.'

'Sorry Ma. OK, now food . . .' Simon wrote down the order, meticulously checking and rechecking what everyone wanted until Becky started banging her foot backwards and forwards against the chair leg with impatience. He then handed the list over to the waiter who smiled with gleaming politeness before rewriting the whole thing on his own pad using his own code. Theresa smirked and Simon scowled and Luke's abrupt giggle got him a glare from Perry. Shirley seemed oblivious, looking around her, absorbing the views from all directions. Lucy watched her, saw her gaze taking in the pink and white cake-like buildings, the banana trees with voluptuous purple flowers and bulging clumps of fruit, the massive hibiscus plants that made the puny specimens from British garden centres look like tragic underfed bits of twig.

It was the hotel's clientele that looked vaguely out of place amongst all the leafy lushness. Most of the guests were British or German, pale and lazy and slightly self-conscious in lurid swimwear. They moved around slowly as if the heat was a burden, glistening with protective lotions and potions and being sure to remind their children constantly to keep their hats on. The Phonetech men, whom Lucy collectively christened the Steves, all kept their chunky steel watches on and wore reflective aviator sunglasses, behind which, she suspected, they were eyeing anything in a bikini. She watched a portly man who must have been in his late sixties, buttoning himself into a shirt that he would probably never wear again once the holiday was over, a pattern of turquoise and lemon zigzags that must have come straight from the cruisewear department of a large city store. She imagined him shopping reluctantly with his wife, being dragged round a vast out-of-town mall where his head would grow light in the dried-out air conditioning and his lost sense of direction would make him panic that he would never find the car park again.

'We aren't very good at hot weather, are we?' Lucy commented to Plum as she watched the man making himself respectable enough to join the tables for food. 'The sun-starved Brits have to have a special separate wardrobe for being hot, and it sits on most of them about as naturally as a posh wedding outfit.'

Plum followed her gaze across the pool. The turquoise man's wife had a lilac cardigan dangling from the back of her lounger, as if she didn't quite trust the sun to hang around reliably. 'Only with older people, surely. Like the kind of men who wear long socks with shorts. The younger ones look all right.'

Lucy didn't comment. Plum presumably counted Simon among the 'younger' men. Simon had been of the student generation that had worn ball-gripping loon trousers and skin-tight T-shirts and now still habitually bought clothes that looked as if they were for someone at least a size smaller. Lucy's contemporaries, on the other hand, had absorbed enough of the punk era to feel at their most comfortable in anything that her mother would think was only suitable to be put in the duster box.

Lucy leaned her head back and pointed her face

straight to the sun. 'Put this on if you must blast your skin,' Theresa said to her, passing over a tube of the children's suntan lotion.

'Give me ten minutes, Tess,' Lucy said, closing her eyes.

'You'll fry.' It was like a curse. Lucy sat up straight and glared at her.

'And if I do, who's to care?'

'You will when your nose is purple and peeling and your eyes are swollen shut.'

'My risk.' But the moment was spoiled and she pulled a bottle of lotion from her bag and smeared it on her face, catching sight as she did of Theresa's little smile. It was just like when Theresa had caught her behind the rhododendron down by the shed in their parents' garden all those years ago. She'd been twelve, smoking her first cigarette with the boy from the classic Cheshire half-timbered house on the corner, the boy Shirley had always encouraged her to play with when she was little because he'd been sent off to boarding school at nine and might be lonely in the holidays. Theresa had crept up, known almost before they did what they were up to and had pounced before Lucy had even managed to inhale the sweet rancid smoke.

'You'll get cancer,' Theresa had hissed into her face. 'If you smoke you'll die.'

'It's one Silk Cut, not a whole habit,' sophisticated Michael up-the-road had sneered.

'If you start now you'll never stop.' It had felt like a challenge at the time. Lucy remembered looking very carefully at Theresa's face, trying to work out whether it was real concern for her young sister that made her so angry or whether she just wanted to pick a fight and put Lucy in the wrong, spoiling her fun. Theresa had been twenty-two at the time, well into grown-uphood by Lucy's reckoning, and her anger had puzzled her. Perversely, it had also put Lucy off cigarettes. She was determined, till Theresa left home a year or so later, that she wouldn't give her the satisfaction of sniffing the air around Lucy and scenting out the hint of smoke, nor would she ever be caught with her finger-ends stained ochrous with tobacco.

'OK, who was the fruit punch and who was the pina colada?' Simon took a tray of drinks from the waiter and started handing them round at random so that the drinks ended up being passed back and forth across the table.

'Mine's the Diet Coke.' Plum reached across and claimed her glass.

'And mine looks like a pina colada but it's without rum,' Theresa said. 'I don't know how people can drink alcohol in this heat.'

'Oh I can.' Shirley chuckled, taking a large gulp of rum punch. 'A lot of what you fancy, that's what holidays should be about. Especially this one. We need to celebrate being all together – such a treat. With you all down south and us stuck back in the frozen north, we only ever get to see you all together at Christmas. There's not even a good family wedding on the cards.' She took another sip and a breath then went on, 'Talking of which, Lucy, what happened to that young man you were seeing, the one you said might have come here with you. What was his name, Joss?'

'Ross.' Lucy felt cornered. They'd all stopped, mid-munch, to listen. Even Sebastian's small round mouth hung open, waiting, showing an unattractive mush of hot-dog.

'Nothing happened. I suppose he changed his mind.'

'About coming here or about you?' Shirley was

57

smiling, as if they were simply having a jolly general conversation about nothing that could possibly be considered remotely personal.

Lucy shrugged. She was too old to have to give love-life explanations to her mother but trying to be private made her sulky. 'I don't know. Does it matter? He isn't here and I don't particularly mind, I mean if he could pass up the chance to come to a place like this—'

'So you won't be seeing him again? When you get back?' Shirley interrupted.

'Mum, give me a break will you! I'm sure no-one wants to hear about my failed romances!' Lucy forced out as much of a laugh as she could manage.

'And so many of them,' Theresa added.

'Yes, give it a rest Shirley love, you're embarrassing the poor girl.' The pat on the wrist that Perry gave his wife looked quite a firm one.

'Woman.' Lucy cursed herself for not keeping her mouth shut. 'I haven't been a girl for a long time now.'

'Well, I expect that's all Mum's on about,' Simon cut in, using what Lucy recognized as his let's-sort-this-out voice. 'You're old enough not to have to put up with disappointments from men. I expect she'd just like you to meet someone.'

'Oh she has already! Haven't you Lucy?' Theresa's voice was bright and sharp. 'That man you met up a tree in the middle of the night? Why don't you tell Mum all about him?'

'Leave it Theresa.' Mark's voice was like a low warning thunder rumble.

Lucy stood up. 'Whatever I do I can't get it right, can I? I don't get myself neatly married off and that's wrong, but when I do chat to attractive strangers, that's wrong too.' Colette was sitting with her elbows on the table, fingers in her ears, looking at the sky and

58

tunelessly singing an old Spice Girls song. Lucy watched her with sympathy, wishing she could do exactly the same. There was a small, waiting silence then Simon briskly rustled his collection of lists and leaflets.

'So, tomorrow then. I thought we could go out and look round Teignmouth in the morning . . .'

'Er . . . not Lucy and me, we've got our first diving lesson in the pool at ten.'

'With the hunky tree-dweller.' Theresa smirked.

Plum leaned forward and touched her arm, then said very quietly, 'Admit you're just a teensy bit envious, Theresa, I know I am.'

Theresa gave her a queenly smile and lowered her voice to something close to a hiss. 'If you're suggesting there's something missing in your life in that department, Plum, then please take it up with Simon, not with me. I certainly don't envy Lucy.'

Which Plum took to mean quite the opposite.

Four

Lucy lay out flat as close to the bottom of the pool as the air tank strapped to her back allowed, figuring out the workings of her buoyancy control device. She felt like Dustin Hoffman in *The Graduate*, hiding under the water from his family. She looked up at the legs of a small child paddling away like duck feet above her. He was way out of his depth and the automatic parent in her scanned the rest of the pool for a set of larger, stronger limbs that would indicate the presence of a responsible grown-up. The child's feet stopped moving and he let his plump legs dangle, trusting his orange inflated armbands for support. He bobbed comfortably, splashing his small hands up and down, the ripples bending the sunlight above her.

It occurred to Lucy that she could do with some support herself. Support of the financial kind, for sure, as ever, but also of the commiserating kind. Colette was far too young to sit with her in the bar or on the beach and sympathize about life's sundry unfairnesses. That was the huge problem with being a lone parent: you had to be wary, make sure you kept some kind of balance about how much emotional sharing-out you inflicted on your child. You had to see-saw between a foolish rosy-outlooked pretence that everything was fine, really, things always turned out OK, and the truth – that life on your own with a kid was a hard, complicated plate-juggling act where you were the only person whose fault the many difficulties, failures and mistakes could ever be. To inflict on Colette the knife-edge day-to-day burden of simply getting by, the constant money-and-work worries, the men (like bloody Ross) who disappointed, and the ever-present rather shameful mild envy of luckier friends and siblings with what seemed to be wondrously sorted lives, would be a dreadful blight on the poor girl's childhood.

'She's only got you, so you'll always have to be the strong one. You mustn't let her see you cry, not ever,' had been her mother's formidable (and hardly realistic) advice the day after Colette was born. Lucy, hormonally poleaxed and already sore from her baby's greedily chewing attempts at breastfeeding, had promptly burst into tears. Shirley had shaken her head slowly, as if Lucy had already earned herself an eternal D-minus for mothering, and then conceded, 'Well I'm sure Plum will always help you out, if you're stuck for advice.' Just as Lucy had been figuring out the implication that her mother *wouldn't* be available for helping out, Shirley had added, 'And there's always me, as a last resort, though when you've ever taken any guidance from me I can't recall. If you had . . .' and she'd sighed, stroking Colette's baby fingers. Lucy, still sniffling into a tissue, had finished the sentence for her: 'If I had, I wouldn't be here now, all alone with a baby.'

'That's not what I meant at all.' Shirley had smiled. 'I know at the time I said you were too young and silly to go producing babies you didn't need to have, but . . .' and she'd paused to swallow and collect her words, 'maybe I was wrong. Prove me wrong, Lucy, I know you can, even if it's only to be bloody awkward.'

As Lucy lay in the water, relaxed, floating, wondering if she was doing the right thing with the BCD, the vision of her clamped van sneaked into her mind. She tried to stop the inevitable express train of thought: by the time she got back the van would have been towed away and scrapped, crushed and pounded to a foot-square parcel of junked metal. The local council was hot on that sort of thing, trying to pass the area off as being a newly desirable one, with hiked-up council-tax banding and generous laxity on the planning rules for extenders and improvers. That would mean she'd have no transport. She'd have no way of getting her ladders and brushes and dust sheets and the rest of her equipment from job to job. No car, no work was the full awful equation. She couldn't tell the family; Theresa would only raise her eyes to heaven in mock despair. Simon would start to flap and worry that she'd turn up on his doorstep seeking refuge, clutching a small bag of worldly goods and Colette's hand. Her mother would mutter about her getting a 'proper job'. Worst of all, her lovely devoted father, still sure that for his younger girl he was the only man in her life to matter, would get her on her own and offer her a spanking new van. It would be so hard to resist, so hard these days to insist that the principle of personal independence *mattered*.

Henry appeared, swimming elegantly in front of Lucy, his thumb pointing up. His eyes behind his mask looked bright and eager. She was about to make the same sign back – after all, she couldn't recall when she'd last felt so physically relaxed even if her mind was racing – when she remembered the instructions about communicating underwater. An upturned thumb meant your dive-buddy was heading for the surface.

She flipped her body over and headed slowly upwards alongside Henry. Mark was already there, partnered with Henry's assistant, Andy. Down at the shallow end, a small collection of swimmers eyed them warily, as if all the equipment attached to their bodies turned them into bizarre water life worthy of only remote scrutiny.

'It all looks a bit Heath Robinson, this stuff, doesn't it?' Mark commented as they peeled off their tanks and weight belts and buoyancy jackets beside the pool. Lucy looked again at the collection of straps and hoses and Velcro and gauges. It did all resemble the kind of contraption that only a crazed inventor with too-easy access to a scrapyard could come up with. In spite of all the Velcro and neoprene, en masse it was ugly, clumsy stuff, emphasizing how dreadfully out of place humans were in the sea. It was pushing their luck, really, to try and intrude into undersea life where fish needed only a set of delicate rippling fins and simple primitive gills to get by.

'It looks as if it's all long outdated, like really old hospital equipment. Shouldn't someone have come up with a streamlined version of all this kit by now?' Lucy asked.

'This *is* the streamlined version. You should check out old movies of underwater divers. This is state-of-the-art, man, no worries.' Henry squeezed Lucy's shoulder. 'You wait till you're out there in the great ocean. Feel yourself floating on the current, at one with the barracudas. Pure grace, *amazing* grace.'

'I'm not sure I like the thought of sharing the sea with barracudas.' Mark looked doubtful as he gathered his equipment together. 'And are there sharks?'

Henry laughed. 'For sure there's sharks, man! But not great whites, not here, just ordinary little nurse sharks and blue ones and hammerheads and stuff. They're just big swimming pussycats quietly minding their own, you'll see.' He winked at Lucy, who grinned back. Henry moved a bit closer to her and spoke more quietly as they all set off along the beach to return the equipment to the dive store. 'OK, so have you got time now for a drink with me? The bar just down the next beach has the best rum punches on the island and I got the afternoon off.'

'Oh. Well, I'd love to, but Mark and I have to rush off and get a cab into Teignmouth to meet the others for lunch. We're in enough trouble with my brother for skiving off to learn to dive as it is.'

'You're crazy. Today there's three cruise ships in and the whole town will be heaving. How about tonight then, after you've eaten *with the family*,' he teased.

'Ah, that would be great but, well, there's my daughter, I shouldn't just slope off . . .' Lucy cursed herself for such pathetic hesitation. Henry was friendly but not pushy. He was about her age and he was fun and he had no connections with home or work or family. What bliss it would be to slip away from the rest of them (already, only the third day in) and spend an hour or two in a bar with an unrelated (and don't forget attractive) grown-up. Colette would say she didn't mind her going, but she would be sure to give her that look, the one that rivalled Shirley's in Conveyed Meaning. Colette's version involved the eyes in raised-to-heaven mode and invariably meant, 'Oh Mum, not another dead-end date.'

'Though Becky could keep an eye on her . . .' But Henry's hands, one holding a weight belt, the other an empty air tank, were already raised in amiable defeat.

'It's OK, I've got a son, ten years old. I know what it's

64

like when you're supposed to be spending time with them.'

Well, that changed things, Lucy thought, feeling an unreasonably and unexpectedly large surge of cross disappointment – after all, he'd only invited her for a drink and she wasn't looking for anything more, definitely not. In spite of herself, though, she felt her voice go hard, as always when the W-word loomed, as it so very often did with attractive men of the right age. If you didn't quite trust your luck when you seemed to have met a good one, you were probably right and the wife-factor would surely be lurking around to wreck things.

'Absolutely,' she agreed, adding, 'and your wife?' They'd reached the dive shop by now and Lucy was glad to get inside, into the cool shade. Glenda was just inside the door and she let out a blast of husky laughter. 'Some wife! Scuttled off to Jamaica when little Olly was two. Visits once a year, always manages to forget the poor kid's birthday. Henry misses her as much as you'd miss a dose of herpes.'

The blast of clammy urban heat that hit Lucy as she climbed out of the viciously air-conditioned taxi almost knocked the breath out of her. The small town, with its narrow hilly streets and its prettily dilapidated Georgian buildings in the soft colours of children's party cakes, seemed to be completely crammed with people. Well, Henry had warned them.

Mark had barely turned from paying the driver before traders scuttled across from their market stalls and started in with the sales pitch. The same question came from several directions: 'You from the ship?'

'No, we're not,' Lucy told a man who was offering to show her the best shop for bargain duty-free emeralds.

'We picked the wrong day for this,' Mark said as he took her arm and tried to get them through the crush without becoming separated and lost. 'Those cruise ships out there in the bay are massive and the whole lot must have descended on this place at once.' He chuckled. 'And I thought Simon had done his homework . . .'

'So all these are the thousands of passengers, all with nothing to do but race around having a frantic shopping opportunity. It's like one of those crazy supermarket trolley-dashes,' Lucy commented. Across the road and up the hill past the inevitable Barclays Bank she could see the big plaster statue of the blue dolphin at the restaurant where Simon had booked a table. Customers clutching drinks spilled out of the doors and across the pavement. Much of the crowd could only be American tourists, the men in baseball caps and fluorescent shirts picked up at the market stalls of other ports and the women dressed to shop in their best shore-going easy-pack viscose trouser suits trimmed plentifully with gold.

'Up here! Lucy! We're up here and we're just about to order!'

Lucy and Mark shoved their way through the crowd and raced up the stairs. The family was at three tables upstairs on a balcony shaded by a palm-thatched awning. The smallest children were with a rather sullen-looking Marisa, well out of sticky grabbing-distance of their mother, an arrangement which seemed to suit Theresa enormously as she was, for the first time, smiling happily and chatting to Simon. Marisa's face, Lucy noticed, was the lurid pink colour of Paignton rock.

Lucy grabbed a seat beside Shirley and took a quick but careful appraisal of her to check if she looked overheated or otherwise out of sorts. The air was so humid, it drained the stamina from even the youngest and most energetic. The night before, Shirley and Perry had gone off to bed early, claiming they needed catch-up time with their sleep. Simon had immediately worried they might be overdoing things and aggravating whatever dire condition one or both of them might be suffering from. It had taken Theresa's astute suggestion that they might just want a bit of peace away from the rest of them to stop him fretting and speculating.

'It's chicken and fries or burger and fries I'm afraid,' Theresa said to Lucy. 'I don't know what on earth the children are going to be like when I get them home if I let them eat this kind of stuff here. They'll be wanting McDonalds next.' She gave a fastidious little shudder.

'No worries. I'll eat anything, I'm starving,' Lucy replied, and Theresa's eyebrows flicked upwards a good couple of inches.

'*No worries!* Doesn't take you long to pick up the local vernacular! How *was* the diving lesson?'

'It was great.' Mark answered for both of them and shuffled out of his chair and made for the stairs. 'Order me chicken with the salad please, Tess, I'm off to the boys' room.'

'No better then?' Theresa glared at him.

'No, no better, darling, thanks so much for your concern.'

Becky felt as if she was with a school party. It was so embarrassing, trailing round the teeming market with her dad chivvying at them all to stay together. He lacked only a games teacher's whistle. Shirley and Perry took no notice of his attempts to keep everyone rounded up, Becky was pleased to see, wandering off together to admire the stalls as if they were in a nice Cotswold village at one of the quieter times of the year. Browsing contentedly, they picked up and inspected samples of the vast ranges of spices and vegetables and leather goods, wooden carvings, jewellery and coconut-shell etchings. Whichever direction Becky turned, steel bands were playing fast thrilling rhythms, patterns of sound that she couldn't quite get the hang of. As she walked between the stalls, men made low, hissy noises at her as if she was a stray tiger cub. She turned in all curious innocence to look at the first few, surprised to catch sight of looks of unexpected hostility. More alarmed than she'd ever thought she would be, for after all she and her mates were well-practised at the sassy 'piss off' rejoinder, she hung on to Luke's arm. He pulled a face but didn't try to extricate himself.

'It's your own fault, you shouldn't have worn those shorts,' he said, eyeing her cropped T-shirt and tiny pink towelling shorts that showed curved little quarter-moons of her bottom as she walked. 'Theresa was right, they're just like knickers. She said little Amy and Ella wear bigger ones than that. Look at the local girls, they're all covered up.'

'Shut up, Luke, you sound just like Dad. How was I supposed to know?'

'I sound like Dad? Shit.'

'Yeah, well.'

'AMY! Where the hell *is* she?' Theresa's shriek cut across the babbling market noises and her face was frantic with panic. 'Becky, Luke, is she with you?' Theresa was in front of them, clutching Ella's wrist tight, her eyes scanning the crowd in terror.

'She was with Marisa and Seb, I thought.' Becky couldn't see Marisa, but Sebastian was holding Plum's hand and kicking at a squashed mango under a stall beside him.

'She was, but Marisa lost sight of her. Stupid girl, she let go of her! You don't *do* that!' Theresa was close to tears.

Mark appeared with a sulky Marisa. 'Can't see her around this bit of the market. I think one of us should go back to the restaurant. Amy might just remember where we were and there was that big blue plaster dolphin thing outside that she liked.'

'I'm sorry. I'm not feeling so good. Is heat.' Marisa's face was blotchy with sunburn and she was fanning her face with her hand. There were oily beads of sweat above her eyebrows and she was breathing too fast.

'And of course you don't get much bloody sun in bloody Montreux do you?' Theresa hissed. 'I did *tell* you: cover up, use the sodding cream, put your hat on, but oh no you had to lie there like a roasting pig . . .'

'Tess, this won't help,' Lucy cut in gently. 'I'll go and see if Amy's at the restaurant, it's only across the square. You stay here with Mum and Dad and if she's not there, Simon and Mark and the rest of us can go round the market and look for her.' She took a few steps and then called back, 'Colette, stay with Becky and Luke.' Colette glared, but Lucy had had to say it, just in case.

She surely couldn't have gone far. A six-year-old child frightened and all alone was surely more likely to stand still and wail and howl than to run off into even stranger territory. There were just so many people: tourists jostling and meandering with no real sense of where they were going, market traders accosting all and sundry and shouting about the quality of their T-shirts and sarongs, their crafts and paintings. Lucy's eyes hurt with the effort of peering through the throng for small, pale Amy in her pink gingham hat. All the worst things crossed her mind, just as they clearly had with Theresa's. Suppose the lost, crying Amy had been noticed and been led away to a car by someone who sounded kind? Suppose one of those comfortable plump cruise-passengers had more sinister holiday interests than deck quoits and minor shipboard gambling? Or what if she'd strayed as far as the docks and fallen in the water . . .

'Hey Lucy! I think this is one of yours!' Just outside the restaurant Henry was sitting on the big blue dolphin, Amy weeping quietly on his lap. Next to him was a miniature version of himself, a young boy with his streaky blond-and-black hair braided into dozens of tiny plaits. 'We told you if we just waited, someone would show up, didn't we Amy? And we were right!'

'Oh poor Amy, did you get a bit lost?' Lucy picked her up and hugged her tightly, almost tearful herself with relief. Over the child's shoulder she gave Henry a shaky smile. He reached out and squeezed her hand, understanding. Amy, instantly recovered, wriggled round and pointed at the boy. 'I like him. I like his hair. Can I have mine like that?'

'This is Oliver, the son.' Henry introduced him to Lucy and Oliver stood up and held out his hand politely, his smile showing the same perfect teeth as his father's.

'Glenda can do it for you, she's my Nana. Sometimes she does it on the beach for people,' Oliver told Amy.

'Can I?' Amy went on, her small fist thumping Lucy on the shoulder.

'Ouch! You'd better ask your mum.' Lucy laughed.

'Ask her as soon as you see her, that way she'll be sure to say yes,' Henry whispered to Amy. 'You OK?' he asked Lucy. 'You must all be going crazy. The one time I took Olly to London he went down one escalator at Oxford Circus while I went up another. I thought that was *it* . . .' Together they made their way back through the crowd across the market square. A ship's siren was sounding, rounding up passengers for the journey to the next day's port. 'Horrid noise!' Amy squealed, putting her hands over her ears.

'About that drink,' Lucy said to Henry as soon as it was quiet again, 'let me buy you one. You're owed, big time. We could go to that bar you were telling me about.' She bit her lip, wondering if perhaps he'd rethought since that morning, changed his mind or met someone else – a holidaymaker with instant sexual fun on her mind and less than thirteen travelling companions to fit in with.

'Sure. About nine? See you in the lobby.'

Theresa's hand shook as she applied her eyeliner. This wasn't supposed to happen. The whole point of taking the au pair was that she and Mark would be able to have some time off, time to be together and recapture – well, something. She wasn't sure what had gone missing exactly (though lately the sex certainly had) but it was as if when Mark went out of the house to work each day he'd left a bit more of their relationship on the train. He was shedding her and the children like a cat moulting away excess summer fur. And now he was always tired too. It was as if the enormous amount of effort that had gone into producing their children had worn his sex drive completely away. There'd been too many years of the mathematical passion-swamping calculation of the ovulation charts, the sex that must be done *now* and the monthly disappointment. But after all the efforts had paid off and the twins had been born, then later the sweet bonus of Sebastian too, it

71

was as if Mark had decided he was now redundant and anything more than minimal bed-effort was pointless. Theresa recalled other holidays, afternoons of Italian heat, post-lunch, post-wine, lying together in cool shuttered villa bedrooms, snatching fast pleasure while their babies slept. Perhaps it was something to do with food, she wondered; maybe fried chicken and iced water didn't have the same arousal effect on Mark as pasta *Puttanesca* and a bottle of Barbaresco.

Marisa was sleeping now in the adjoining room, her face a lurid pink mess against the white pillow. At least she'd stopped being sick. The taxi driver hadn't been too pleased, having to stop twice for her on the short trip between the town and the hotel. 'It was food, maybe, something I eaten,' Marisa had said, wailing quietly but persistently as if she was gently keening for something lost and making Theresa want to slap the silly suffering girl.

'It was too much sun,' Theresa had snapped back.

'Leave her, she feels bad enough,' Mark had said quietly. It was all right for him, he didn't have to look after the fat Swiss slob. As if absolutely nothing was going wrong, he'd gone off to slaughter Simon at tennis. Where had he been when she was calling room service for all those bottles of mineral water, at the same time trying to supervise the children's baths and sort out beds for the twins in their room alongside Sebastian? In fact where was he now?

Theresa got up and went to look out beyond the balcony towards the beach. It was almost dark, night fell so fast out here. You hardly got any time that could be called 'evening'. Out under the trees people were still strolling around in the warm air, packing up from staying late on the sand or taking the last swim of the day as the massive, surely too big, sun went down fast behind them. This was the time when they were all advised to keep their terrace doors closed against the foraging twilight mosquitoes. Theresa couldn't be bothered. Let the bastards bite. Her eyes smarted: everyone she could see out there seemed to be in pairs. There was that young couple who were forever groping each other in the pool kissing passionately beneath the gazebo. Everyone looked so happy, as if all the things that were supposed to define a Proper Holiday – no rows, lots of best-ever sex, the forgetting about trivial niggles of home life – were well in place and the whole thing was going right. She and Mark should be together, snuggling their clean, contented children down for a story and sleep, then getting ready for dinner, having an early companiable drink and being two grown-ups leaving any child-hassle to the girl who was paid to see to it. Too much *Peter Pan*, Theresa thought, briskly dashing a tissue across eyes which now threatened to stream. The bit she'd liked best in that book, reading it aloud recently to the children, had been when Mr and Mrs Darling had kissed their children goodnight and gone off out together (to the theatre, or was it dinner?) all dressed up. That was the treat side of being a parent, having the delights of children *and* the pleasure of a separate adult life. At the moment, considering Marisa's uselessness, it occurred to her that she couldn't have done worse if she too had left her children in the care of a big furry dog.

Theresa pulled the terrace door shut, closed the curtains then chased a couple of mosquitoes, thwacking them dead against the wall with the Baedeker Caribbean guidebook. Amy and Ella sat on the bed guzzling down room-service pizza, ignoring her mood and engrossed in an all-American version of *Family Fortunes*. She looked at the over-exuberant contestants and sighed: what kind of a team would her family be able to put together, she wondered.

'So what was tonight's menu special?' Henry walked close to Lucy on the sand. Ahead of them, like an oasis in the dark and showing up cartoon-like silhouettes of leaning palm trees, were the lights of the beach bar they were heading for.

'Oh, it was an all-Caribbean barbecue night. Swordfish and spare ribs and spicy chicken, salads and rice and sweet potatoes, that sort of thing. Pretty delicious actually, I ate stacks.'

Henry laughed. 'And don't tell me, a limbo-dancing demonstration with burning torches and the diners invited to join in, though none of them do till they're really drunk and they don't care about falling over and making prats of themselves.'

'You're right. But I refuse to be amazed because I suspect this is the pattern for the whole season. If it's Thursday, it must be limbo. Tomorrow we get a gospel choir and Saturday it's steel band.'

'You should get out more,' Henry teased.

'We're all-inclusive. The parents don't mind what we do but Simon says every meal not eaten here is a huge waste of their money. Anyway, I'm out now. Colette's hanging out with Becky and Luke. I think she hopes they'll be a bad influence.'

'And will they?'

'Probably.' Lucy didn't want to talk about children. This was time off from being a parent, an aunt, a daughter. What was it Simon had said as she was leaving? Oh yes, 'So you're sloping off are you, Lucy?' as if she was a naughty teenager wriggling her way out of some important family bonding session. And there'd been the other thing, the cutting one, this time from

Theresa, snidely telling Shirley and Perry, 'Lucy's going out for a drink with one of the locals.' Shirley for once hadn't sat passively but had replied sharply, 'Only the "local" who took care of your daughter, Tess. I think we all owe him a debt, especially you.' Theresa had bitten her lip and looked to Mark for comfort, but he'd been oblivious, studying the wine list.

The bar was bustling and crowded with a rowdy mixture of holidaymakers and residents, most of whom greeted Henry loudly, eyeing Lucy and grinning in a way that suggested she might well be his several hundredth conquest. She didn't care, she felt no pressure to do anything but talk to him and spend some time relaxing with a drink or two. It was one advantage of having decided men were no longer worth looking for: you didn't even bother with the lipstick if you didn't want to, nor did you get all geed up about what would happen, how far would you take things. If she was dressed more smartly than she had been for the beach – loose black linen trousers, floppy white shirt – it was because she'd made the effort for the hotel restaurant's dress code, not for Henry.

'This is Dexy's famous rum punch with a secret ingredient.' Henry put a massive glass on the table in front of Lucy. She picked up the cocktail stick and dipped the row of cherries in the drink, licking at them.

'I can guess what the secret is: more rum by the taste of this.' She grinned and took a large sip. It was sticky, sweet and potent, the kind of drink Lucy would never have chosen at home.

'So, what do you think?' Henry was smiling, waiting for her to admire the local poison.

'Wow, strong stuff. A drink for steering clear of if you're looking at a day's work tomorrow,' she told him.

'What would you have had back home?'

Lucy thought for a moment. There were all those hopeful wine-bar first dates with men who'd had some kind of potential. And there were girls' nights with shrill don't-care laughter and some lurid cocktails.

'I go for a white wine spritzer, usually,' she said. 'A thin sad shot of sour cheap wine with the built-in safety of too much water.' Some of the 's's' were already tangled. She'd have to take care.

'Sparkling water, though.' Henry laughed.

'Soon flattens out.'

'Not like life, I hope.'

'Well I keep hoping that too, but . . . heavens, look there's bloody Becky, what's she doing here? She's supposed to be with Colette. *Becky!*' Lucy was instantly out of her seat and pushing her way across the bar.

Becky was half-lying across the table in the corner, her raucous laughter the loudest in the bar. Her face was scarlet with smeared lipstick and too much drink and the boy who'd been selling jewellery on the beach had one arm round her and his other hand somewhere under the table. One of the straps on Becky's skimpy little top had slid so far down her arm that her left breast was threatening to show itself off to the entire bar. Opposite this pair was one of the many young couples from the hotel, sipping beers and looking as if they weren't quite sure they were comfortable.

'Becky, what the hell are you doing in here? You promised you'd keep an eye on Colette for me.'

Becky's eyes were barely focusing on her. Lucy remembered she'd had a glass of wine with dinner, but then had gone to her room before the end of the meal taking Luke and Colette with her. She must have raided the minibar before coming out. Becky's face was deep in exaggerated thought for a moment, as if remembering how to put a sentence together. 'Colette's with Luke,' she said carefully. 'They're watching *Raiders of the Lost Ark* on telly. Perfectly OK, see.'

'No it's not perfectly OK. *You* definitely aren't.' She reached across the jewellery boy, wishing she hadn't caught sight of his hand extricating itself from beneath Becky's tiny skirt, and hauled the girl out of her seat. 'Come on, I'm taking you back to the hotel before you have to be carried there.'

'But it's nearly my birthday!' Becky wailed, pulling herself back into the corner.

'Not till next week it isn't, now *get up.*'

'I'll get her.' Henry's hand reached across, hauled on the girl's wrist and hoisted her out of her seat. Before Becky had time to protest she was out of the bar and standing, albeit shakily, on the sand between the two of them.

'God Henry, you must think this family is totally out of control!' Lucy said, taking Becky's arm and guiding her in the darkness along the beach towards the hotel's lights. Behind them was the sound of pounding luscious reggae in the bar, while ahead, Lucy noted with despondency, was the dispiriting din of the hotel entertainment: a lacklustre rendering of 'Yellow Bird', on the gentle undemanding upbeat considered suitable for the mass tourist trade. Henry's hand reached across behind Becky's lolling head and brushed lightly against her face. 'Don't worry, stay happy,' he said. Well, she'd try.

Five

The rain woke Plum. It was still dark but that didn't mean it was the middle of the night as it would on a hot night in England. In half an hour it could be fully light and she would start tormenting herself with the temptation of a mountainous breakfast.

The torrent of tumbling water was pounding hard on the corrugated verandah roof over the balcony and Plum wished she'd remembered to take the swimsuits off the rail and bring them into the room the night before. They didn't dry properly out there anyway, not unless you hung them in the scorching noon sunlight; the air was just too humid.

'They said this was the rainy season, but just how much of the stuff can the sky hold?' Simon, next to her, was already awake with his light on, propped up and reading a gory Patricia Cornwell. 'It's been going on for well over an hour. Becky or Luke or both are awake: I can hear their television through the wall.' He made a face. 'Cartoons, by the sound of it.'

Plum laughed. 'I suppose you think if they've got their eyes open they might as well be doing a spot of maths. They're on holiday, Simon, let them relax.'

'They've only just gone back to school after the

summer. You know what I think of them having this extra time off.'

Plum climbed out of bed and went to slide the terrace door open to see for herself the astounding downpour. 'It's no good grumbling to me about it. If you didn't want them to come then you should have made it clear to Shirley and Perry.'

It was easy for her to say, Simon thought, as he tried to settle back into his book. Plum's parents had been of the liberal, easy-going Hampstead intellectual sort who had carefully considered and valued the opinions of their children right from the moment they'd begun to put thoughts into words. But, for him, the habit of doing as you were told in the good old-fashioned Northern manner was a hard one to break. Perry had never actually said that children should be seen and not heard, but Simon would be willing to bet that somewhere in the back of his mind that idea still lingered. He remembered when he was about nine, informing one of the Devon landladies, serving dinner, that no thanks, he didn't want mushroom soup – in fact he really hated it more than any other food in the whole world. His father had taken him out into the hallway with its swirly green and orange carpet and smell of damp umbrellas and given him a lecture on rudeness and manners. It had been the first time he'd realized that his parents weren't necessarily always right; for he hadn't been rude, he was sure. You had to have a cross thought in your head for rudeness. He'd just been chatty and truthful. Chatty though was bad, it seemed, even if you were smiling at the time, and even truthful was sometimes a bit more than people really required. This holiday, the way his father had said, 'I'm booking us all a fortnight away, all the family together,' had been a statement, not an invitation or a question. He hadn't left any scope for saying no. It had reminded Simon of Latin lessons, of being taught how to translate a 'question requiring an affirmative answer'. He'd had a lifetime's practice.

Simon's head was pounding. He didn't want to admit, even to himself, to having caught too much sun, or drinking too much of the Sugar Mill bar's gluey pina coladas the night before. He'd enjoyed a good three of those after dinner, fooled (easily) by their puddingy sweet taste and almost syllabub-like texture into discounting the sizeable rum content. The young couple, the gropers, who had caught him watching them in the pool had been in the bar too, still kissing and touching, fondling each other when they thought no-one was looking in places that would be better kept for times of more privacy. He and Plum had taken their last drinks down the steps to the beach in the dark, lying flat out side by side on a pair of sunloungers and staring up at the stars that seemed so outrageously close. There'd been no sign then of the deluge to come. The clouds must have been gathering from the Atlantic side of the island.

'What's that noise?' Plum, coming out of the bathroom, said.

'More rain? Wind?' Simon suggested.

'No. It sounds like someone throwing up.'

'Probably the plumbing.' Simon was now engrossed in a particularly gruesome autopsy in his book and not at all interested in plumbing or nausea.

Plum was standing stone-still in the middle of the room, her head cocked and listening hard. 'There it is again. It's Becky, I'm sure. Poor girl, I'll go and see if she needs anything. First Marisa and now this. Perhaps it really was something they ate . . .'

It took a while for Luke to open the door. Plum could hear his bare feet slap-slapping reluctantly across the tiled floor. He looked furious, standing in the doorway in his blue tartan boxer shorts and a torn and faded yellow T-shirt that looked ready for lining the dog's basket. For the first time, Plum registered that Luke was no longer even the slightest bit child-shaped. His tall, lean, rugby-player frame almost filled the doorway and he wasn't moving aside.

'What?' he demanded, as if she was the fifteenth visitor that night and he was thoroughly bored with door-duty.

'What's wrong with Becky? I could hear through the wall — is she ill?'

Luke scratched his head and opened his eyes wide. 'What? Becky? Dunno, no don't think so.' He still hadn't moved. Taking a quick glance beyond him, Plum then swiftly took advantage of him following her gaze and sidestepped him into the room. It was a mirror image of hers and Simon's, though with a pair of beds instead of the generous king-size double that they had. This room had been trashed into a typical teenage shambles of clothes, magazines, school books and empty Coke cans. The scent of stale cigarette smoke tainted the air. Becky's bed was empty, the sheet and blanket tumbled onto the floor and the pillow missing. There was a groan from the bathroom.

'Oh, great, the bloody cavalry. Thanks a whole bunch Luke,' Becky called, catching sight of her mother.

Becky was slumped on the floor in the classic position of the penitent drunk hugging the lavatory. Her pillow was beside her as if this was the only place she could trust herself to spend the night. Plum tried to haul her gently up but she pulled back, staying where she was as if it was the only possible position for comfort.

'She just got in, OK? Nuffin much I could do. Don't see why I should cover up for her.' Luke shrugged and went and got into his bed, pulling a sheet over his head.

'Becky, whatever's wrong? Have you had too much sun, because if you have, we need to get plenty of water into you.'

Becky's reply was to retch again, bringing up a thin weak stream of beige liquid.

'Too much sun! Huh!' Luke re-emerged from his nest. 'Too much booze. Ask her where she's been, go on, ask her, 'cos I wouldn't mind knowing so I can have my turn bein' out clubbin' or whatever.' He appeared at the bathroom door, his glare of grievance reflected in mirrors on two of the walls.

'Luke, you shithead!' Becky started to cry, a sad little whimpering sound full of self-pity.

'Well what j'expect? I agree to share a room with you even though we're too old, *way* too old for sharin', just to help out 'cos Dad's moaning on and saying we can't sting Grandad for the extra for single rooms, though we all know he wouldn't mind, and what do I get? I have to look after Colette and watch stuff on telly that won't give her crap dreams, and then you come in banging on the door 'cos you've lost your key and then you start bloody throwin' up all over the place. You should have been put in with Marisa or with Theresa's brood.' He stopped for breath and looked down at his sister with an expression of frank disgust that Plum recognized as being one of his father's specialities.

'Why were you looking after Colette?' she asked. 'Where was Lucy?'

'*Out!* Like Becky. Everyone's bloody out having a

great time. 'Cept me, of course. Being as how I'm just a *kid*, and just a *mug*.' He turned and stalked away. Plum heard him getting back into bed, thumping his pillow as he turned it over and sighing as loudly as he possibly could. She'd have to deal with him in the morning, talk him through his grievances which might well be justified. For now, though, Becky needed some care and attention.

'What did you drink, Becky? Just tell me the truth and I won't be cross.'

Becky wiped her damp hair across her face and tried to focus. 'Rum stuff. Cocktaily things. Not many though, truly. I wasn't out that long. Ask Lucy.'

'Oh I'll ask her, trust me.' Plum went to the minibar and found it denuded of all soft drinks except water. She poured some into a glass and took it to Becky, who had recovered enough to sit on the side of the bath.

'Thanks Mum. And . . . Mum?'

'Yes?'

'Don't tell Gran will you? Please? I don't want them to think—'

'Think you're a drunken slag who gets totally off her face?' Luke's grumpy voice interrupted.

'Yeah, something like that. And Dad . . .'

'I'll deal with your father, don't worry.' Plum grinned. 'If he gets difficult I'll remind him of something he told me about one of those precious bloody Devon holidays, the key words to which are fairground, rifle range and a bottle of Scotch. Now try and get some sleep, and till you do, just sip at the water a bit from time to time. This will pass.'

'It'd fuckin' better,' Luke growled.

Lucy could see a selection of the Putney Mothers running in stages from their rooms towards breakfast, first to the shelter of the big tamarind tree by the gazebo and then making a fast onward dash with their small children across the open area past the pool, heads low against the stabbing rain. They were doing what Colette called girly-running, awkward in strappy little sandals or flip-flops and with their hair flopping free from slides and into their eyes. At the section where the aromatic turpentine tree and hibiscus overhung the path, the children squealed and giggled as the sodden leaves brushed against their bare arms. Under shelter on the dining terrace the mothers flapped uselessly at their children with tissues, trying to mop the worst of the water from their heads so it wouldn't drip into their breakfast cereal. The dads, Lucy noticed, simply headed straight for the buffet.

Shirley and Perry, looking as calmly accepting of the state of the weather as only those used to living close to Manchester and accustomed to holidaying in England can, were already sitting with Simon and Plum at the enormous table which had been moved away from the edge, out of reach of the water that still cascaded from the palm-thatched roof and gushed down onto the huge fat greedy leaves of the philodendron plants below.

'Oh. Hi you two, slumming it with us today?' Theresa arrived towing Sebastian and the twins. She looked tousled, as if she hadn't slept much. Her sun-streaked hair was twisted and pinned up loosely, making her almost indistinguishable from the other half-dozen London mums in the hotel. Shirley approved. She'd heard those strident Home Counties voices – well, you couldn't miss them – commanding their children's activities on the beach and she liked the idea that Theresa, her most socially ambitious child, could now be taken for what she defined as a

Surrey Lady. If she only paid a bit more attention to her nails, proper manicures and some shiny polish . . .

'We thought it might be a good idea to come over and join you for breakfast so we could all plan the day together. Otherwise everyone skitters around not getting organized,' Shirley said.

Mark, arriving with a big plate full of watermelon and pawpaw for the children, grinned at her. 'Lucy and I have got our first open-water dive later this morning. So that's us fixed up I'm afraid, for now.'

Theresa frowned. 'Well I don't suppose we'll want to do much anyway, if this rain keeps up.'

'Oh it won't,' Perry decreed. 'Rain before seven, fine before eleven . . . Oh good, here's Lucy and Colette.' Theresa noticed how much his face brightened at the sight of them. Scanning back towards her childhood she couldn't recall his face ever lighting up that much at the sight of *her*. Probably all the delight he'd felt at having a new child had only lasted with the final one of the three of them. Ridiculous, she told herself, still to mind.

'Hi Dad, morning Ma.' Lucy sat down beside Perry and kissed him. 'I'm not sure the sayings of north country English shepherds count over here. Someone in reception said there was a big storm coming next week and that this is the beginning of it.'

'Bit of rain, what a fuss.' Shirley tutted. 'We didn't used to let it spoil our plans in Devon, now did we? There was always a museum to see or some nice shops to look at. You'll see, by the time we're loaded up and halfway to the sugar plantation or the rainforest or wherever we're going it'll have stopped. We'll go this afternoon. You divers won't want to be out in a downpour in a boat for too long.'

Lucy looked across at Mark and grinned. 'Hey, it'll

take as long as it takes and maybe a little bit more. It's a local saying, Ma.'

Luke still felt aggrieved and childishly pleased that the glowering skies matched his mood. Becky had woken up late with no hangover and no regrets and, amazingly, was her usual maddening bumptious self. 'It's the best way, drink what you like then sick it all up, the way bulimics do only with them it's food,' she'd said. She shouldn't be like that, he thought. She should be sorry for keeping him awake all night, sorry for leaving him with Colette (whom he was quite happy to be with, apart from when he'd rather be watching *Death Wish 2* on the movie channel), and sorry for having a good time that she hadn't let him join in with.

He sat on the damp stone with his feet dangling over the end of the small jetty at the end of the beach, the opposite end from the headland where his grandparents' villa was. He'd taken a bread roll from breakfast and was breaking off bits to hurl into the sea. Fish were gathering to feed on the crumbs: bright, luminous creatures that reminded him of the crazily vivid colours of children's drawings. With what felt like a mighty clout of nostalgia, he could visualize and almost smell the present his gran had given him when he was ten, a set of a hundred multicoloured felt-tip pens, all arranged in a circle in their pale wooden box, a delicious spectrum. He'd kept the colours in the exact order that they'd arrived in, thrilled by the barely visible progression of one shade into the next. Once, Becky had got at the box when he'd been out at a Sea Scouts event, and she'd muddled them all up. He'd pretended to be furious, as if she'd destroyed something, but he'd lain on his bed for hours, rearranging them into their proper order, amazed and fascinated to be so nearly caught out so often by the minute differences in shades.

'That's a parrot fish, that blue one.' There was a shadow on the water. Luke looked round at the speaking boy and recognized the ginger-haired son of the gold lady, the one whose bracelets jingled so you knew where she was without seeing her, like a cat with a bell. He was about twelve but had the kind of know-all authority in his voice of someone much older. Luke guessed he was hated at school for being clever and could only practise it on strangers like himself.

'How do you know?' Luke asked.

'Easy. All these bright ones here are parrot fish. Then there's the little black and silver striped ones, they're sergeant majors, and the yellow and blue things are angel fish. There's a chart in reception. I learned it.'

'You must have been really bored.'

The boy shrugged. 'Not really. It's something to do.'

'You *sound* bored,' Luke ventured. The boy was dressed head to foot in Gap Kids, he noticed. He could imagine the gold mother coming home with the dark blue bags, chucking them on the boy's bed and saying, 'Put these away now, Oscar,' (or Algernon or whatever poncy name he'd been given), 'they're to wear on holiday.' No choice, no say, as if he was still six.

'Well I am a *bit* bored. There's just me and my mum and she lies around reading all the time. I've had mumps.' His face cheered up as he said it.

'So've I.'

'Yes but *badly*, and recently. The school didn't want me back yet. It's all boys, and boarding, so you can understand them.'

Luke couldn't. At his school (comprehensive, his mum being posh enough to believe in state education as a *principle*), a bus ride away and a swirling sea of both sexes, if you were ill you stayed off for as long as possible and had to fend off the school secretary ringing up all the time to see if you were bunking off. They certainly didn't encourage convalescence on a Caribbean island. And what was special about mumps and boys? He'd have to ask Becky, if they were ever on talk-terms again.

'We could take a pedalo out if you want.' Luke stood up and shoved his hands deep into his pockets, trying to look diffident. It might be quite good to hang out with someone else, be independent. It would show Becky, anyway, plus give her a chance to do a girls-together bonding stint with Colette.

Together, Luke and Tom (whose hand had twitched out as if to shake Luke's as he'd introduced himself) sauntered back along the soggy beach to the water-sports shop. Lucy and Mark were there, having their pre-dive briefing in the room at the back with Henry and Andy and the rest of that morning's pupils. The shop smelled of damp wetsuits. Glenda was outside hanging up sarongs under the almond tree, now that the sky was safely cerulean again.

'OK boys, what would you like? Are you taking a Sunfish out, or a canoe? There's plenty here, most folks have gone into town.' She laughed. 'They don't understand island weather. A grey sky in Tunbridge Wells, that can be a day's worth of misery. Not here though!'

'Could we just have a pedalo please?' Luke thought he should take charge, make it clear he was easily the elder.

'Sure, help yourselves. Not the blue one though, OK? Oh and take snorkel vests just in case . . .'

Tom raced ahead to the line of pedalos on the sand, eager and puppyish and Luke wondered if he should have asked Colette to come instead. She was calm, not so childishly excitable. She didn't wear him out and knew when to keep quiet and just let him think.

'She said not the blue one,' Luke reminded him.

'This isn't blue, it's purple,' Tom said. 'And it's the best one, it's the biggest, a real two-er. Most of the others are just singles. We'll go faster in this.' It was true. Probably someone else had already taken the blue one away, perhaps it needed fixing. This one was definitely purple, or at least purple-ish. If he was fitting this colour into his spectrum wheel of pens, it would be just as close to the red ones as to the blue. Together they pushed the big plastic thing down to the sea and launched it, splashing into the shallows in their trainers. Tom looked down at his feet as if remembering something his mum had told him, but said nothing.

'We haven't got the float things, the snorkel vests,' Luke said as they clambered aboard. 'Can you swim OK?'

'Course I can. Anyway we're not going that far, are we?'

It was amazing how fast they left the shore behind. With both of them pedalling they quickly picked up speed and aimed the craft round the headland out of sight of the hotel's beach.

'We could go anywhere. Right round the island,' Tom said.

'Or to Barbados, or down to Trinidad.' Luke felt it was important to establish a wider view.

'Or Venezuela or the Falklands.' Tom was getting giggly.

'Don't be stupid.'

For a while the two of them paddled hard, each keen to be thought strong and tireless. They kept parallel to the shore, following the beach up towards the next headland beyond the bar which Luke assumed was the one where Becky had got so drunk the night before. It was quiet there now, with just a few holidaymakers sitting under thatched sunshades sipping an early beer.

'The sea here's much warmer than it is in Portugal,' Tom suddenly said.

'I know,' Luke replied. He didn't, he'd never been to Portugal. Plum and Simon preferred holidays in Cornwall or Scotland, places where the unpredictable weather was likely to provide a huge part of the fortnight's adventures. Competing with gale-driven rain was the thrilling possibility of instant death from falling out of a dinghy into the glacial water of a fathomless loch, or tumbling from the treacherous shifting mud-slide that made up the Cornish Coast Path. On balance, pedalling along on the warm Caribbean, Luke was pretty grateful to his grandparents.

'I thought you didn't get your feet wet in these things. You don't in Greece,' Tom suddenly said. Luke looked at his own feet. The pedalling was getting quite hard now and Tom was right, the water level did seem quite high, his knees were almost under.

'It's sinking.' Tom peered over the side. 'We might have to swim.'

'Yeah I suppose, but . . .' They were further out than he'd thought. That must be because of the current. Venezuela no longer seemed out of the question; and Lucy had said that Henry had said there were sharks.

'OK, stand up.' Luke pulled his feet up from the pedals and clambered up onto the seat.

'What?'

'Stand up and we'll shout to those people at the bar. There's canoes and stuff, someone can come out and give us a tow.' Luke hadn't been a Sea Scout all those years for nothing, even if most of his practical boat experience had been on the unexotic reservoirs round Staines beneath the Heathrow flight path. 'And be *careful*.' Tom was trying to be too fast, too eager and the pedalo was rocking.

'I *am*. It's the waves, not me.'

'Hey, you lot! Over here, come and get us!' Luke waved and yelled and a young couple at the café waved back then went back to their conversation.

'Oi, you dumbos! Give us a sodding lift!' The water was higher now, lapping over his toes.

'Yeah, fuckheads! Come *on*!' Tom was competing, Luke realized, determined to be more insulting than he was. The couple got up and strolled away, holding hands and talking close together.

'Jeez! You stupid git!' Luke accused Tom. 'Now you've driven them away!'

'Great, blame me.'

'Well . . .' There wasn't any point. They were going to need their breath for the long swim. Luke was sure he could make it to the shore, just so long as no monster, no jellyfish, giant octopus, shark or devastating undertow got to him. He was worried about Tom though. It would be a hard slog for someone so much smaller than him, for someone who'd been ill enough to need a holiday to recover. But there wasn't any choice. 'OK, Tom, let's go. If we hang on we'll drift further away.'

Tom looked at him and grinned. Luke's stomach turned over, recognizing an awesome and terrifying expression of trust.

'All the way to the Falklands?' Tom said.

'Quite bloody possibly. OK, one, two, three, JUMP!'

'So they're not with you?' Glenda, in her flowing dress made out of a pair of sarongs printed with repeated heads of Bob Marley in black and red, stood in front of Shirley, Simon and Theresa as they sat beneath an almond tree on the beach. The gold lady, sprawled close by on a lounger, lit another cigarette and listened.

'Well no, Luke wandered off in a sulk soon after breakfast. Haven't seen him since. I don't know if he was with anyone.' Simon could see no reason to be agitated. This woman seemed to be implying that Luke and another boy had stolen a pedalo, unless he'd misunderstood. How far could they go on it?

'Well, he was. He was with a smaller, gingery boy. They took the wrong pedalo, a leaky one that I'd specifically told them not to take, and no life preservers. I *told* them.'

The gold lady sat up, suddenly anxious. 'Was the gingery boy about twelve, in navy shorts?'

'He was.' Glenda had her hands on her hips. She was angry, Shirley could see, but there was more than a trace of worry. She gave Glenda her most reassuring Cheshire smile.

'Oh, they'll be all right. I'm sure they can both swim. I expect they're lurking about on the beach somewhere, plucking up courage to come and admit they've sunk your boat,' she said. 'Boys are like that.'

Glenda's temper snapped. 'God, how can you be so complacent! People like you remind me exactly why I left England! They've taken a leaky craft out on the sea. They've been out for hours and all you can say is "boys will be boys"! I bet you wouldn't be this bone-headed if they'd gone missing off Newquay. You'd have the bloody coastguard out before your sodding ice cream had melted.'

The gold lady glared at Simon and pointed her cigarette at him. 'I shall blame you,' she accused, 'if anything's happened to my Tom it'll be all your fault.'

Hotel guests who had been at the sea's edge were now drifting closer to listen. Earpieces from personal stereos of apparently comatose sunbathers were being removed for better hearing. Theresa slunk further down on her lounger, mortified. She felt as if they were collectively accused of being the holiday family from hell. Surely that was what happened to Other People, the sort who had drunken fights on planes and stripped down to their cellulite at ghastly vomit-laden theme nights. And once again, where was Mark when he could be useful? Out on the sea, or under it, with no cares in the whole bloody world.

'Now we're not going very deep, no more than ten metres this first time and it's only for half an hour, though you've got enough air for much longer. That's because you'll be nervous and when you're nervous you use a lot more, gulping it in like you can't get enough.' Henry was going over the lessons again as Andy sped the boat away from the shore. Lucy and Mark grinned at each other, both apprehensive, both excited. The boat swerved round the end of the head-land sending waves skittering into hotel guests dawdling along in canoes or taking the chance to get the hang of windsurfing in sea that didn't half-kill you with cold if you fell into it.

'Look at those kids on the half-sunk pedalo,' Mark said. 'What the hell are they doing? Abandoning ship?'

'Where? What kids?' Henry looked out across the boat's prow. 'I told Glenda not to let anyone have that one!' He tapped Andy's arm and pointed. Just then, the two boys jumped into the sea and Andy swerved the boat round fast after them.

'One of them looks a bit like Luke,' Lucy said, peering over the sea. Seconds later, the two boys were being hauled over the side onto the boat and they stood dripping and grinning cockily at the divers and crew.

'You'll have to come out with us, it's too late to take you back.' Henry looked at his watch. 'I've got a snorkel group at twelve. No-one was supposed to take the blue one out. The guy's coming to take it for repair.'

'Sorry,' Luke said, 'but you've got to admit it's more sort of purple.' He grinned and Lucy thumped his arm. 'You could have got yourselves drowned, stupid. This is serious sea.'

'And you're supposed to be wearing life vests too. Wait till I get back and see Glenda.' Then Henry smiled at Lucy. 'Am I going to spend the whole of this fortnight rescuing your family?'

A turtle was swimming past Lucy and giving her no attention at all. Captivated, she swam after it but the creature, so cumbersome on land, was too fast and graceful for her to chase. Then Henry pulled on her hand and pointed to the seabed as a ray, three feet or so across, fluffed its way out of the sand and rippled slowly away. Nothing down here seemed afraid, Lucy realized, nothing seemed to feel they were a threat. She and the divers were accepted simply as extra sea-life with their own unfathomable and unquestioned part to play. If only the humans in the world were as tolerant. She felt an overwhelming sense of privilege at being allowed this look at the hidden habitat of so much life. Two-thirds of the earth was covered in sea, two-thirds of it a habitat for animals and plants that most people could never hope to see in their natural state like this. Henry was beside her. She knew he was sensing her feeling of wonder. She looked at her pressure gauge – time to go to the surface. She looked at Henry and raised her thumb.

Six

Simon had forgotten his sunglasses. He kept forgetting things and seemed to be constantly plodding the cool terracotta-tiled corridor between the lobby and his room collecting his book, his hat, the suntan lotion or cash. The rest of the family were annoyingly quick to catch on to this which meant he was also asked to remember to pick up Plum's book or a CD of Becky's as well, and then got shouted at when he came back to the pool or beach without them. His brain was being addled by the sun, though the rest of him seemed to be in remarkably pert working order. Even walking felt different here, springy and light, though his breath was running short, gasping in the heavy, humid air.

The worry about Luke had unsettled all of them so much the day before that the afternoon trip to the rain forest had been put off till the next morning. As minutes and then an hour passed after Glenda had told them the boys were missing, the possibility that some-thing dreadful might have happened started to become real. When she'd calmed down and done a little think-ing, and just as they were all starting to feel the beginnings of panic, Glenda had concluded that the dive boat must have picked them up: so many hotel guests were out on the sea swimming or racing about in sailboats and jet skis that someone would be sure to have spotted a couple of floating bodies.

Later, Plum had spent most of the afternoon in the sea, snorkelling slowly over the reef and avoiding contact with both the gold lady and Shirley. And then she hadn't wanted dinner at the hotel but had taken Becky to the pizza café in the precinct across the road. Simon assumed the idea was to get her alone and give her a bit of a talking-to about the dangers of drink and men in hot climates, but the two of them had returned mildly plastered and giggly in the kind of way that made him think he (and probably All Men) been a major part of the evening's jokes.

The door to his room was open. Outside was the trolley full of towels, sheets and cleaning equipment which always seemed to be parked somewhere in the corridor. In the room, the maid, whose name badge said 'Carol', was stripping the bed. Carol moved around in an unnervingly slow way, as if she might come to a permanent halt at any second, suiting energy conservation to the climate. She smiled at him and said a cheerful hello, asked him his plans for the day. Simon mentioned the rainforest and she laughed and told him she'd never been there, just as London residents will admit, often to their own surprise, that the Tower of London is somewhere they've never got round to visiting.

The sunglasses were in the bathroom. Simon rinsed stray specks of toothpaste off the lenses then looked at himself sideways in the mirror – how paunchy did this loose shirt make him look? Should he tuck it into his shorts or would that just draw attention to his waistline? His hand went up to his hair, for the usual quick run-through to see what fell out, but just as fast came down again. Why give himself the grief? He switched off the light and came back into the room. Carol was now bent over the bed, tucking in a sheet. Her broad round bottom, with the shiny pink uniform overall pulled tight across it, was pointing at him, almost wagging in invitation. Simon caught a glimpse of the back of a gleaming black knee beneath the skirt as she leaned further over to deal with an awkward corner. His hands didn't feel part of him and his head was swimming with thoughts that were too lasciviously fast and furious to have any real form. This was how it was when the body was lively but the brain was limp (and how often, in the dull drab forever-February days at home, had it been the other way round). Without conscious awareness of how it happened, his hands found themselves stretched over an expanse of taut slippery fabric, and his body squashed against the outline of malleable flesh beneath. The shock of contact as he realized what he'd done coincided with Carol's shriek of surprise.

'I'm so sorry!' Simon backed away instantly, his hands in the air. 'I tripped on the rug! I'm sorry!' Carol stood upright, her hand on her hip and a knowing grin on her face. 'Tripped huh?' She didn't even pretend to believe him. Simon waited to be clouted across the face, for her to storm out and holler for Security, for even as he'd spoken the words he'd recognized them as pathetic, inadequate and patently untrue. Instead she stood still, considering, with a seen-it-all smile. One hand rested on her ample hip. Simon saw her suddenly as a big, motherly, cushiony creature, someone he could weep on, confide in. His heart was racing, wondering if he was right to think like this.

'I'm used to you English guys, smouldering in sexy heat ya don't get back home,' she told him, her expression switching terrifyingly fast to a formidably stern one. Then she prodded him hard in the chest with a pointing finger and he backed towards the open door, praying to escape. 'But if I hears *anything*, just one single *word* about you losing it with one of the younger girls, you're gonna be outa here and off this island so fast. Got me?'

'Got you.' The words fell out in one fast, frightened breath. 'Sorry, very, very sorry.' Simon nodded so hard he thought his head would roll over the floor. He stumbled backwards through the door, desperate to be with Plum and the children, be a good husband, a good parent, a good son again.

'And watch out for those rugs, take care where you're walking.' Carol's grin was back in place, and as he walked away he heard a whooping cackle of laughter, possibly, he thought as he trudged towards the lobby, at the thought of sharing this sorry tale with the rest of the staff during their coffee break.

Lucy relaxed against the headrest and closed her eyes. It was cool and peaceful in the minibus, without Theresa's brood and their constant nausea-provoking flapping that Sebastian might get carsick. 'Hey, don't go drifting off to sleep, you might miss something.' Lucy snapped her eyes open again and marvelled at the spooky parental sixth sense that had her mother, way down at the front of a twelve-seater minibus, knowing that Lucy was thinking of snatching a quick doze four seat rows away at the back.

'You were always the same,' Shirley went on, though this time smiling at Victor the bemused driver, including him as if he'd be thrilled to hear their family reminiscences. 'Even as a baby, the minute you got in a car when you were little, off you went. Some nights, we'd drive round the block a few times in the Rover (remember the Rover?) just to get you off.'

'She'd always bloody wake up again when you put her back in the cot.' Perry was joining in now. Lucy smiled but said nothing. If she encouraged them, they'd be well away, recalling aspects of potty-training unfit for public hearing and moving up through her infant food fads and the time she got threadworms. She wondered sometimes how many other afterthought children ended up being forever cast in the role of The Eternal Baby. Only a few months ago, visiting Shirley and Perry in Cheshire, she'd amazed her mother by cooking and serving spinach along with other Sunday-lunch vegetables.

'But you don't like spinach!' her mother had declared, put out that Lucy had dared to change her tastes, colour in her mother's picture of her in a different way. She smiled again as she thought of that spinach and how she'd managed not to retort that she certainly would still hate spinach served in Shirley's boiled-to-the-death way which bore no resemblance, apart from the colour, to the leaves she'd barely warmed through in sizzling butter and then dusted with nutmeg.

The bus was climbing, up away from the coast and into the densely wooded hills. Lucy opened the window and could smell warm wet scents of musky leaves. There were few houses now, but here and there she could see glimpses through the trees of homes painted in the island's characteristic turquoise, pink or vivid blue, the fronts set on stilts to accommodate the steep hillside. Some were simple, barely more than slatted huts knocked together from aged, mismatched planks with rusting corrugated iron roofs and windows with louvred shutters but no glass. Others were more substantial, still low-built in the local, almost bungalow, style but constructed from sturdy brightly painted concrete. Every house, even the smallest, had a verandah with wicker chairs, tubs of flowers and a couple of snoozing cats, and frequently a sleeping man, face obscured by a hat, as well. They passed thatched shady stalls set up on the roadside selling fruit, vast bunches of bananas, breadfruit, grapefruit and watermelons, everything so much bigger and more lush than at home.

'Imagine living here,' Lucy muttered to herself. The thought of her soon-to-be-homeless state had burrowed its way back into her mind. She pondered gloomily the dismal prospect of looking over dingy, neglected west London flats. They would be so far towards the outer edge of her price range that the cost of tarting up the rooms to an acceptable level of pleasing decor would be pretty much out of the question. They would smell of stale cheese. The carpets would be shredding at the edges and stained with old sour wine and spilled ground-in food. What looked like shadows in the ceilings' corners would every time be darkened paint, discoloured by smuts of neglected dust and the greasy webs of countless long-dead spiders. Perry would offer her money, as he did every time she moved flats, in the hope that she'd buy a place of her own. She would refuse, as she always did, on the increasingly shaky grounds that she was far too old to be relying on her family for handouts and preferred to be independent. Perry would sigh and tell her she was stubborn and he was only thinking of Colette. Shirley would also sigh and say 'It's high time you settled down with a nice man' (as if it was that easy . . .), a situation that ideally required someone with enough of what she called Sterling Qualities to keep her in the manner of Theresa and Plum. As far as Lucy was concerned, she *was* settled (apart from the ending of the flat's lease and the demise of the van, which she certainly didn't want to think about *now*). Adding a Mr Possibly to the equation wouldn't necessarily help.

'Hey, surely that's not a grave, is it? There in that garden?' Mark, just in front of Lucy, leaned across and commented quietly to her as the bus slowed for a road junction. Lucy peered through the foliage into a neat garden planted with exuberant geraniums and a mass of tangled plumbago and the kind of lobster-claw flowers that she'd only previously seen in the most exotic London florists. Chickens were scrabbling around. A litter of half-grown puppies, the colour of dusty camels, was dozing between the house's stilts, and just as the bus started moving again Lucy caught sight of a dark wooden cross marking a patch of raised earth that did look exactly like a grave.

'I'll ask Henry when I see him,' Lucy said to Mark. 'It might be a local tradition to keep your loved ones on site or it could just have been a specially loved dog.'

'Bloody big dog,' he muttered.

'A cow then.' Lucy giggled.

'You don't bury a cow, you eat it.' Mark was now chuckling too, but slightly nervously as if he'd sensed that the Grim Reaper himself might be hanging around the premises, keeping an eye on his investment.

'I'm starving. Anyone got any chocolate?' Luke, up at the front close to Shirley, was getting fidgety.

'You can't last five minutes without an input of junk can you?' she teased him.

'I'm just hungry, s'all. What's the problem?' The driver turned and grinned at him, swerved the bus rather abruptly to the edge of the road and stopped. Saying nothing but still smiling, he opened the door and leapt out, disappearing among the trees.

'See, now look what you've done Luke, whingeing like that.' Shirley poked Luke hard in the ribs, laughing at him. 'Now we're stuck.'

''S'not my fault. Anyway he's probably just gone for a slash.' Lucy sensed his irritation, watching his teenage body hunching down, the shoulders rounding and his head hanging. If she could only draw that attitude, that posture, she thought, capture so exactly the awful adolescent shrinking of confidence mixed with angry bravado, she'd give a copy to every insensitive grandparent on the planet, just to remind them . . .

'So you're hungry, man. Who else?' The driver jumped back into the bus clutching a handful of neat small bananas, which he handed round the family.

'Thanks. Oh, they're so dinky!' Becky unpeeled one delightedly and ate most of it in one go.

'Special, extra sweet, extra small and straight off the plant. We call them rock figs. You don't get so many of those shipped overseas. We keep the sweetest here for us!' Victor laughed, starting the engine again.

The road became a track, bumpy and narrow, climbing through the trees. It was deeply shady and there was a constant smell of slightly rotten sweetness. As he drove, Victor identified trees and shrubs, stopping to pull a piece of bark from a tree ('Mmm, cinnamon on the hoof!' Theresa said, inhaling the fresh sharp scent) and to pick fresh nutmegs, peeling off the pulpy yellow flesh and exposing the scarlet net of mace surrounding the nut.

'So if this is a rainforest, where's the rain?' Becky asked Victor as the bus lurched now over ever-narrower, more bumpy track.

'About ten minutes away,' he told her. 'About the time you'll be swimming in the waterfall pool. We're nearly there. But if you want real rain, you be here next week. There's a big storm coming, it's that time of the year.'

'Do you get hurricanes? What's it like?' Luke was leaning forward, interested in the possibility of a spot of danger. 'And how do you know when they're coming?'

Victor laughed. 'Sure we get hurricanes, usually the tail end of someone else's bad time, though the last one, Hurricane Georges, that was one destroyer.' He tapped the side of his nose and grinned back over the seat to Luke. 'And how we know they're comm', man, well . . .' His voice dropped and Luke leaned forward, fascinated. 'Well,' Victor went on, 'what we do is this thing. We listen to the weather forecast! OK, here we are now at the waterfall. Take some time, enjoy!'

Mark climbed out of the bus and stretched. Every bit of him ached and he hoped it was simply from being in the minibus as it lurched and juddered over the last couple of miles of track. He'd wanted to do the driving, suggested simply hiring a couple of Jeeps and following the map. It had been Simon (typically) who'd been cautious, lecturing him on the inadequacy of island road signs, doing his usual old-woman what-ifs, running through all potential disasters from a simple puncture to the certainty that the cars' canvas roofs would be torn apart by crazed monkeys intent on ripping them all limb from limb.

'Who wants to swim?' Plum went to the wooden platform at the side of the road and peered down steep stone steps into a dizzying canyon. Over the sound of the cascade she could just make out the shrieks of swimmers in water that fell fresh out of the rocks and could easily be near-freezing compared with the humid soupy air. The thought of diving into such refreshing chill was dangerously attractive. It occurred to Plum that if any of the family was harbouring a secretly dodgy heart, an enthusiastic leap from soggy clogging heat into instant cold could be fatal. A small nasty worm of devilment had Plum privately betting with herself as to which of them would be taking the biggest risk. Lucy was all right, being slim and fit and still on the safer side of forty. Theresa, too, although fraught and nervy, never knowingly consumed anything that was going to trouble her cholesterol level and probably had blood pressure that was so used to crashing up and down that she wasn't going to have her aorta panicking over a splash of cold water. Simon, though, he was another matter. He was becomingly alarmingly apple-shaped around the middle, something she'd read was a dangerous pointer for future heart attacks. And he worried a lot about getting older, too. On the basis that you were sometimes unlucky enough to get what you wished for, it was possible that the gods had lined up for him an imminent opportunity for not actually having to *get* any older. Perry and Shirley would go on for ever, she could tell, in spite of Simon watching for every hand twitch (Parkinson's), sweating brow (heart failure) or stumbling gait (imminent stroke). They were halfway down the steep and uneven chasm steps now, Simon holding Shirley's arm and trying to slow her pace, and then he settled her on a bench under a palm-thatched shelter before vanishing with Mark beyond the door of a hut signposted 'Changing Men'.

'If only you could,' Plum heard Theresa mutter behind her as they went in through the 'Changing Ladies' door.

'Could what?'

'Change men. Just hand one over like something that

didn't fit you from Marks & Sparks and get them to give you a better one.'

'Is Mark really that bad?'

'I don't know, Plum. He doesn't say anything much, just drifts around as if conversation is something he used to do but doesn't need to any more. I've forgotten what he's like.'

'Maybe it's the antibiotics. They can make you a bit down.'

'Down? He barely speaks. He's practically comatose. Oh, unless he's out learning bloody *diving* with bloody *Lucy*. I've seen them, with her new friend *Henry*, strolling back up the beach and laughing about this and that and nothing. Never shares the bloody joke. Of course if we'd gone to Italy we'd have the usual things to talk about, things in common. Art and food and stuff. Real things.'

'Couldn't you have that here? Rent a car and go out on your own. There's a couple of galleries in town, I noticed in the guidebook, with some amazing Caribbean art collections.' Bloody snob, Plum thought as she tugged her swimsuit up over her bottom. Probably thinks nothing worth looking at was painted after the sixteenth century. She could imagine Mark, trailing round Tuscan galleries having museum guides read to him by Theresa in her best Home Counties aren't-we-cultured whine. He was probably just as uncommunicative wherever he was, but Theresa, woman with self-improvement on her mind, wouldn't notice.

'Not swimming?' Lucy sat on a rock next to Mark and dabbled her feet in the water. It was incredibly cold; in minutes her feet would be numb. Colette, Becky and Luke were tiptoeing in the shallows on the slippery rocks, daring each other to leap into the icy water, just as she, Theresa and Simon used to do in the freezing grey sea in Devon.

'No, no swimming. I'm not up to having my balls frozen off, even if it would be a fitting punishment.' Lucy looked at him, wary. Clearly there was something on his mind that he might be about to offload on her. 'Please don't,' she wanted to say. He was staring down the path at Theresa, who glared back then dived expertly into the pool. When she came up she didn't gasp and splutter at the cold as others did, but simply pushed her hair out of her eyes and duck-dived neatly under the water again.

'Nerveless, isn't she?' Lucy commented. Mark grunted. He was looking very boyish, she thought, sprawled on the bench in his linen shorts and baggy black T-shirt, and his mood seemed appropriately tetchy and teenage to match.

'She might be nerveless,' he said eventually, fidgeting with a fern leaf he'd picked out of the bank, 'or she might not. I daren't test.'

'OK, I give up. What are you talking about?' Lucy wasn't sure if she wanted to know about some row they'd had, but it seemed, just now, polite at least to give him a chance to tell her to sod off and mind her own business.

Mark turned and studied her face. He looked as if he was working out the level of confidence he could trust her with, which rather made her want to get up, run down the remaining steps and hurl herself into the water with the others. Even Shirley was paddling about, carrying her Dr Scholls in one hand, holding her skirt out of the way with the other and enjoying the refreshing chill on her toes.

Then Mark was off again. 'Have you ever done something bad, not that it would hurt anyone else, not

106

really, so long as they didn't know, and you were sure you'd got away with it, so truly *no-one* was hurt, and then found much later that you hadn't been quite as lucky as you'd thought?' Lucy considered. Well of course she had. Wasn't that what being young and experimenting was all about? 'Yeah, years ago,' she laughed, hoping against instinct that she could keep this light. 'I snogged my best friend's bloke while she was on the school ski trip and then the stupid sod went and confessed all to her about three months later.' Lucy chuckled. 'He said he felt "guilty". I reckoned at the time he was just showing off. Nobody came out of it too well. Sue and I were never the same after. Silence would have been better all round.' Was that the kind of thing he meant?

'Silence isn't going to work with this.' Mark himself went quiet for a long moment then added, 'I've caught something.' Looking down at the water, Lucy for a few seconds thought he was talking about fish. She pictured him with a smart whippy salmon rod, up to his thighs in green waders, a helpful Scottish ghillie standing by with a landing net and a congratulatory smile. Mark wasn't smiling.

'Caught what?' she asked, thinking with dread: please don't let it be AIDS.

'A nasty, persistent little bug, non-specific urethritis to give it its proper title. NSU.'

'Oh.' Lucy nearly added 'is that all?' because compared with The Big One, surely it wasn't that much of a problem. 'Not from Theresa presumably.'

Mark let out a blast of laughter. 'Theresa? God no! Can you imagine . . . ?'

Lucy frowned and looked at him. 'No, I can't, but then she'd probably say the same about you. I bet it never crossed her mind that you'd have an affair, though only because she doesn't have enough imagination. It crosses every other woman's mind.'

'I haven't been having an affair. There's no-one.'

'Then how . . . *Was* it a woman?' Well, you never knew, Mark might well have gone to that kind of school.

'Yes of course it was a bloody woman! Some hooker, no-one I actually knew.' Mark was running his hands through his thick fair hair. It was blonder now, after a few days in strong sun. He was looking perplexed, hot and pressured and scared and resentful, now that he'd weakened and *told*. Good, Lucy thought on behalf of her sister, let him sweat for more reason than just tropical heat.

'So are you going to share this bad news with Theresa or are you going to do the grown-up thing – get yourself fixed and try and keep your dick in your pants from now on?'

Mark sighed and looked at the ground. His feet were now surrounded with shredded fern leaves. He scuffed them into the earth. 'That's the problem. I thought that's what I'd done. Then normal relations, as they say, were resumed with Tess and this bloody sharp pain started up again. Apparently it's not that easy to fix. I'm on the second round of treatment and I might have given it to her. I've got to tell her, otherwise we'll be reinfecting each other for ever.'

'Ah. Well, I guess you have to. Why though, Mark, are you telling me?' Lucy was genuinely curious. She'd never been that close to her brother-in-law, or even to her sister come to that. If they weren't related to her, this was a couple she wasn't likely to have got to know at all, not even in her capacity as a decorator. When Theresa talked about having The Men In (and they frequently *were* in: laying a maple floor in Mark's study, replacing a perfectly good pink bathroom suite with a plain white one simply because pink was so *naff*, measuring up for smart aquamarine decking where the paved kitchen terrace used to be), she *meant* men.

'I think I'm using you for a practice run. I'm waiting for you to call me a lousy cheating heap of shit. I think I'm waiting for you to hit me and tell me to fuck off back to bloody Surrey.'

Lucy shrugged. 'Sorry Mark, I can't oblige, because whatever you've done it just doesn't even begin to affect me, not really. I don't think you're any worse or better than I did before because I simply didn't have any expectations about you. Though . . .' and she swallowed to suppress a threatened giggle, 'I am a bit surprised. I didn't think you were that, well, adventurous, I suppose! Sadly for you, I can't do the other thing you're hoping for either and tell you that it'll be OK, that if you just tell Theresa you love her and that you're sorry it'll all be all right.'

'Yeah, I know. I'm on my own then.'

'Aren't we all though, Mark, aren't we all?' Whyever did he think it needed saying?

Ethan was on the beach in front of the hotel, stretched out under an almond tree. Becky could hear the wind chimes he was selling before she could see him. Then, as she approached, she could smell him, the rich tang of burning marijuana wafting towards her on the warm air.

'Got some for me?' She plonked herself down beside him, watching his eyes as they flickered at the view under her small skirt. He thought she'd simply sat down beside him and he'd sneaked a look. She knew better. Every move she made around him was calculated. She could have sat down smoothly and modestly, carefully folding her legs down beneath her, but it was more fun this way, teasing and tempting to play at being sexy, but pretend she wasn't making any of the running. He handed her the joint and she inhaled, long and deep. The lady who always wore gold was on a nearby lounger, glaring at her. Becky grinned and waved cheekily.

'She'll tell your mom,' Ethan warned.

'Who cares?' Becky lay down and leaned back with her head in his lap. 'She'll probably tell her this too.' Ethan bent and kissed her, lightly on the edge of her mouth, too quickly for her to taste him properly. It left her sensing that the control point had shifted, that she was suddenly feeling a sheer *want* that she hadn't quite bargained for. Oh *God*, she thought, almost squealing out loud, for fuck's sake *do that again*.

Seven

It was the lazy centre of the afternoon. Holidaymakers exhausted from doing nothing lay snoozing on loungers like corpses stretched on slabs in a busy mortuary. Around each one was the debris of fervent relaxation: bottles of suntan lotion gritted with sand, dog-eared paperbacks, bleary snorkel masks, frisbees and tatty straw baskets bought in a last-minute rush at Britain's regional airports, which now had their decorative plaited flowers fast unravelling. The only speedy activity was from the tame black birds that scurried around, close to the dozing holidaymakers, scrabbling noisily for bits of dropped chocolate or crisp crumbs.

The Putney mothers, exhausted from an energetic stint in the children's play area, watched their infants digging soggy sand in the shallows and wondered how on earth they were supposed to keep them from frazzling in the sun. The children threw their hats in the water, hauled off their T-shirts and wanted to roll naked in the sea. Little voices constantly shouting 'Look, Mummy!' were answered with increasingly lethargic 'Yes, darling, lovely!' as the women wondered why it was that men always seemed to need to spend hours making just that one call to the office, exactly at a time when they were most needed for family duty.

The gold lady lit her twenty-fourth cigarette of the day and felt glad, on the whole, Tom wasn't still three years old. The disadvantage was that he tended to count her drinks every evening (and announce the running total rather too loudly) and that he'd noticed a nice young man called Steve was paying her quite a lot of very welcome attention. This had paid off well: Steve had allowed Tom to go with him and his colleagues on the Pirate Adventure cruise, which kept him safely away from that Luke boy who seemed to be an influence not entirely for the good.

Lucy and Shirley strolled along the beach in search of a new place to find a cooling drink. Half a dozen of the beige stray dogs that seemed to live on the shore ran around them, pushing to get close enough to nip at their ankles for attention, and Lucy shooed them away, shouting and clapping. Shirley took no notice but glided along elegantly beside her, turning now and then to watch the day's cruise ships starting to head back out to sea for the overnight journey to another island. She was wearing a flowing loose flowery sleeveless dress and a straw hat with a silk scarf tied round the brim, reminding Lucy not so much of a casual holidaymaker as a lady in the English shires, in search of a genteel tearoom after an afternoon looking round a National Trust manor house and garden.

It seemed to suit Shirley, this heat. The humidity forced her to slow down, to temper the brisk pace at which Lucy remembered her always dashing through life. She'd been one of those speedy mothers who did everything so fast it was next to impossible for a small child to keep up and avoid being told off for dawdling. Shirley had had no truck with shoelaces that got themselves into knots, with shirt buttons that became mysteriously fastened in the wrong holes or with zips that somehow picked up a stray thread and got themselves stuck. Lucy remembered the curt 'Tch, come on, let *me*!' and the strong capable hands wrenching everything into its right place at double any speed Lucy could manage. She'd been a demon with a hairbrush too. Lucy remembered the daily agony of the morning brushing, attacking the stubborn knots in her long hair with swift impatience, as if going at it hard and fast was bound to get better results more efficiently than slow and careful disentangling would have done. 'Quick, come on, we haven't got all day,' was a kind of maternal motto that all three of them remembered well. Sometimes, as at one Surrey Christmas when Mark had been a bit slow with the turkey-carving, one of them would say those magic words and reduce the others to a fit of juvenile giggles. Theresa had once said those words would be on Shirley's tombstone.

'I can get Coca-Cola at home,' Shirley was complaining mildly, 'I fancy something else. Not another fruit punch though, I find them a bit sickly.'

'You could try a lemon and lime drink I read about somewhere. It's called a Bentley.' Lucy laughed, 'Appropriate for a car dealer's wife.'

'*Ex* car dealer's wife. Do you know, that land the last showroom was on was worth a mint. The developers wanted it for an Oddbins with a customer car park. I was glad to be rid of it. It's about time, he's supposed to have been been retired a good twelve years, but you know what he's like, has to keep his hand in. Just as long as he's not under my feet all day.'

So that was *one* of the things they were to be told. Lucy was hugely tempted to ask what else there was on the list. Simon would be hopping mad if she Knew All before he did, though with his reticence, full of certainty that any news could only be the dreaded worst, he was pretty sure never to get round to asking. 'I can hear children. It sounds like playground noise,' she said instead. They were well beyond the hotel boundaries now, and this area at the town end of the beach had only a few buildings, stalls selling the usual beaded jewellery and coconut-shell carvings, pottery and tie-dyed swimwear, the bar where she and Henry had found Becky and a restaurant with a sign that promised 'Best fresh dolphin'. Shirley shuddered. 'Don't let Becky see that, she'll go mad. Half the world is doing dolphin conservation and the other half is eating it.'

'It isn't that sort of dolphin, Ma,' Lucy explained. 'Not the smiley sort, just an ordinary fish. I think it's called dorada.'

'Well why don't they write that on their blackboard then? Confusing people like that.'

Beneath the shade of the next clump of almond trees was a local family picnicking with a selection of cool boxes, crate of beers and pounding reggae music. Lucy recalled summer after-school picnics she and other mums had taken their children for in the local park. There'd been a park-keeper with a passion for peace and quiet, who'd shouted at any children who dared to indulge in noisy ball games on his precious flat-mown grass. Once, when someone had brought along a radio, he'd threatened them with severe repercussions from the bye-laws. She watched as a pair of schoolgirls, not much younger than Colette, joined the group. They were dressed in their school uniform: dark red pleated skirts, white shirts and socks and straw boaters just like the one she'd had to wear in the short summer terms at her own school.

'If we'd had weather like this I wouldn't have minded about my school hat,' she commented to Shirley as they passed.

'I remember you used to get detention for not wearing it on the bus,' her mother laughed.

'Well what was the point? There wasn't exactly an overdose of Cheshire sun for it to protect me from, and half the time it rained anyway and ended up smelling of rotting hay. Colette's school has the same kind of stupid hat, can you believe. I should have sent her to the comprehensive.' The question of Colette's education was one that she rarely felt comfortable about. Her father, when Colette had got to the age of eight, had cornered her at a weak moment and insisted that if she wouldn't take money towards somewhere to live, then at least the best she could do for her daughter was to let him pay for her education. Lucy, typically, had refused and stuck with her decision for the next couple of years. But then, in the ludicrous unlucky dip that is secondary-school allocation, Colette had been refused a place at any of the local schools Lucy would have been happy to see her settling into for the next seven years. In a panic, she had accepted her father's offer. Colette was therefore a pupil at a smart London day school, with a uniform that included a waxed jacket that could only be bought in Harrods but which, apart from its pink and grey lining, looked identical to any that could be found on countryside market stalls at a tenth of the price. Lucy, meeting other new mothers at the first parents' evening the year before, had mentioned that it seemed a peculiar garment for London streets, something more suited to rambling across fields, and had been depressed to be met by blank incomprehension. It occurred to her then that Colette might well be the most impoverished pupil in the entire school, an opinion backed up by Colette coming home one day with a new friend called Isabelle, who nosed around opening every door including the one fronting the gas meter and commented that she lived in a building just like theirs, but in the *whole house*, not one that was divided into six cramped flats.

'Oh look, how pretty, this must be the school for the little ones,' Shirley said as they rounded a bend on the beach. Lucy stopped and gazed at the pale yellow wooden building, brightly painted with a circle of jolly dancing figures holding garlands of flowers. It was about the size of a big Portakabin, surrounded by a sky-blue picket fence. A woman in a green and white checked dress was collecting up infant-sized chairs and taking them inside for the night. Close by, beyond the fence, was a collection of larger wooden buildings, all with thatched verandahs and with doors painted with a single flower and the name of it printed beneath.

'So you've found our school!' Henry emerged from the shadow of a clump of trees, Oliver by his side.

'I was just thinking how wonderfully different this is from schools back home,' Lucy said with a sigh. 'I mean, there's no reason why we should have to put up with dull grey old bricks is there? We should paint things up a bit too, give the more boring buildings a bit of life.'

'They do at some of the nursery schools in the town,' Shirley protested. 'It's nice for the little ones but wouldn't do for a great big comprehensive though, Lucy, be sensible.'

Lucy and Henry grinned at each other. 'It would make sense to me,' Lucy said.

'You'd only get graffiti.' Shirley frowned 'Not just words and stuff. If you painted pictures of *people*,

116

they'd only add rude bits on. You know what kids are like.' Then she turned to Henry and said, 'We're just going for a cool drink, would you like to come with us?' She looked at Oliver approvingly. Lucy could see her assessing how clean and neat his maroon trousers, white shirt and properly knotted tie looked. She was probably, Lucy guessed, contrasting him with the grubby fray-edged boys who fought and jostled at the bus stops close to her home. Shirley disapproved of scruffy loud schoolboys whose shirts hung out of their trousers, who slopped fizzy drinks and shards of chocolate bars down themselves as they swore and bickered in the bus queues.

'Where do the big ones go to school?' Lucy asked Henry as they set off back along the beach.

'There's a senior school in the town. Oliver starts there next year. But after that it isn't like in England where so many folks get to go on to university. Here it's a lot down to how much money you have, or who you know. Unless you're a genius,' he grinned. 'That helps.'

'Helps anywhere,' Lucy agreed, thinking about Colette and her dogged acceptance of her long daily bus journey through traffic-stacked suburbs, a journey that in summer could be stifling with smoggy dust and in winter meant both leaving the house and returning to it in grim darkness. Then there were the hours of homework, pointless repetitive maths exercises and lists of French verbs to learn by heart as if nothing had progressed in the world of education since her own schooldays. There had to be a more interesting, more modern way of learning. The school liked to claim they were 'maximizing each girl's potential' but on the days when Colette fell asleep with her head on a history book Lucy suspected it was more to do with the school maximizing its chances on the educational league table. She should move out to the country, she thought, to where at least in the spring and summer months they could appreciate the changing seasons, feel that nature had some kind of relevance to their lives.

Henry led them all through what looked at the front like a dilapidated beach bar, constructed from loose rough slabs of multicoloured corrugated iron. There was a patchy bird-chewed palm roof and the name 'Yellow Poui' roughly painted over the doorway. Shirley eyed the place with deep suspicion and gave Lucy one of the famous Looks, but she followed Henry through the dark tatty little bar room and out to a shaded garden behind.

'You wouldn't have known all this was here, would you?' Shirley said, looking round with surprised delight and marvelling at the array of immaculately arranged cacti, the eponymous yellow poui flowers, enormous agaves and low-growing palms set into cool gravel. Tables were arranged around a small pool with a fountain in the centre.

The only other customers were from the hotel, the young couple that Simon called the Gropers. Their fingers were interlocked on the table and Lucy managed (just) to resist looking at their legs to see if they too were twined like twisted hazel twigs. It was a long time since she'd had someone wanting to be so literally attached to herself. She smiled across at them, hoping they couldn't read a reluctant flash of envy in her eyes. That kind of never-let-me-go pop-song clinch was strictly for those under twenty-five, fresh new lovers, the ones who hadn't been worn to cynicism by disappointments and failed false starts. Rotten Ross, as she now thought of him, had preferred a distinctly hands-off arrangement, never so much as putting a friendly arm round her crossing a busy street in the pouring London rain. Lucy had assumed it was because he thought they were both a bit past all that surface affection, that it was too teenage and smacked of insecurity. Now that she'd been so casually jettisoned from his life she realized it was simply that he hadn't liked her enough. Sitting opposite Henry, watching the easy relaxed way his body arranged itself between her and Oliver, she wondered what the hell had ever made her think she and Ross had even liked each other at all. At a table in the local Pitcher and Piano, where the noise level had made conversation something that you had to get seriously close together in order to enjoy, he'd sat looking round, his left leg flicking up and down restlessly like a drummer in a very bad rock band. His eyes had been forever darting about watching women coming into the bar, eyeing up the short-skirted groups of them before turning back to her and asking (as if it was simply noise level that drowned her out, as if he was almost interested), 'You were saying?' No wonder Colette had come up with her most cynical yawns when she'd put on make-up and fluffed up her short yellow hair for dates with him. She should have listened when her daughter had written him off (in a brutal ten minutes) as 'not bad-looking but won't last'.

'It's so lovely to have all the family together like this. I can't think when Perry and I were last on holiday with the children. And never with all the grand-children, unless you count Christmas or Easter get-togethers, that sort of thing,' Shirley was saying to Henry, drinking her lime and soda through a red and white straw as contentedly as a child having a teatime treat in McDonald's.

Lucy experimented with a bit of mental distancing.

If anyone had told her a year ago that her mother would be happily chatting in a Caribbean bar in the middle of an afternoon with a young(ish) attractive dreadlock-haired black guy, she'd have dismissed the prophet as totally nuts. Shirley's usual afternoon companions tended to be a collection of golf widows, real widows and ladies heavily involved in charity committees and the few Masonic jollies that women were allowed to attend. They were women who dressed for respectability, never omitting a lace-edged silky slip beneath a skirt, even in the height of summer because it didn't do to risk showing a leg-outline against the sun's glare. Saggy upper arms were always covered with discreet cardigans or a smart pale jacket from Country Casuals. Now, though, Shirley was leaning against the back of her chair, fanning her warm face with her straw hat. She'd removed the silk scarf from the brim and given it to Oliver to use to tease a small tabby cat that reached up and grabbed as he dangled it just out of reach of its unsheathed claws. If Becky or Colette had played like this back at home, they'd have been told pretty firmly to find something a lot less valuable to mess about with.

'There's just Glenda, Oliver and me,' Henry was telling Shirley in answer to a question about his own family. 'Pa died a couple of years back.'

'Did your mother ever think about going back to, well, home?' Shirley wanted to know.

'Glenda? Back to the cold? Are you serious?' Henry laughed and banged on the table. 'My dad was fine working in London when they got together, he'd saved for just about ever to get there and then he meets her and she wants to drag him back to live here.'

'Succeeded, though,' Lucy teased.

'Wasn't it ever difficult though, being . . . er . . .' Lucy recognized Shirley's generation's difficulty with the vocabulary of sensitive race relations.

'A mixed-race family?' Henry supplied for her. 'No. If you want to make it a problem, if you're that kind of ignorant, then you can. Same as the rest of the world. We do have one thing that's the other way though. Glenda paints – you should come and see her work, there's a lot of hers in the big gallery in town. Living here for thirty years doesn't count you in as a Caribbean artist. The big attention's on ancient lifetime residents like Michael Paryag or Canute Caliste who've hardly been further than the next island. Look around you here though, there's Hispanic, Asian, European, African. Most of us here are imports one way or another. There's hardly any Carib Indians left.' He chuckled. 'Blame the Brits, the slave importers and the sugar trade that's rotting the world's teeth.' He grinned, showing his own perfect set. Oliver's were the same.

'I just wish our Lucy could find a nice young man to settle down with. Then it would all be perfect,' Shirley leaned forward and confided to Henry.

'Mum! Do you have to?' Lucy laughed but felt furious inside. It probably hadn't crossed Shirley's mind that she sounded exactly as if she was angling to make Henry her son-in-law before the fortnight was out.

'Parents!' Lucy grumbled to him, glad she was tanned enough to cover a blush. 'At what age do they stop being so embarrassing?'

'Hey, Glenda's just the same. "When you gonna get that boy a little sister?" she says, just when there's the maximum number of single women around.'

Shirley smiled, pleased with herself. 'You see? It's what we're for, all over the world. You two will be just the same with your own children.'

Henry and Lucy looked at each other and grinned. 'I

121

doubt it, Ma,' Lucy said. 'After all, aren't we supposed to learn from experience?'

At the time it had seemed like a good moment. The children were splashing happily in the paddling pool with Marisa (in her new straw hat and thickly slicked with Factor 24) and Theresa had actually said she'd had a lovely day. After he'd told her, he'd planned, they could have a drink alone together at the beach bar, watch the sun go down and start getting on with the good times again, the way cleared, forgiveness and contrition in the air.

He held her hand as they walked along the beach and down to the end of the pontoon to watch the brilliant fish feeding just below the sea's surface. Two of the Phonetech Steves were racing and yelling on jet skis out in the bay. Below there was a school of the stripey sergeant majors, barely visible, rippling with the current, just letting it take them with no effort. Mark wished he could be like that, give himself up to a life with no striving. There were just too many things that had to be kept up. Not only the mortgage, which wasn't as hefty as those of many of his friends: working for a bank did have some perks. It was more a question of that dreaded word: lifestyle. Way back when he was at school – studying for A levels he supposed he was, looking back – he'd assumed that you simply fell into whatever kind of existence you could afford. It had seemed obvious, then. Really rich people lived in whopping great houses, sent their kids to smart expensive schools and drove cars so new they never had to think about checking for tyre-wear. Non-rich people didn't, but they just got on with life. Simple. But he'd reckoned without Theresa who had Aspirations in the same way that some people had eczema: usually dormant but lurking ready beneath the surface to flare up at the slightest provocation.

It had been all right before the children, at least for him. There'd been two incomes, a peaceful, chic home, long French and Italian holidays savouring food and wine. For Theresa, though, the years she'd put in working at the Ministry of Overseas Development were almost entirely years of lost time, of disappointment. The worst days had been those when she'd trailed home and reported, tearfully, that yet another junior colleague had just gone on maternity leave. Of course with two good incomes they could afford the IVF treatment. What they couldn't really afford, on Mark's income alone, were the resulting children, wonderful though they were.

First there was the move to a bigger house at the smart end of Esher (though, Mark wondered, did it actually *have* an unsmart end?) The private obstetrician ('Such precious babies' the clinic had said, as if some babies weren't), the simple delighted abandoning by Theresa of her job (at last with her own baby-swag from the maternity-leave office whip-round) and announcing that she never intended to go back but to dedicate herself to these long-awaited children. 'It's the least they deserve,' she'd said, when he'd tentatively questioned whether child-care alone would be quite as fulfilling as at least a part-time career. The twins were already at a pre-prep school that cost an arm and a leg. His remaining limbs would be on the line after Christmas when Sebastian joined them. He'd suggested checking out the local primary schools and received a Look that rivalled the best of her mother's specials. 'Plum and Simon's are state-educated,' he'd pointed out.

'That's because Plum's inherited peculiar Hampstead principles,' she'd said. Mark couldn't see a problem with Principles. They came a lot cheaper than Aspirations.

'But Luke and Becky have turned out all right.' He tried, weakly, to make a fight of it.

'A matter of opinion,' she'd stated, leaving him in no doubt that his own didn't count.

'There's something I've got to tell you.' Mark started slowly now with a safe enough cliché, he thought. The idea was that she'd guess something far worse than the truth and possibly be relieved. Perhaps she'd react like Lucy. No, of course she wouldn't.

Theresa said nothing, just looked at him and waited. She was supposed to say something along the lines of 'You're having an affair?' and burst into betrayed, dismayed tears. He stuffed his hands into the pockets of his shorts and looked at her eyes which were mystifyingly trusting and lacking in foreboding.

'I've done something very stupid and I'm really, really sorry.' At last a flicker.

'Is it money?' she asked. 'Have you done a Nick Leeson at the bank?'

Mark laughed, then abruptly stopped. 'No, no nothing like that. I've, well I'm not, well.'

'Not well what?'

'That's it, I'm not well. I've caught something and, and I know you'll hate me for this and I don't blame you, I'd feel the same, sort of disgusted and cheated on and all that, but I do love you, really I do and I'd do anything not to be having to tell you this.' Mark stopped wittering on and shoved his hand through his hair. He knew his gesture looked ludicrously schoolboyish on a man of nearly fifty.

Theresa's eyes, when he dared risk looking at them,

were quite steely now. 'You've caught something? I suppose you don't mean a bad cold? So is it herpes, AIDs, *what*?' Her voice rose, panic setting in as she voiced the possibilities.

'God no, nothing that bad. It's NSU. I had to go to the clap clinic and get treatment. NSU's not as bad as—'

'Not as bad as *WHAT* exactly? Jesus! I can't believe this! You said you'd got cystitis.' Theresa put her hands over her ears, then her eyes, blocking him right out.

Mark scuffed his feet and looked at his bare brown toes. He felt as if all of him was contaminated, that he sweated toxins.

'Why?' Theresa howled the word, then added, 'And *who*? What filthy little tart have you been having it off with?'

Mark shrugged, a dangerous gesture but dreadfully appropriate. 'Er, yes. It was, actually. A tart.'

Theresa gazed at him, puzzled, not understanding. 'I haven't been having an affair,' he insisted, as if he was giving her the good news. 'I wouldn't do that, I wouldn't . . .'

'What? You wouldn't be *unfaithful*? So you've been *paying* for it? And that's not as fucking *bad*? Shit, I feel sick.' Theresa wrapped her arms across her stomach and stared down at the pretty fish. 'Always the same one?' she then asked.

'No. I didn't even know their names. Only once or twice.'

'Is that supposed to make it all right, because if you think it does . . .'

'No. No I don't.' There was a silence.

'Why weren't you more careful? I mean haven't you heard of condoms?'

'I was.' He shrugged miserably. 'One split.'

Theresa gave a brief laugh. 'Oh well it would. You always were *such* a *big* boy, weren't you?'

'I'm so sorry,' he ventured.

'Sorry doesn't come close,' she muttered. 'Just tell me, what did you go out looking for that you couldn't get at home?'

He shrugged again. 'There's nothing, just, oh I don't know. The risk, the secrecy, just *different* . . . I won't do it again, not ever.' She glared at him, her face full of hate. 'Why the hell not?' she sneered. 'You sure as fucking hell won't be doing it with me.'

'What's a clap clinic?' Colette hoped it was all right to ask Luke, that it wasn't something that a girl of her age should know by now. She'd known most things ahead of others at her school, probably still did know some stuff that all those nice little good-at-netball girls would never need to find out about, like where to get a pregnancy-test kit in the middle of the night when everything was shut and your mother was tearful and scared. And she also knew that just because your mother had the kind of boyfriend (once, and very briefly) who was really friendly and bought you a PlayStation didn't mean he couldn't also be the sort who liked to stroke under your school skirt to the top of your leg just when you'd got to your best-ever level on Final Fantasy Seven. The police had come about that one, and then they'd moved on to another flat, fast.

'It's where you go to get fixed up when you've caught clap,' Luke told her blankly, as if he could hardly believe she was asking this.

'But what's clap?'

He folded his arms and gave her a superior smile.

126

'It's a sexually transmitted disease. Haven't you done that lesson in school yet?'

Colette laughed. 'At my school? I don't suppose we ever will,' she told him, hoping, stalling, praying that he wouldn't ask her why she wanted to know. She'd have to say it was something she'd been reading, not something she'd been accidentally overhearing down on the rocks at the end of the pontoon. After all, she quite liked Mark.

Eight

It was raining again. Becky complained that if she'd wanted to get soaked right through to her knickers she could've stayed in England and walked very slowly to school every drizzly morning without a jacket. Shirley told her, quite sharply and in front of everybody in the bar after dinner, that she was a spoilt brat who didn't deserve any holiday more luxurious than a cold rainy week in a leaky tent in Wales.

In the daytime after the clouds opened and rain hurtled to the ground, steam rose when the sun scorched through and the heavy soaking bougainvillea dripped and sweltered. Plum said she could almost see it growing as she watched. She wished her garden flourished like this. At home in Wimbledon, heavy rain followed by generous sun always meant an extra helping of slugs and snails with newly sharpened appetites.

In the evening the wind became brisker and blew welcome gusts of cooling air across the verandah along with more stinging blasts of rain. At dinner, every table occupied by British guests had at least one question for the waiters about what the weather was going to do the next day. The staff shrugged and smiled and reminded them it was the rainy season. The words 'What did you expect?' hovered, politely unsaid. The young couple that Simon called the Gropers were barely on speaking terms. Lucy could read, from their slumped and miserable bodies as they sullenly and silently chewed their jerk chicken and rice, that something in their holiday had gone seriously wrong.

'They're getting married on Tuesday,' Plum told Lucy, following her gaze across the dining room, 'and that's about when the big storm's due.'

'What, they're getting married here? Just the two of them with no family?' Shirley looked horrified.

'Probably cheaper. A proper English wedding can set you back a fortune,' Perry chipped in, then added, winking at Lucy, 'not that I'd grudge it. It's what a girl's father's for, saving up for her big day.' He patted the area on his chest where he kept his wallet. 'I've had yours gathering interest for a long while. There's more than enough to do you proud.'

Lucy's smile was a strained one. 'Dad, just do me a favour and lose it on the horses or give it to a cats' home, will you? You know I'd hate that kind of wedding, all meringue frock and a sit-down rubber-chicken lunch at the Masonic hall.'

Shirley frowned. 'Chances of seeing you in a proper frock. Mind you, if you had the kind of job where you didn't wear paint-stained old overalls, you might . . . well, I won't go on but you don't do yourself any favours.'

'Come on now, leave her alone, she's all grown-up,' Simon pleaded.

'And doing perfectly well without a man in her life,' Plum chipped in.

'And your hair used to be so long and feminine.' Shirley, on the outside of three glasses of white wine, was on a roll now.

'Shit, I don't believe this.' Lucy flung her napkin on the table and got up. 'Sorry, but I'm losing my appetite. I think I'll join Theresa in having a migraine.'

Colette stared after her, wondering if she should show she was on her side and get up and go with her. She was cross with her grandmother because she was being exactly like Lucy had thought she'd be before they left. Lucy had so nearly said no, had only given in because Theresa had rung up and said she'd be spoiling things for everyone if she didn't come on this holiday. Colette, though, had seen Tom at the next table eating slices of mango and banana with ice cream and chocolate sauce and she wanted to stay and have some. She leaned across and asked him if it was as nice as it looked and he told her it was loads better than that. His mother, the gold lady, glared at her, which made her feel even more that life wasn't fair. Luke saw and grinned across the table at her. 'We'll have a game of table tennis later, if you want to,' he offered. She felt grateful but depressed, like she had at school the time Samantha Cotton invited her to her birthday party after Isabelle had been such a cow and told all the class that Colette lived in a titchy flat the size of their dog's basket and that her mum drove a beaten-up old van. She'd felt quite shocked that anyone could make any big deal of it and realized she'd discovered real snobbery for the first time in her life. Even Theresa didn't sneer at people for being rich or poor. What had bothered her though was the same as what bothered her now: would Samantha Cotton have invited her to the party if she hadn't just wanted to get back at horrible Isabelle whom nobody much liked? Would Luke really want to spend the evening playing table tennis with her if he hadn't been sure the gold lady would hear him being nice to his cousin?

*   *   *

Theresa lay on her bed flicking through the TV channels. She kept veering between hunger and tooth-clenching nausea and if she could get the energy organized she knew she should order something light from room service. She felt like a sulking child: everyone else was in the restaurant having a lovely dinner and here she was pretending to feel awful because she couldn't face, yet, playing the Happy Wife with Mark. Annoyingly, she could feel a real headache coming on, which might be connected with drinking all the miniature bottles of gin from the minibar and then finding that somehow she'd got through all the little vodkas as well. She wanted to cry and cry, but she was too angry for tears. Each time she managed to feel sad enough to produce some, adrenalin-fuelled fury stopped them coming out and made her stamp across the room and back, like a prisoner pacing out a life sentence, trying to thrash out the bitterness.

The worst thing was the wondering why, the feeling of being so sort of *passed over*. She was chewed up inside with curiosity. What had Mark wanted to do with a paid stranger that he hadn't done with her? Was it leather, bondage, or simply a sleazy in-car blow job, parked where it was public enough for the thrilling risk of being caught? She could have done all that. All she'd needed was the hint that safely marital in-bed sex was getting a bit uninteresting. Or was that true? Perhaps there had been hints that she'd chosen to ignore. Perhaps when she read magazines at the hairdresser she shouldn't always skip past the articles that promised things like 'Scorching sex tips for burnt-out lovers'. It had been easy enough, convenient enough, to assume that if Mark didn't actively complain then he wasn't unhappy the way things were. And besides,

131

she didn't want Bernard, retouching her highlights, to catch her avidly reading (even jotting down notes) about how to slide her tongue round previously unthought-of corners.

Theresa went to the window, pulled back the curtains and opened the sliding door. Great sheets of rain were pouring from the domed roof of the white iron pergola by the pool, like a power shower off a bald head. There was no-one in sight and, feeling childishly as if she was now so alone that no-one would miss her if she went out and drowned herself, she stepped onto the terrace, climbed over the balcony rail, wandered out into the downpour and onto the beach.

'I didn't think you'd be here.' Even as Lucy said the words she realized they sounded both senseless and ridiculous. Henry obviously thought the same and laughed loudly. 'Right, so who *were* you looking for down at the dive shop in the dark and in the pouring rain?'

'Hey, no-one! I was just walking on the beach and I saw the light was on. I only looked in because someone could have been robbing the wetsuit store!'

'And you'd have done what? Fought them off with your bare hands?'

Lucy didn't mind him teasing her. He wasn't trying to score points, to put her down. Ross used to tease her about forever being dappled with flecks of paint. She'd thought he'd just found it funny, endearing even, but then once, in a restaurant with friends of his – glossy air stewardesses and various airline staff – he'd grabbed her hand and held it up to show them all, pointing to traces of the Paint Library's Elizabethan Red down her nails, saying wasn't it lucky she wasn't a surgeon, she'd be coming home covered in patients' blood. The slick stewardesses had smirked and giggled, putting their delicately manicured hands to their sheeny pencil-outlined mouths in a gesture of calculated prettiness that Lucy was sure must have been taught at flight-crew school.

'I'd have sneaked away and pretended I'd seen nothing,' Lucy teased back. 'And in the morning I'd have told you I'd had a strange dream, all about burglars making off with your entire stock. You'd have been astounded at my prophetic powers.'

'Seriously, you'd have done the right thing.' Henry went to the fridge at the back of the shop, pulled out a couple of Carib beers and handed one to Lucy. She settled on an upturned crate that in the morning would contain the day's diving equipment for the boat. Henry went on, 'Theft on this island is usually to do with drugs. There's a lot of real poverty here, it's not all just smiling, pretty natives and welcome-to-paradise stuff that you tourists see. When you look at those smart yachts anchored just off the reef, sometimes you have to think about where they've come from and what they might be carrying. I don't ask any questions, I don't want to get shot.'

'That bad?'

'No, not that bad. Just a little bit close to that bad, just sometimes. Ninety-nine per cent of sailboats are American charters for the vacation trade. But for those few that aren't for real the holiday trade's a good cover. Anyway,' Henry pushed the door open to see how much rain was still falling, 'most of the yachts are on their way out of here now, heading up to a safer harbour in Barbados before the big storm gets here.'

'How big does a big storm get?'

'They're talking hurricane level. We don't get that many, but when they hit . . . wow!'

'So what do you do?'

133

'You board up, dig in and wait! All bad things pass.'

'Not as quickly as good things.'

'Well that's OK,' he laughed, 'it means you have every excuse to make sure you really enjoy them while you can.'

'We had a sort of hurricane in England once, back in the Eighties. Colette was a baby. I think it was the first time she slept through the night.'

Henry laughed. 'She wouldn't sleep through the ones we get here, I promise you.'

'Yeah, well you would say that wouldn't you?' Lucy mocked him. 'It's the "everything's bigger in Texas" principle.' But Henry wasn't smiling any more. 'Hey, seriously, if we do get a warning, you do what the hotel management tell you, like *exactly*. You don't go outside and pick fights with the bad weather we get here. People die, but they're usually people who don't follow the rules.'

'You're cheery tonight. Nothing but warnings, "don't do this, don't do that", you sound like my dad.'

'Your dad's cool, I'll take it as a compliment.' Lucy groaned and he laughed at her. 'So that's why you're wandering around on the dark, wet dangerous beach by yourself; getting away from the family.'

'That obvious? I love them but . . .'

'And I love Glenda, but . . . It's the same here. Why do you think I'm down here sorting tomorrow's boat stocks when I could be home watching Glenda teach Oliver how to appreciate the finer points of vintage Flintstones cartoons on channel 48? She lives above her studio just along the street but she's always stopping by. That's the way family is here, but sometimes a man just needs peace.'

'So here we are, a pair of exiles.' It didn't sound too bad, Lucy thought. It was a bit like running away, but only as far as the garden shed when you're a child with a small but satisfyingly niggly grudge against a parent. You felt safe enough, but just distant enough too. Then Henry was next to her, close enough for her to scent the salty sea on him. She closed her eyes, relaxed and waited.

The rain had almost stopped and the sand beneath Theresa's bare feet felt like smooth wet concrete. She couldn't see very well where she was going and assumed it was a mixture of the rain and the tears which had, eventually, decided to let themselves out. She, like Lucy, was actually quite enjoying herself now. There was something about thoroughly justified grief and anger. This wasn't some petty row, some silly argument about a triviality like who'd forgotten to pay the Amex bill: this was the real, dramatic thing. It was almost sexy. If Mark turned up on this beach now . . . if he was just the other side of that row of palm trees, she couldn't swear she wouldn't wrestle him to the sand and show him there was nothing he could buy from any lousy impersonal money-grabbing hooker that he couldn't get for for no price at all from her. Of course he wouldn't be there, but she'd walk on anyway and look.

Theresa tripped over the trunk of the first tree, the one that lay almost flat out along the beach, curving gracefully skywards only halfway along. She swore, and lay sprawled on the gritty soaking sand, her leg painfully grazed on its matty leaf-stalk trunk. The tree, in daylight, looked like the sort on every travel poster, half-reclining lazily on the sand, its magnificent spread of vast glossy leaves vivid against a brilliant blue sky. Theresa thought it was a fraud, appealing so gorgeously, grandly upwards like that, luring people to come to paradise and then lying there tripping them up in the dark.

Theresa lay on her back and let drops of rain, reduced now to lukewarm drizzle, fall into her open mouth. From the circular palm-covered beachfront games area back at the hotel she could hear the click-click of a table-tennis game and bursts of young laughter. There was more laughter closer to her as well. Keeping completely still and concentrating, she identified low, intimate, sexy murmurings, sounds she really didn't want to hear just now. She rolled over, grabbed the shaggy hostile palm trunk and hauled herself up. It was no way to treat a pale blue linen Nicole Farhi dress, it occurred to her, covering it in wet sand. The rest of her felt dirty too, filthy inside and all over with some unknown, uninvited germ that Mark might have let loose in her. She padded towards the sea and splashed about in the warm cleansing shallows. The soft waves washed over the hem of her dress and she flicked at the fabric, rinsing off the sand. She'd thought the beach shelved gently here but her feet seemed to be pitching steeply forwards. Peculiarly detached, somehow, as she went deeper and deeper, not quite sure what she was doing and unable to aim herself back towards the lights on shore, she started swimming awkwardly as she plunged on out of her depth, hampered by the clinging shift dress that hadn't exactly a generous width for walking, let alone swimming. So this is how people drown, she thought vaguely to herself, they just drift off into water in the wrong outfit.

The water felt colder as she moved out deeper, and jolted her senses. Theresa didn't at all want to drown. She didn't want Mark to think that for the sake of his bit of tacky off-limits sex she would go to the trouble of destroying herself and her family. She was determined, suddenly, not even to let him see her sulk. She wouldn't give it the importance it didn't deserve. How hard that would be she didn't yet know. What she did know was that it was getting hard to reach the shore. There were lights everywhere: at the hotel, on the end of the pontoon, in the villas on the far headland where her parents were staying, lights out to sea on tankers and cruise ships and lamps swaying high on the rigging of moored yachts in the bay. Further away the town of Teignmouth blazed the night away. She swam in a circle, tired now but warmer and strangely elated. Her head drifted beneath the water and she didn't fight hard to come back up. When she did surface, there was someone beside her, a girl with flowing yellow hair. She thought of mermaids and smiled. Mermaids never drown. She'd read that on a Cornish gravestone and felt sad about the grave's occupant, who presumably had. Perhaps the sea was heaven.

'Come *on*, you thick dumb tart! Swim with us, don't just give up!' There was a man as well. Mer-man, mer-bloke? What? Theresa thought. He was pulling at her arm, the girl had the other one and they'd taken her over, towing her towards somewhere safe. She let go and trusted them, floating in her unsuitable, but clean blue dress towards the hotel lights.

'You'll be all right now.' The girl sounded kind, as if she felt gently sorry for Theresa.

'When she's sober,' she heard the man mutter.

Theresa giggled. 'I'm glad I wasn't skinny-dipping,' she said, pulling her dress down over her thighs as she staggered out of the shallow water onto the beach.

'Aren't we bloody all?' said the girl.

The return of the blazing sun that all the guests felt entitled to made breakfast a slightly overexcited time, shrill with the voices of the bossiest planning the day's structure for the meeker or lazier. Simon was pleased with himself for having got up early and been busy making arrangements. The family were to go out, for the whole day, on a trip around the island on a catamaran. A barbecue lunch on a deserted beach was included and he was as certain as he could be that no-one would object.

'Not all *day*!' Becky screeched. 'I'm supposed to be—'

'What? Supposed to be what?' Plum was quick to ask. She'd seen the hunky young jewellery-seller close to Becky on the beach, the two of them giggling with their heads together. He was too old for her, Simon had said, and for once she'd been inclined to agree. The tawdry reputation of some British girls on holiday was common knowledge at exotic destinations all across the world, and Plum was well aware that Becky in her skimpy bikinis and sexy little midriff-baring tops looked exactly like a sweet and tempting piece of easy meat. Plum herself was pretty sure that Becky was still a virgin, though she certainly wasn't going to ask her. After all, what could she do with a worrying answer?

'I just said I might see someone, that's all.' Becky quietened as fast as she'd flared up. For once they were tempting her with something that she might actually mind missing out on and she wasn't going to argue, and it still rankled that her gran had called her spoilt. 'I'll maybe see them later.' Plum smiled to herself, recognizing the skill with which Becky managed to avoid giving away even the sex of her appointee. Such crafty teenage tricks would be handy to keep for use later in life.

Simon was relieved to be escaping the environment

of the hotel. He'd become highly nervous of accidentally meeting the maid he'd so stupidly (and clumsily)
goosed in the bedroom and was sure that behind every
staff member's polite smile was the powerful and terrible knowledge that He was The One. The worst thing
was, he couldn't, hand on heart, swear it wouldn't happen again. Those high swaying bottoms, the leisurely,
provocative walks and the glistening intricacy of the
black multi-plaited hair aroused him quite extra-
ordinarily. The pale feeble flicker of a tan that the
European women lying slab-like on poolside loungers
were so pleased with themselves for acquiring simply
didn't bring even the smallest glow of lust to his loins.
Plum, bless her, assumed he was simply drinking too
much to be capable. A couple of times he'd made a
courteous sexual effort and constructed for himself a
rather smutty but pretty effective fantasy that involved
the room maid, a bottle of baby oil and a locked laun-
dry store, but he could tell that Plum was glad enough
to get back to the book she was reading.

'You'll be coming, won't you? Not going off diving
with your new friend?' Simon asked Lucy. After she'd
stormed out of the restaurant the night before, and with
Theresa not even turning up for dinner at all (migraine;
since when had she suffered from migraines?), he wondered if he was the only one in the family with a
suitable sense of team spirit.

'Yes I'll come,' Lucy told him. 'Though if Mum
thinks that by getting me for a full day on a boat she's
got me captive for another dose of nagging about settling for Mr Take-What-You-Can-Get-at-Your-Age then
I swear I'll dive overboard and swim to shore, even if
there's sharks.'

'I don't think she'll dare.' He grinned. 'Colette told
her off after you'd run away. Announced loud and

clear something like "Mum's decided she doesn't actually like men very much." That shut her up, you could see the cogs turning while she started wondering if you'd turned into a lesbian.'

'I knew those painting overalls were good for something. By the way, how's Theresa's headache? Is she coming?'

'Theresa's fine. And yes, I'm coming.' Theresa looked slightly bizarre, Lucy thought, out in the bright morning air with full eye ma ke-up and glossy lipstick. The words 'brave face' came straight into her mind. Mark must have told her, but Lucy knew she was the last one her sister would confide in. She rather wished Mark hadn't either, some things you'd just rather not know.

The smallest children weren't coming with them. Sebastian's unreliable digestion when it came to travelling was given as the reason, but Mark had admitted to Perry that he felt abject terror at the thought of being responsible for making sure three such small children didn't fall off the catamaran. Marisa was taking them to see a puppet show at a hotel further along the beach and had found a friendly Norland nanny in charge of one small baby to share her gripes about her employers with.

They were all assembled on the pontoon with supplies of bottled water, sunhats and plenty of high-factor suntan lotion. Luke and Colette sat on the edge, dangling their feet into the water and watching the fish. The boat was on its way; Mark had spotted it rounding the furthest headland. Shirley felt apprehensive: she was sure she could hear music coming from the boat's direction and trusted that it would be switched off once they were on board so they could have a calm, peaceful trip.

'Theresa! Have you recovered?'

'Lord, it's the Gropers,' Simon muttered to Lucy.

Theresa scuttled quickly away from her family group and tried to head off the young couple further along the pontoon. She almost hurled herself at them in her eagerness to keep them out of the family's collective sharp earshot, but Plum and Lucy, perhaps slyly suspecting entertainment value, were beside her.

'After last night – we were worried about leaving you to go back to your room all alone like that.' The girl's voice, unfortunately for Theresa, was a vibrant and carrying one. She touched Plum on the arm, a friendly, confiding gesture. 'State of her, had more than a few, but then don't we all now and then? Only human! Thought she'd drown though.'

'Leave it, Cathy,' the man mumbled at her, 'you're being mouthy.'

'Sorry Paul,' Cathy said, then turned back to Theresa. 'But next time you go for a midnight swim, take a friend just for safety. Hope your dress was OK. You going on the boat trip?'

Theresa's smile was a tight, fraught one and her reply was a clipped 'Yes', which Lucy thought rather inadequate and rude in the circumstances, as it seemed serious thanks for the saving of life might be more to the point. Lucy looked at Mark but he was gazing out to sea, studying the approaching boat. So he'd definitely confessed all to Theresa, then. Whatever alcohol-soaked trouble Theresa had been rescued from the night before just had to be a reaction to his news. Unless, of course, Theresa had a secret double life as the night-wandering gin-monster of Esher.

The catamaran was enormous, with decks on each hull, a full-scale bar and small galley below in the centre. Lucy held Shirley's arm as she climbed aboard and found her somewhere to sit on the deck as far as she could get from the booming effects of the pounding reggae music. Cathy and Paul clambered across the deck and made straight for the bar area and there were several passengers already settled aboard, which didn't please Perry. He said to Simon, 'I thought you'd booked a whole boat, not just seats on some kind of disco ferry.'

'That would have cost a fortune, Dad. These things take up to thirty people.'

'I keep telling you, Simon, money's not a problem. If we'd had the boat to ourselves we could have got the bloody music turned down.'

Lucy felt sorry for Simon, who'd simply been doing his best to get things right. He sat near the back of the boat with his shoulders slumped, reminding Lucy of when she was little and he decided that the role of Middle Child was a hard one to have been dealt. He must have been close to fifteen, growing so fast that she, at five, thought he looked like a pale skinny ghost. She remembered him nagging at Shirley to let down the hem on his grey school trousers and how she'd kept saying she'd get round to it. In the end, mortified by the constant sight of the top of his grey school socks, he'd had a go at doing it himself, hacking at the stubborn stitches with Shirley's stitch-ripper and managing to slice a massive hole in the fabric. 'I was only trying to help,' he'd claimed, justifiably, hunching miserably on their big maroon Dralon sofa with the unwearable trousers hanging like the lifeless legs of a ventriloquist's abandoned dummy across his lap.

The sun was scorching, reflecting off the sea and doubling its damage potential. There was no shade on the boat, but the breeze was cool, deceptive in making the passengers feel that the sun wasn't doing its worst.

Lucy could see Cathy and Paul settling to put away as many bottles of Carib beer as they could manage, and Becky drifted off to chat to them and sneak a couple of bottles for herself at the same time. Shirley sat watching the palm-fringed coastline as they sped past craggy hillside villages, small fields of brown and white goats and curly-horned thin cows that were tethered singly under shade close to brightly painted homesteads.

'If this was English coastline it would be nothing but horrible off-white bungalows,' Plum commented, admiring the hot, vivid colours of the houses dotted around on the hillsides. 'And I've never understood the dreary British obsession with net curtains.'

'You need them for privacy.' Shirley was a great believer in nets and felt they were a tradition that deserved defending.

'Even when you put them on the Velux windows when you had the roof space converted, and the only people who could see in would have to be in a passing helicopter?' Lucy teased.

Shirley gave her one of the Looks. 'We haven't come all the way to this beautiful place to argue about net curtains,' she said. 'We can do that at home.'

'What *have* we come here for, actually?' Simon asked. Lucy looked at him. He was staring at the sea as if he wished he hadn't, at least not yet, released this particular bull into the ring for Shirley to fight with.

'We've come to be together, as a family, Simon. To remind ourselves of what that means. That's all,' she said. 'I know you, I know you've been angling for a deep dark motive since the day we told you we were making the booking. Just relax, just enjoy yourself.'

It was on the way back later that afternoon that Shirley started to tremble. Amazingly, it wasn't Simon who first noticed, because he was occupied being seasick over the back of the catamaran. The Atlantic side of the island didn't have the placid leisurely waves of the western, Caribbean side. Here the sea rolled and heaved and fat rollers crashed to the shore and spumed high off the rocks. Only Plum remained completely unperturbed, absorbed in the final chapter of Ruth Rendell. Cathy and Paul huddled together for warmth in this much cooler wind. Mark and Theresa, sitting silently on separate hulls like a pair of seagulls, focused against nausea on the horizon. Becky, Luke and Perry were in a row holding tightly to the deck ropes, with Colette in front of them and Perry praying she wouldn't feel sick and be put off boat trips for ever.

Shirley and Lucy were comfortable on proper seats up by the galley. Music was still booming out, but they were too tired now to be anything but oblivious to it. Shirley had done a lot of swimming, during the lunchtime stop on the shore. The beach had been stunning, a stretch of deserted, pale sand that glinted as if diamond shavings had been grated over it. More shelter would have been good – wherever she sat beneath the young and wispy palms she hadn't managed to get the whole of her in the shade at any one time. She'd taken refuge under the sea. She'd never tried snorkelling before and had enjoyed the strange sensation of being among, not above, fish as they went about doing whatever fish do. She hadn't seen the dolphin, which she rather regretted, though it was nice that it had let Becky swim along with it, stroke it even, because that seemed to be what the younger ones liked to do. She couldn't imagine wanting to stroke one herself, sure that it would be a slimy, greasy-skinned thing and also that, really, it wouldn't like it. They might bite. You couldn't trust just everything (or everyone) that smiled.

When she started to shiver, Shirley at first thought she was getting chilled. The sea was rougher now, but as she'd never been on any kind of British boat trip that had involved anything less than a force five cross-Channel wind she didn't feel queasy. She worried mildly about Simon, though, who had once managed to get seasick in a canoe on Lake Windermere, and who had eaten a vast amount of the barbecued prawns with chilli sauce at lunchtime.

'Are you all right?' Lucy asked. She was sitting close beside her but her voice sounded as if it was miles away, like someone down a telephone back in the days of trunk calls. 'You're looking a bit pale.' This was disappointing, Shirley thought, especially as she'd looked in the mirror that morning and seen a tanned face that the younger women of Wilmslow paid a fortune in sunbed fees to acquire every winter. She put her left hand up to move stray hair out of her eyes and found that the hand didn't quite know where to go. It waved about, lost for a moment, forgetting where it was supposed to be, what it should do. A prickle of confusion warmed the back of Shirley's neck, then the hand recalled what was asked of it and she pushed the strand of hair behind her ear beneath her hat.

'You're cold. You're shaking.'

'No, I'm not cold,' she protested. The hand was back in her lap with the other one now and she raised both sets of fingers a little. They trembled, hard, as if they were seriously afraid of some terror that the rest of her hadn't yet discovered. Lucy's hand came down over the two of hers and stilled them.

'I'm just a bit tired, that's all,' Shirley told her. Her head ached too, a delicate but persistent throb slightly below the surface of her right temple. She would be all right with a couple of aspirin and a sleep.

Nine

Early in the evening the bar was noisier than usual, with the guests assembling before dinner to discuss the notices about the approaching hurricane that had been placed on their beds while they were out enjoying the day. The air was buzzing with against-the-elements jokes along with reminiscences about the Last Lot, for everyone British thought they'd seen the worst a hurricane could throw at them, having witnessed the odd BMW crushed by a falling oak, along with a Sussex hillside of struck-down pines. There was talk of battening down hatches and Dunkirk spirit (this last followed by behind-the-hand sniggers, guilty looks round for German guests and hissings about 'Don't-mention-the-war').

Several anxious souls murmured about contacting tour reps with a view to arranging an earlier flight home, but they were witheringly accused either of a ratlike abandoning of ship or of missing out on a potentially thrilling experience, as if it was merely another unmissable local attraction, rating five stars in the guidebook. A frantic Italian couple were avidly questioning the hotel manager, wanting more precise details than he was able to give. However hard he insisted he didn't yet know if the hurricane was even heading for the island, the couple pressed him to tell them more, as if he had a hotline to the elemental gods and was deliberately keeping the truth from them.

Simon brought his hurricane instructions into the bar with him and perched on a stool next to Lucy. 'I suppose we've all got these,' he said, waving the sheet of paper.

Lucy grinned at him. 'Well I expect so, Simon, unless you think God is directing a special storm just at you.' Simon frowned. 'You shouldn't joke about it, Lucy. There could be serious danger.' He was in his own element now, she realized, getting ready to orchestrate the family's survival in the face of disaster.

'Listen to this,' he said, reading aloud. '"Pack all your belongings in a suitcase, put the case inside the plastic bag provided and place high in wardrobe . . ."'

'Amazing, isn't it?' Theresa interrupted, arriving just in time to claim the last bar-stool. 'Surely they don't really expect us to pack *all* our stuff up, do they? All the stuff in the drawers, everything off the hangers, I mean if it's already *in* the wardrobe . . .'

'If that's what it says . . .' The gold lady leaned across and helped herself to cashew nuts from the bowl in front of Lucy.

'Absolutely.' Simon was delighted to find an ally. 'You must do just what it says; after all, the people here have gone through all this before and they know what they're doing. We've got no idea.'

Theresa gave him a look that would have crumpled a non-relative. 'Thank you Simon, yes I do realize that, but I wonder if it might be a bit over the top, possibly connected with avoiding tricky insurance claims?'

'We're all *doomed*!' one of the Steves mocked loudly from the far end of the bar. Everyone laughed except Simon and the bar staff, who were too busy dealing with the extra drinks orders that the overexcited guests seemed to need.

'And what about this bit, about actually *getting in* the wardrobe?' Theresa's perfect cherry-varnished fingernail stabbed at the paper. 'How are we supposed to get in if it's full of luggage? Tell me that, Simon.'

'They're quite big,' he ventured.

'Depends how much luggage you've got,' she countered. 'And I do have three children and an au pair to cram in as well. It would be like one of those silly student charity stunts they used to do: how many geographers can you cram into a phone box.'

Lucy felt fidgety. The others would be arriving in a few minutes and there was something on her mind that she wanted to share with just Simon and Theresa. 'Listen, I want to talk to you two. Come outside onto the terrace.'

'Oh a mystery, I could do with some distraction.' Theresa picked up her daiquiri and followed, tripping along smartly on her kitten-heeled scarlet mules. She really did look supremely glamorous tonight, Lucy thought, as if this was a special occasion. As well as her nails being wonderfully manicured, her hair had been glossily blow-dried and Lucy knew she must have put in an hour or two in the beauty salon on the top floor. Her dress was spaghetti-strapped, sleek navy blue and fluted a little just below her knees. Lucy guessed it was by Ghost, and probably cost a good percentage of what she herself earned in a week. She tried not to mind, reminding herself that after all what she had *was* what she earned, not what she'd married. Somehow it didn't feel quite as comforting as usual.

'So what's the big secret?' Simon settled himself at a small ornate iron table, tracing his fingers over the leaf shapes on the surface.

148

'It's not really a secret. It's Mum.' There was no point skirting round it. 'On the boat she was really shaky, and she sort of, well, she sort of lost it a bit . . .'

'Lost what?' Theresa sipped her drink and looked puzzled.

'It was rather choppy. She probably felt dodgy,' Simon contributed, but he was frowning, considering.

'Not as bad as you did. I saw you chucking up over the side.' Theresa giggled. 'What a waste of all those lovely prawns!'

'Back to Mum.' Lucy glanced round. Soon the others would be looking for them. 'She doesn't get seasick. She's got a stomach like cast iron. Don't you remember that time when we went to the Isle of Man in a force nine and she calmly carried on knitting while everyone else was groaning and dying and praying around her? No, this was strange, as if her brain had gone walkabout and she couldn't quite find it. And she shook so much, really trembling, and when we got off the boat she was wobbly. Dad had to hold her arm. I watched: he was still holding on to her all the way back to the villa. It's the first time I've seen her looking frail.'

'So what are you saying?' Theresa had finished her drink and she waved to a waiter across the terrace for a refill.

'I think she got seriously dizzy, had a bit of what she'd call a "turn". I think maybe we should ask Pa about it, in case it's not the first time. Simon might have been right all the time, there might be stuff about her being ill that they aren't telling us.'

'I knew it,' he said, 'I thought they'd have told us by now too. I was just beginning to relax.'

'But what if it is?' Theresa pointed out.

'Is what?' Simon asked.

'Is the first time? And she's perfectly all right now? Old people do have things like this, very mild strokes that are all right till you scare them witless by giving it a name. What's the point of making a big fuss and worrying them both when there's not a lot they can do till she gets home?'

Becky flipped a coin. She'd delved into the bottom of her purse and pulled out a two-pence piece especially. It was important to use English money: the local currency might be biased in favour of Ethan's require-ments. She brushed out of her mind the logical consequence of this train of thought: whichever way the coin fell, she knew deep down that having sex with Ethan was something that she wasn't entirely sure she wanted to do, even though he'd made her feel more randy than a springtime fox. The thing was, it was time she had it with *someone*; she would be seventeen in a couple of days. Everyone else at school had had sex and mostly with more than one person. Some of them were practically at old-married-couple level, es-pecially drippy Delphine who started every sentence with 'My Nick says . . .' Becky didn't want that, but she did want to have a clue what sex was like. She listened in on the morning-after discussions, perched on the counter in the girls' loo, looking as if she knew just what they were all on about, laughing in all the right places when they giggled about squelchy con-doms or stuffing their knickers under the sofa when a parent came home too soon. One day, and it was creep-ing nearer all the time, someone would realize she never actually had anything to contribute to these shrieky tell-all sessions. This must be peer-group pressure, she realized, and she'd always prided herself on refusing to succumb to it. She was still determined it wasn't just that causing her to stand there with a coin in her hand and a decision to make. It was simply sheer curiosity and the ripe, right time to dispose of her virginity. It was like when she'd been younger and had a wobbly tooth, the moment had always come when she'd known that the one final neat twist was all it needed to get it out.

There was no-one back home she really fancied. They were all pale, clumsy big-footed boys with sick-making acne eruptions and soft stupid-looking fleshy faces and thick necks that reminded her of toys that had been a bit too tightly stuffed. Not one of them had any sense of personal style, even the ones from the university (actually those were worse: they were the dreggy ones who couldn't pull a fellow student and resorted to easier pickings among the kind of school-girls who were pathetic enough to give them some status as Older Men). Ethan was different. He wasn't that tall, but his whole body swaggered up the beach with effortless sexual confidence. His baggy shorts swung perfectly on his hips, not wilting at half mast as if he needed a Mummy figure to pull them up properly. His shoulders were broad and straight under his T-shirt, not apologetic and shivery like those of boys in England.

The chorus of a song kept coming into her mind; the word 'horny' repeating itself over and over. It was exactly how she felt. When his warm soft mouth had grazed across hers on the beach, Becky's body had been overwhelmed by a kind of liquid lurch, a longing to roll beneath him and be pressed hard into the sand. No-one at home had ever made her feel like that. Snogging boys at parties or crushed up in the crowded dark at various clubs, all she'd felt was mild nausea at the taste of recent hamburger or the stench of belched beer. They shoved their eager swollen crotches in the vague direction of her pubic bone, neither caring nor even aware that half the time they were rubbing themselves frantically against her handbag or the unresponding soft centre of her lower intestines. Until Ethan, the only good sexual experience she could count on having was spread out in a warm, scented bubble bath, by herself.

The coin came down in Ethan's favour. Becky picked it up off the cool terracotta floor and shoved it back in her purse, feeling a tweak of encouraging excitement. She wasn't sure, on the whole, that a spot of hot-weather lust was the best reason to do it, but it would be OK, it was good *enough*. If the whole thing was a disaster at least she could just go home and forget about it, delete it from her memory and decide it didn't count. And if it wasn't disastrous, if it was just the best thing she'd ever had, well – she'd left herself enough time to get in a few more goes at it before the holiday ended.

She picked up the piece of paper that had fallen off the bed and skimmed over the list of instructions on it: a hurricane sounded thrilling, though the hotel management seemed to be taking it horribly seriously. 'No alcoholic drinks will be served in the hours before the storm' she read. She slid the page between the mirror and its frame, where the list of rules stared back at her as she smoothed on some lipstick. Spoilsports.

'You shouldn't read anything into it, Simon. They are quite old and they've been out with us in that frazzling hot sun for the whole day.' Plum watched Simon as he gazed at the two empty places at the table.

'And there was no shade or shelter on that boat. They're probably exhausted,' Mark chipped in. Shirley

152

and Perry had phoned the restaurant and left a message: they were having a light snack in their villa and an early night, a message which effectively fended off the possibility of after-dinner visitors.

'It must be awful being old. Everyone sittin' around waiting for you to snuff it.' Luke reached across and helped himself to a hunk of bread, which he ripped apart, scattering crumbs across the tablecloth.

'Luke! That's a terrible thing to say! No-one's wanting them to die!' Theresa slapped his hand hard, knocking the remaining bread to the floor.

'*You* did that!' he accused her, pointing a knife. '*And* you didn't listen. I didn't mean you *want* them to die, just that you all hang about, looking for signs of it. No wonder they've pissed off to their own space.' His voice faded to a mumble as he added, 'Bloody wish I could.' Theresa heard him and glared at Plum, waiting for her to tell her son off, but Plum simply smiled fondly at him and took no notice. Bloody floppy wet liberal, Theresa thought, no way will *my* brood get away with that kind of talk.

Becky also heard what Luke had said and felt sorry for him and a bit guilty. If she hadn't got these sensational sexy plans of her own for the evening she would have offered to play table football with him in the games room. He liked playing it with her because she was just as good at it as he was and worth having as an opponent. Perhaps the Tom-person with the gold mother was around, or perhaps Colette would take him on. When she got up after the meal and went off to meet Ethan, poor Luke would be stuck with all these boring adults while they wittered on as they always did, disagreeing oh-so-politely about education or acupuncture, or chatted to some of the Steves and got told how much they'd been ripped off for the catamaran trip. The Steves did that every night; she'd heard them in the bar bragging on about how much they'd saved by shopping around for cheap car hire and making sure they got well tanked up with cocktails during half-price Happy Hour. She'd seen one or two of them eyeing Lucy's legs as well, as if they were wondering how much of a discount she was likely to offer for shagging them all at once. In their bloody dreams.

Theresa was on show and sparkling and Mark was confused. She'd left him to help Marisa with the children's tea and baths, swanned off to the hotel spa on the top floor and come back with her hair done, body aromatherapeutically massaged, nails perfectly painted and a look on her face that he hadn't seen since they'd set off for Paris for a weekend of so much scintillating sex that they came home having seen nothing of the sights. That had been a long time ago. Pre-children, definitely. He couldn't work out what she was up to. She'd smiled at him as she shimmied naked between the bathroom and bedroom, put on scarlet lace underwear and then those red shoes as well, as if that was all she intended to wear that evening, then she'd sat at the mirror to do her make-up, legs tantalizingly apart, calves and thighs tautly braced on those sexy heels. She'd got him to fasten her chain of silver hearts round her neck and she'd watched his face in the mirror as he'd stood close, breathing in her perfume and fumbling with the clasp. It had driven him crazy, wanting to stroke her, touch her and take her there and then but knowing sex was now completely forbidden. She was doing it on purpose, watching him, teasing him with what she was definitely not going to let him have. Eventually, when all the rest of her was ready, she'd dropped the sleek

154

blue dress casually over the top, like a protective cloth over a precious ornament. And all the time she'd chatted on, bright and brittle, telling him how wonderful it had been to see the dolphin and the turtles when she'd snorkelled with Becky and how much the children had enjoyed their day with Marisa.

Theresa was looking rather different now she was drunk. After three pre-dinner daiquiris she'd made steady progress through the best part of a bottle of white wine and her glossy veneer was sliding off. Her lipstick was smudged beyond the corner of her mouth and her mascara had settled into tiny furrows beneath her eyes. Before what he now thought of as The Telling, Mark would have reached across and stroked the black smudges away. Now he was terrified to make any gesture towards her in case, in this drunken state, she slapped him hard and yelled at him to keep his filthy diseased hands to himself. Then they'd all know. Sober, the humiliation he'd inflicted on her kept her silent. Pissed, she could say anything. Keeping it as something to sort out just between the two of them was Mark's only chance, he was sure, of mending all that he'd smashed.

'Goodness, your three are up late!' It was Simon who first spotted Marisa making her way across the restaurant towards the table. 'What?' Theresa spun round and took in the sight of Marisa leading Amy, Ella and Sebastian, in their Teletubby pyjamas and clutching their cuddly bedtime toys, towards them. Sebastian was rubbing his eyes and looking as if he was sleepwalking. The two girls were grinning at everyone, delighted to have the entire restaurant staring at them. Ella stopped to pull up her pyjama top and proudly show Cathy and Paul her tanned tummy.

'What on earth are they doing in here? They should

be fast asleep by now!' Theresa was on her feet, head to head with Marisa, who stood stolid and silent before her.

'I want this night off. I meet someone, my friend in the hotel with the one baby.'

'But . . . well, you can't! This is your *job*!' Theresa protested. Guests at surrounding tables fell silent. Women pushed their hair out of the way of their ears for easier, shameless listening.

'But I work all day, with no rest. Now I want time.' Marisa was immovable. She picked up Sebastian and sat him on Mark's lap and sent the girls to sit where Shirley and Perry should have been. 'My friend, she says I have time off just like at home. That is what she has with her family.'

'But we've brought you on *holiday*!' Theresa's pretty red shoe managed a petulant little stamp on the floor.

''S'not a holiday for her if she has to work every day,' Luke contributed.

Theresa rounded on him, hissing like a cross cat. 'I don't need any input from you, thank you very much.'

'Marisa's got a point.' Lucy joined in, bravely, Mark thought. 'I mean surely she should have some time to herself. Looking after three young children is hard work.'

'Thank you Lucy, I do know that actually. It's why I brought help with me. It's what she's for,' Theresa snapped.

Mark, trapped beneath the dozing Sebastian, knew he was being worse than useless. Theresa was trembling with alcohol-fuelled fury now and clearly heading for the kind of mood where she'd say something irretrievably awful, probably fire Marisa on

156

the spot and send her straight back to Switzerland in the morning. That would be hugely expensive, he calculated, possibly a figure not unadjacent to the cost of Sebastian's entire first year's school fees. He stood up, clutching his son to him, and offered Theresa his most charming smile. 'Look, I'll take them back to the room and stay with them while Marisa goes out for a while, shall I? Surely that will solve things. And Marisa, we'll talk again in the morning, OK? Sort something out?' He told the girls to come with him, took Amy's hand and led the little troop out of the restaurant. Marisa followed. There was a daring ripple of applause and Theresa sat down heavily, fuming.

'It's that bloody Norland nanny she's met, giving her ideas about entitlement.' She stabbed her spoon hard into her melting peach sorbet and it splashed cold orange dollops down the front of her dress. 'Oh fuck,' she said, laying her dispirited head slowly down on the table and surrendering to sad, silent tears.

Lucy had tried not to think about Henry all day, even out on the boat when there were long lazy hours of nothing to do but watch the waves. She didn't want to waste any time thinking about men at all, not since she'd promised herself that Ross would be the last to make her feel like any kind of pathetic victim. That way, at her age, lay a cursed lifetime of Bridget Jones-hood, comparing Disasters and Disappointments over too much appropriately sour wine with similarly afflicted girlfriends. At least Colette would be happy. When she'd been little it had seemed important to try and find her a kind and loving Daddy figure, someone who'd stay around at least long enough to catch sight of any children he might be responsible for producing. For a long time now, though, the seeking of the perfect male had been as if Lucy was trying to keep on pretending to her child that Santa really did exist, long after Colette had come cheerfully to terms with the truth.

So all that meant that this wasn't like going out on a date. It definitely wasn't. As she cleaned her teeth – convincing herself she wasn't being over-thorough with the mouthwash – she wondered why there wasn't a different word for Going Out With Men that grown-ups could use. 'Dating' was so very Australian TV soap, or American early Sixties high-school.

Henry was out at the front of the hotel, waiting in a white Suzuki Jeep with its roof down. Lucy saw him before he caught sight of her, leaning back in the seat with his eyes closed, one foot up on the dashboard, his hand hanging out of the window and beating out a rhythm to whatever music he was listening to. Lucy felt peculiarly nervous, with butterflies dancing about in her stomach. She waited to collect herself for a moment, lurking behind a feathery palm in a pot by the doorway. On that upturned crate in the dive shop the night before, he'd kissed her – just once but properly, as if laying out his intentions extremely clearly. The butterflies did a formation flip inside her as she hovered behind the plant, considering those intentions and what she wanted to do with them. They'd clearly been what her mother would call less than honourable. Pure sex. Well that was OK, Lucy decided, for now that she'd given up on settled relationships, she would settle for good old sex, honest if not honourable. This could be a classic Holiday Thing. Just for tonight she would be one of those notorious English-girls-abroad who behave disgracefully and then forget about it on the plane home before the stewardess has finished explaining the emergency drill. There were condoms in Lucy's bag, as ever. They were from way back, from pre-Ross. He'd preferred his own choice, rather ludicrous ridgy black ones that had made her feel as if he was trying to dress up his penis as something else, a cartoon policeman's truncheon came to mind. She wondered if condoms had a 'use-by' date stamped on the packet and, if she got run over and killed, would a mortuary attendant going through her bag feel sorry for her for clearly having had them so long?

She smoothed down her dress, which was an ancient faded Liberty lawn wrapover that she'd had for so many years it had come back into fashion again and appeared in a four-times-the-price version in *Vogue* that summer. She was far more used to wearing trousers and felt strange with the warm night breeze wafting the fabric around her thighs, almost as if she wasn't wearing anything at all. The dress was pretty but not actually very sexy. If she wanted serious instant sex appeal she would have to ask Theresa if she could borrow the outfit she'd worn for dinner tonight.

'Hey, Lucy!' Henry had seen her, was out of the car and strolling across to meet her. He took her hand, kissed her cheek quickly and smiled, then led her over to the Jeep.

'There's a restaurant on the edge of the town up a hill. I thought we'd—'

'Oh! But we just ate . . .' Lucy felt dismayed.

Henry laughed. ''S'OK, me too, a TV supper with Olly and his homework. But this place has a great bar, quieter than most places – I thought we can get a drink, talk?'

'Fine! That would be terrific.' Lucy hated the sound of her own voice, gushy and silly-girlish. She tried again. 'We went out on a boat trip round the island.' She sounded worse and stopped. 'Sorry,' she laughed, 'that sounds so like a typical junior school "what I did on my holiday" sort of stuff. Anyway, I can't tell you anything new about a trip round the island. I think I'll just keep quiet.' She slid down lower in the car seat, feeling foolish. Hell, he'd kissed her once. It wasn't supposed to turn her into a pathetic quivering heap with mush for brains. Probably if all the holiday women he'd screwed were laid end to end, they'd stretch from here to Barbados, possibly back again too.

'No, you can tell me,' he said. 'After all, none of the versions I've heard so far have been *yours*. Did you get seasick? It's rough round the Atlantic side, especially now.'

'Simon did. I'm fine. Why is it worse now?'

'The storm. We're already getting the swell from where it's churned up out in the ocean. The last cruise ships are pulling out tonight and there'll be no more till it's over.'

Lucy shivered. The vagaries of British weather-forecasting seemed pretty trivial compared with what could happen here, more a form of take-it-or-leave-it entertainment. The words 'a bit of a damp start to the day' could mean anything at home from a spot of minor drizzle to a full-scale thunderous deluge, it didn't matter much which. Here, getting it wrong might well mean life or death to the residents.

The restaurant was an old converted sugar mill high on a hill, still with the stream and a wheel. Huge lilies grew in a pool up on the terrace, fat fleshy leaves crowding together and enormous pale flowers, as big and smooth as alabaster vases. There were tables on the deck, which was on a level with the tops of banana trees growing on the hillside, so the air was damp and languorous, heavy with the scent of coconut and vanilla. Lucy breathed in slowly.

'On a hot day in London, all you can smell is traffic and chips,' she commented. 'This is bliss. It will be hell to go home. I shall probably cry.'

'So don't go.' Henry shrugged.

Lucy laughed and sipped her beer. 'If it was that simple . . . I've got people's houses to paint, a daughter to educate and . . .' She couldn't think of anything else.

'Is that it?' Henry waited, laughing at her hesitation.

Lucy thought for a moment, looking out at the lights of the town below, at a ship heading for a safer horizon.

'I suppose it is, really. Jesus, it doesn't exactly add up to a whole bag of good reasons.'

'There are schools here. You can paint houses here. You'd have no trouble finding work, though you'd miss home I expect.' It sounded so simple.

Well, would she? Lucy thought aloud. 'There's friends of course, I have got people I'd miss but not desperately. And family, well, you've seen them, but we all live scattered separate lives. We don't usually go round in a herd like this. This is a mysterious Proper Family Holiday, some kind of last-chance bonding effort.' She laughed, thinking of Theresa over dinner, and spluttered a bit into her drink. 'Though of course for that you need a Proper Family.'

'And what's that?'

Lucy didn't hesitate this time. 'One that leaves you in peace. One you can check in with just now and then without them greeting you with unsubtle accusations like "Well hello *stranger*" when you phone.'

'Wait till Colette goes to college. See if it's really that easy.'

'Yeah I know. But it's not just that. My parents wanted the best for us all. Nothing wrong with that, but it's *their* best. Simon managed it, he's successful, big house, posh wife, all that. And Theresa too, she did the thing girls are supposed to do, or should I say *were*, and married the perfect Surrey man. I'm the one that they still think is the underachiever. I mean I support myself, I have a job I like but, Jesus, in a few years I'll be forty and Ma still looks mildly disappointed every Christmas when I don't bring along a Mr Nice Man that she can serve up to the rest of them along with the turkey.'

'Sounds like you've got one of those families you have to join,' Henry said.

'What, like a golf club with rules and a waiting list?'

'You got it. I reckon with families there are two sorts,' he went on. 'The family that's happy to see you set sail on your own, do your stuff and be pretty casual about when they see you and when they don't. Then there's the sort that wants to keep you on strings. Like anyone you get involved with has to join the clan, not claim you for themselves, and kind of almost abandon their own folks so the control stays in the same old hands. Seems to me you got one of those.'

Lucy thought for a moment. 'You could be right. Those who are happy with it call it a close family. With Plum and Mark, my parents got a pair of highly suitable candidates to join the family, not people who would remove their kids to an alien world. But don't forget they live a couple of hundred miles from all of us. It's not surprising that when they come down that motorway they want some sort of gathering that will let them go back home reassured we're OK. Anyway, what about yours? Joiners or quitters?'

Henry laughed. 'Quitters. Glenda and I have our own lives, which means we're free to be close. This island is completely my home. Apart from a few years I've been here all my life. Glenda could go back to England

and fit right in but she likes it here. It's choice.' He leaned close to her and stroked her wrist. 'You should come and see her work.'

Etchings time, Lucy thought, her insides lurching a bit.

'You could come maybe a couple of nights from now, the night before the storm's due say? I'll cook. Bring Colette,' he said. Lucy's stomach resettled itself. Just when she was up for a spot of stolen sex, he turned out to be A Friend. Well, maybe that was OK: she liked Henry, so friends would have to be fine. She thought about the condoms in her bag and smiled. She would throw the damn things away, she decided. They didn't seem to be required.

Becky scrubbed at her teeth for at least ten minutes, rinsed and slooshed with half a bottle of mouthwash and could *still* taste Ethan. She felt used and furious. It wasn't enough, it wasn't what she'd wanted and she'd been had, but only in the sense of being conned. She looked at herself in the mirror. Still a fucking virgin. Or rather *not* fucking. It would go down all right in one of the morning cloakroom sessions at school. She could picture herself combing her hair, doing her mascara, saying breezily, 'Oh yeah and I gave him a blow job on the beach, under a coconut palm, *completely* stoned.' Definitely it would be a worthy contribution, it would sound great. She wouldn't tell them it had been about as interesting as chewing the gearstick on her mother's Volvo, and tasted like something that had been too long at the back of the fridge. Nor would she tell them that the only bit of her he'd wanted to get hold of had been the back of her head, and then, painfully, a grip on her ears, making sure she kept going, couldn't even come up for bloody air. Still a virgin. God. She snapped the bathroom light off and dived into her bed, landing on the TV remote control. There might be something on, she thought, fishing it out from under her tummy and flipping through the channels. And she wasn't giving up yet, there was still time. After all, he owed her now.

Ten

'They want the girls to be bridesmaids.' Theresa thought that if she just announced it over breakfast she could find out whether this actually sounded like a good idea or not. She didn't think it was; these people weren't really her type. The girl had a gold ankle chain with a dangling tiny padlock and he had one of those walks that flicked out from the knee, reminding her of a very cocky plumber she'd had in when the downstairs loo gave up flushing.

'Who wants bridesmaids?' Colette asked, adding quickly, 'Yuck, frilly sticky-out dresses,' to fend off anyone who might consider recruiting her for the job.

'That young couple, the ones that are always kissing. Cathy and Paul, I think they're called, the ones who are getting married on Tuesday,' Theresa explained. 'The ceremony is in that gazebo thingy down by the pool. They asked me just now. What shall I say?'

'But we don't even know them,' Shirley pointed out. 'Haven't they got any family they could have asked? And isn't it all a bit late?'

'I don't think that's the point,' Lucy said. 'I expect they've come away to escape from all the hectic organization you usually get and now they've met some cute little children and thought it would be jolly for them.

Maybe not knowing them is part of the fun. It's spontaneous.'

Theresa bit her lip. Cathy and Paul had dragged her out of the water that stupid night. Just because they claimed they'd saved her life, now they'd decided they could claim her. They'd been laughing about it when she'd met them just now in the hotel lobby on her way to breakfast. 'You can't say no, we saved you from drowning so we own you!' Cathy had laughed. 'You're our slave!'

'It's an old Chinese tradition,' Paul had joined in. Theresa had smiled, rather stiffly, but had refrained from pointing out that as none of the three of them had even a smidgeon of blood from anywhere east of Epping Forest, it was hardly relevant. The night-swimming episode was one she'd hoped to forget. Marisa was with her, too, listening with her inexpert ears, quite probably picking up completely the wrong impression. It was hard enough getting au pairs to come out and live in Surrey – commuting to an exciting London nightlife being just too expensive – the last thing she wanted was to find that her name was mud at the agency when she called up to replace this one.

'What are we going to wear, Mummy?' Ella pulled at Theresa's arm.

Perry laughed. 'Well there's your answer, I think the girls have already made their minds up.'

Theresa frowned. 'I can't imagine, darling. I expect the bride will think of something.' She looked around and aimed her smile at Lucy. 'I suppose they might as well, it might be the only chance they ever get.'

'Oh I don't know, Theresa,' Plum said, 'you could always divorce Mark and give it another go with someone else.' Startled into silence, everyone immediately looked at Mark.

'Hey, don't ask me!' he said, managing a charming but unconvincing smile.

'Sounds like Plum's getting sour,' Theresa commented with a warning smirk.

'Goodness, I am sorry.' Plum was flustered, thrown by the lack of easy laughter that she'd anticipated. 'I didn't mean anything, it was just one of those flippant things you say.'

'*You* say.' Theresa wasn't going to let it go.

'Yes, all right, if you like, one of those things *I* say.'

She reached across the table for another comforting croissant. It was getting hard, being so nice, so even-tempered, to this same collection of people every single day. They were all, as a family, terribly good at Not Mentioning. A few hours' sleep and deleted from the collective memory was the sight of Theresa head-down in her pudding. All smiles at breakfast, and not one of them asked the poor woman if she was feeling better (or rather – for let's not join in the pussyfooting – recovered from her drunken tantrum), not even Lucy. That was probably in case Shirley and Perry got to hear about it. They couldn't have that, oh no, mustn't upset Mommy dearest, who might respond with another little 'turn', though of course no-one was going to get Shirley on her own and ask her about her dizziness, just in case it Spoilt Things. Had none of them noticed that Theresa was drinking herself silly or that Mark was wandering around in a daze or that Lucy was leaving Colette in the care of her cousins while she went slinking out at night like a cat going mousing, and Becky . . . where did she disappear to last night? And worse, why did she come scuttling back so early and start running the shower for such a very long time?

Plum had tried talking about it to Simon but all he could think about was the symptoms of heart failure and whether his mother was spending too many hours in the sun. If only all this consideration extended beyond his precious parents. They were supposed to be the family he'd grown up and *left*. Surely his first concern should be the family he'd *made*. Plum had found a stunning little gallery in Teignmouth, with a painting of the harbour that she'd love for the dining room at home. It was expensive enough to need a second opinion, but dragging Simon away from his parents to come and look at it with her was even harder than getting straight answers out of Becky.

Plum took solace in food. That was the best thing about a buffet system, no-one noticed how much you were putting away. She could go up for a small, modest plateful, the kind of amount that would keep her safely on the foothills of the Shape Sorters' calorie mountain, but then, if she felt stressed enough, it was so easy to pop back for another go. 'Just a tiny bit more of those spicy sweet potatoes,' she'd mutter, as if anyone was counting, adding the smallest extra spoonful of curried swordfish to go with it, and then possibly another. After all, you didn't get to sample much of that kind of thing at home, so you had to, didn't you, while you could. It wasn't as if being abstemious was going to shift the weight right now and turn her into a sylphlike beach-babe at this late stage in the holiday. And whatever she gained, well, you didn't balloon overnight. It wouldn't need to be dealt with till she got home.

'Mark and I are going diving at eleven,' Lucy was saying. 'And then I want to take Colette into the town, so she can buy presents for friends.'

'And there's a museum I'd like to look at,' Theresa joined in. 'So I could come with you if that's OK. We'll take our Jeep.'

'We might as well all go,' Shirley decided. 'I wouldn't mind getting one or two bits and pieces. And I haven't sent any postcards.'

'Good idea,' Simon agreed. 'Plum wanted to show me a painting she's found. We could all look, give it the all-clear. All right Plum?' It would have to be. Plum sighed. She'd only wanted a second opinion on the painting, not a third, fourth and fifth. She piled more guava jam on her croissant. When she got home she would sign up to help out as an extra body on the college biology field trip. She was getting plenty of practice at travelling mob-handed, she'd be quite good at it.

The notice summoning all the guests to a meeting that morning was on a large board, propped up against the wall and blocking the hotel's main doorway, so unless guests had made a very early start on their excursions, they couldn't pretend they'd missed it. Those who looked as if they were inclined to treat the situation lightly were being hauled into line by tour reps, who hung around the reception desk clutching clipboards and looking bossy. Lucy was passing through the lobby with Colette on her way out to the shops across the road in search of chocolate, but was firmly turned back. She sat on the big pink sofa by the reception desk to wait for the others.

'Have you seen the notice?' One of the Steves plonked himself down next to her. 'We've all got to be there, half an hour from now. It's like a three-line whip. The management's called a meeting.'

'I have seen it. It's about the hurricane I suppose, unless we've been naughty guests and we're all going to be told off,' Lucy said.

'I haven't been naughty. Have you?' he asked,

putting his mouth closer to her ear than she'd have liked. Without actually moving, she could feel her flesh creeping away from contact with him. Back home, if she'd never met Henry, Steve might look reasonably appetizing, say at a party, or to chat to in a bar. He was tall, had a body that probably owed its shape to an expensive gym membership, and he had boyishly appealing fair hair, floppy like Hugh Grant's. His skin, though, compared with the rich ripe brown of Henry's, reminded her of the greyish dull tint of cheap gravy granules. In winter he would resemble a giant maggot.

'Is there really going to be one?' Colette broke into thoughts that were beginning to alarm her.

'A hurricane? Looks like it!' Steve seemed pleased.

'Well, there might not be . . .' Lucy didn't want Colette to start worrying before they found out if there was anything to worry about.

'Oh, I think we're for it, no question. Doom and destruction! That'll give everyone something to write about on their postcards!' Steve got up and wandered away, pleased with himself, looking for someone else who would listen to his gleeful tidings.

Simon wondered if the awful possibilities had crossed anyone else's mind. This hurricane could be the death of all of them. It wasn't a joke: they didn't call this kind of thing Extreme Weather for nothing. They might all be crushed by falling buildings, roof tiles could slice through their skulls. Deluges of wild water could cascade down the hillside behind them, sweeping the hotel and its frantic residents into the sea. The sea itself, perhaps, would come pounding up the beach and simply not stop. Did hurricanes involve tidal waves? It would not surprise him. He doubted any of this had crossed anyone else's mind, not in such calamitous detail as he was capable of imagining. Most people didn't see disaster looming the way he did.

He'd been blighted with this vast capacity for expecting the worst ever since his mother's terrifying kerb drill when he was about six. Other mothers held their children's hands firmly, simply stopped at the roadside and guided their little ones across without any fuss. Shirley hadn't been like that. She'd always let him run along the pavement like an unleashed puppy. He'd enjoyed that, having both hands available for pulling on bits of hedge and jumping to grab the lowest branches of the sycamore tree on the corner by the fish shop, being able to swing round lamp-posts. He'd race and whoop and jump past his envious class-mates, every one of them being clutched by the hand and marched along as if the only thing that mattered was the simple speedy getting home. Sometimes he'd just run backwards, all the way from school to the big crossroads. That was where the trouble was. He knew to slow down as he got near the heavy traffic, but he was never slow enough, never decelerating quite soon enough for his mother.

'*STOP!* Stand *STILL!*' The order, which came every day and was loud enough to scare the sparrows from the trees, wasn't even bordering on negotiable. The other children, with their good little hands grasping their careful mummies, used to turn and smirk as he cringed at the traffic lights, waiting for death to bear down on him with every family saloon. Even then, when the crossing-time came, Shirley didn't hold on to him. 'You've got to learn,' was her dubious reasoning, as Simon trotted terrified into the street, as close to her side as a champion poodle in Cruft's obedience trials, pretending there was a thread linking the two of them, like mittens on a string. Awful things could happen on roads, the very worst things. A boy in Theresa's class had had his head crushed under the wheels of the brewery lorry because he'd run into the road chasing a football. Theresa had whispered to him, just when he was trying to get to sleep, that some of his brains had trickled away down a drain, all mixed up with beer. Shirley had said he should let that be a lesson: that boy hadn't *STOPPED!* or stood *STILL!* when he'd got to the kerb.

The dining terrace had been hastily rearranged, with the tables all pushed to the wall and rows of chairs facing the sea. There was the lingering scent of grilled bacon. Another noticeboard, easel style with a large pad of drawing paper clipped to it, faced the lines of chairs and there was a stubby blue crayon ready in an ashtray on the table beside it.

'It's like a bloody sales conference,' one of the Steves called from the back row. 'Where's the overhead projector?'

Shirley bustled into the room and went to sit next to Lucy and Colette, a couple of rows from the front. She smiled past Lucy at her granddaughter and then half-whispered, 'You don't want Colette listening to all this. The poor child will get frightened to death.'

Lucy smiled and gripped the edge of her chair in an effort to keep herself quiet. Nothing changed, certainly not her mother and her 'You don't want'.

The possible response, 'Oh but I *do* want' was just too juvenile. She felt tense with frustration that she couldn't come up with an instant something-smarter. After all these years, she should have a well-rehearsed collection of them at the ready. Ironic, really (not to mention maddening), that just at the point where she'd

172

decided she didn't mind too much giving her mother a sharp dose of the truth, Shirley's health should start to be vulnerable.

'She likes to know what's going on, and anyway it might be important for her safety that she listens, that way she won't take risks,' Lucy replied with simple truth.

'She doesn't know what she wants at that age.' Shirley leaned past Lucy again and said, 'Colette love, why don't you pop down to the pool? Marisa's there with the little ones, so you won't be on your own.'

'No thanks Gran, I'm OK.'

'You don't want her being clingy like this.' The half-whisper was back.

'I am *not* clingy.' Colette was leaning across Lucy now, her head so close Lucy could smell the Sainsbury's Sun and Swim shampoo she'd been using every evening. 'I'm just interested, OK?'

'Hoity-toity! There's no ice creams for little madams.'

'Oh God, I'm not five.' Colette sighed. Lucy nudged her arm and gave her a private calming grin.

The room was now full. Simon and Plum were the last to arrive and had to scuttle to empty seats on the front row, like embarrassed last-minute cinema-goers. Shirley looked around for the rest of her party and waved to Mark, who was sitting near the back next to the gold lady. She couldn't see Theresa or the teenagers and concluded that very sensibly Simon had told them not to come. They'd only fidget and start chatting any-way.

The hotel manager was tall and businesslike in a smart navy suit and a tie with the hotel's green and white leaf motif. He wore heavy-rimmed oblong glasses and his expression of grim foreboding reminded Lucy of Trevor McDonald on the news when he had a major disaster to announce to the nation. Using the blue crayon, he sketched a rough map of St George and the surrounding islands. Out on the pale blank right side, he then added what looked like a big Polo mint and an arrow.

'Hurricane Susie is heading this way,' he announced simply, pointing to the blue arrow. 'Right now there is still a small chance it may miss the island altogether, but equally we have to prepare for the possibility that it might not.'

'Oh well, if we don't even know . . .' Perry murmured, folding his arms and waiting to hear something that had more impact.

'A hurricane is like a doughnut, or a flying saucer if you like. The wind forms spirals round, forming the central hole, which is the calm eye of the storm. At the moment the speed of those wind spirals is 120 mph, while the whole thing, the mass, is moving this way at eighteen mph. That is a category-three hurricane, and if it continues like this it will reach here sometime during Monday afternoon.'

'Is category three the worst?' the gold lady asked.

'No. And we have to hope and pray it stays at three. Even then we're going to have serious structural damage. It will be worse if the whole thing slows down. The slower the storm travels, the faster the wind speed will be when it hits.'

Colette took hold of Lucy's hand. Lucy squeezed her fingers gently, trying to give a reassurance that she didn't actually feel. The tone of the manager's voice made her feel as if the end of the world might well be coming. Perhaps her mother had been right, perhaps Colette should be diving and swimming and carelessly having fun while she could. Perhaps they all should, enjoying their last couple of days on earth in happy but unwise ignorance.

'Buildings are replaceable,' the manager went on. 'People are not, so it's vitally important that you follow any instructions that we give you. After Sunday you should not go out of the hotel grounds. You should try to return any hire cars and read all the notices we put up in the lobby.' He looked around the room and grinned for the first time. 'And get to know each other, you might be spending a lot of hours in small rooms with strangers!'

'Just what I've been trying to do all week,' quipped a voice from the back. There was a burst of nervous laughter and then the sound of sobbing. Cathy got up and rushed from the room, dripping tears on all she passed.

'What about my *wedding*!' she wailed as she ran. Paul, looking embarrassed, shuffled out after her.

'Well there you are, you see,' Shirley said to Lucy. 'That's what happens when you mess about getting married abroad.'

'It's all a bit serious, isn't it?' The gold lady was on the pontoon waiting for the boat to take her across the bay to Teignmouth. Lucy and Mark were waiting for the dive boat to pick them up.

'It's like those programmes about holidays from hell that you see on television,' Mark said. 'I bet there'll be dozens of people craning out of windows with camcorders, hoping to flog a video of flying coconuts to some crap TV company.'

The gold lady moved closer to Lucy and lowered her voice so Lucy could barely hear. 'What do you think we should wear?'

'Wear? What for?'

'Well, for the storm of course. It might be life or death—'

'Clean knickers then, obviously,' Lucy interrupted, giggling.

'No, seriously. I mean it would probably be a good idea to wear something you can run fast in, and of course it would have to be something that doesn't matter getting wet. And will it get cold? And suppose you end up swept away into the sea, you wouldn't want to be wearing something bulky that would pull you under.'

'Perhaps you should ask, next time the manager calls a meeting.'

'Do you know, I might do that.'

The dive boat pulled up to the pontoon and Lucy clambered down into the seat next to Henry. 'This has to be the last dive,' he said. 'Sorry but the sea's starting to cut up too much. Visibility down there is getting worse all the time and it's too risky. I need to take the boat round to a safe place too.'

'Don't apologize. The ways of the weather aren't your fault.' She thought for a moment, watching the herons preening on the headland, then went on, 'Henry, the people at the hotel seem to think the storm is going to be completely catastrophic. Are they right or are they covering themselves?'

Henry frowned. 'They're right, or at least they could be. We might not be at the centre of the actual hurricane, but whichever way, the island's going to take a beating. If anyone tells you to hide under the bed, just do it and stay there till they tell you to come out. Don't ask why.'

'OK, I won't.' She looked back at the shore, then asked, 'Where are all those boats going?' Behind them a long line of fishing boats was making its way across the bay. They lacked only strings of flags to make them look like the beginning of a seaside regatta on the Devon coast in August.

'They're heading for the mangrove swamps round the other side of the island. That way they'll be protected from the worst of the battering. That's where I'm taking this later.' He looked at her and grinned. 'And after that, how about ditching the family and you and Colette coming out to eat with Oliver and me tomorrow night? There's a great little restaurant that might not be standing this time next week. It's called my place, I'm not a bad chef.'

'It's all right, you don't need to do the hard sell! I'd love to. If we're on a forced lock-in after tomorrow, the family will have plenty of time to get sick of my face.' Even so, she would have to put up with the wrath of Simon, the raised eyebrows and pursed lips of her mother, the scowl of Theresa (envy, she wondered?) and probably a leery suggestive wink from Luke, but it would be worth it. After all, with the apocalypse booked in for Monday, it was time to cram in the fun.

Simon was watching the girl who watered the plants. Her intricate hair fascinated him. It shone so much; in fact her skin, everything about her glowed. Her large mouth, slick with a deep grape lipgloss, seemed to have a perpetual smile.

'There's a nest up there,' he commented, as she caught him watching her.

'Yes sir, it's a hummingbird.' Her smile widened and was just for him. He knew it was a hummingbird. He'd seen the tiny bird, its wings beating faster than he could focus, flying from the nest in the twining creeper that spread under the roof of the lobby all the way from the reception desk to the edge of the verandah roof by the pool area. The nest was the size of a golf ball, woven from grass and stems of dried leaf. It must have been one hell of a building job for such a little bird.

'There are three baby birds,' the girl said. Her name was Tula, her badge told him.

'There's another nest on the terrace just outside my room, but I don't know what kind of bird it is. It's a bit like one of our English sparrows, but more green. Do you know what it is?'

Tula smiled. 'I might. You'll have to show me.' Simon's heart started to speed up. Did she mean now? Alone in his room with him? Why would she want to do that unless . . .

'Er, it's this way, if you'd like to . . . Are you sure?'

'All part of the service, sir.' Tula left the watering can on a ledge by the reception desk and followed him along the cool corridor. Simon didn't feel at all cool. He felt as if he'd caught a prize-winning fish but wasn't sure how to land it, or, with his hands, body and the back of his neck sodden with nervous sweat, if he'd be able to. At least there really was a nest to show her; if the stuff of fantasy failed him, and that was more than halfway likely, he'd come out of it knowing a bit more about the island's bird life.

'Here we are.' It sounded so stupid, because of course they were *there*, though it didn't really matter, as his voice no longer felt as if it was his. Simon fumbled with the key and flung the door open, half expecting to see Plum inside, collecting some suntan lotion or her umpteenth bloody book. There was no-one there. The maid had been and the room was immaculately tidy and clean. He went to shut the door, but then left it slightly ajar, in case Tula got nervous and fled.

'So where's this nest?' She turned and smiled at him

as she walked to the terrace window and slid it open. So many straight white teeth, he thought, such a lush wide glistening mouth.

'It's just up there.' He pointed to the creeper that hung below the terrace verandah. There was the nest, and, disturbed by human presence, a small greeny-brown bird flew away fast.

Tula laughed. 'That's just a common old finch! We got thousands, man! Doncha get those back home?'

It was the worst thing. She was laughing at him. He could see right into the stretched pink mouth. Perfect: no fillings, no overbite, all molars present, the ortho-dontist in him couldn't help noticing.

'Yes, yes we do. I suppose I just hadn't looked at it too closely.' He felt as if, without so much as brushing against Tula, he'd managed to strip himself of all dignity. She was no fool, but he was. She turned to leave, still giggling, and gave his arm a squeeze as the door suddenly flew wide open. Carol, the room maid, stood firm and square in the doorway, her arms folded and no smile on her face.

'OK. Now I warned you before,' she accused him, stepping inside the room and closing the door. Simon backed onto the balcony, terrified of Carol's angrily waving finger and advancing bulk.

'Actually, we were looking at the bird's nest.' Simon tried his best to sound outraged. 'Tula has been very helpful.'

'It ain't her job to be helpful, not that way.'

'It's fine, Carol, no problem.' Tula tried to placate her colleague. 'He didn't take any advantage.'

'Not with you maybe,' Carol told her, 'but with some.'

'He did? With you?' Tula switched sides, literally, and went to line up next to Carol. The two of them glared at him and he could see them figuring out what to do next.

'Way I see it,' Carol said to Tula, 'kind of woman he's after, he should be out paying for on the street, not mishandling the likes of us.'

'You're right, for sure.' Tula nodded.

Simon now *was* outraged. 'Now wait a minute, I didn't . . . I wasn't . . .'

'No?' Carol came up close and, to his amazement, slid her hand down to his crotch. There was a waft of sweat, not unpleasant. She grinned. 'Like to try black pussy, would you? The idea make you horny?' The strong firm hand fondled his balls. Simon was frankly terrified and nothing in her grip was daring to stir. Behind Carol, he could hear Tula starting to giggle.

'Well, before we island girls buy the goods, we like to check over the stock,' Carol said. 'So come on, let's see what you old white guys got in your pants.'

Before he could work out what was going on, Simon was upended on the bed. Tula and Carol, shrieking with laughter, easily pinned down his feebly thrashing limbs and stripped off his shorts and swimming trunks in what seemed like less time than it took to peel a banana. He feared for the stripe of tender pallid flesh where the sun hadn't been, for his penis, craven and lifeless, that they stared at, pointed at, howled and hollered with laughter at. Carol was even wiping away tears. He couldn't recall such humiliation since the diarrhoea day at his infants school, and the even worse day after the following fortnight when Miss Jenkins had compounded the awfulness by telling the assembled class that they must *not* call him Shit-leg Simon.

'Sorry man, but it's no competition with home-grown!' Carol called as she opened the door and hauled Tula out after her. Just for good measure, she left the door wide open. Simon could hear voices in the corridor: Carol and Tula saying polite, professional good mornings to a group of guests as they passed his room. He closed his eyes, as if that made him invisible, and so missed seeing Colette and the gold lady's son Tom passing by his open doorway. With his hands now over his mortified eyes, he also missed Colette looking in and taking in the sight of his rumpled bed and sad, exposed penis. It was a good thing he missed this because, instead of delicately pretending she'd seen nothing and averting her shocked young gaze, she ran off down the corridor, convulsed with laughter that was even louder than Carol's.

Out by the pool at lunchtime everyone was talking about the hurricane. Plum tried to read her book but the sound of all this chatty semi-panic was making it hard to concentrate. There wasn't anything any of them could do about it, and it was still a couple of days away so they might just as well all carry on enjoying their holiday. That daft girl Cathy wouldn't stop crying about her wedding, an event that could surely go ahead as planned, so long as any fallen leaves and coconuts and bits of branch could be kept out of the photos.

Lucy, back from diving, had some news for everyone. 'Henry says that a hotel on one of the other islands is closing till after the storm and transferring some of its guests over here. One of them is a major celebrity apparently.'

'Ooh, Henry *says*. We are getting pally,' Theresa commented. Lucy ignored her.

'Leave it, Tess, he's a very nice young man,' Shirley said.

'I hope he or she won't expect celebrity treatment,' Perry grunted. 'Who is it anyway?'

'I don't know,' she said. 'But it's someone who travels with their own staff, cook and driver and stuff, so they won't be in the restaurant bagging the best table and having us all pretending not to stare.'

'It'll be Madonna,' one of the Steves suggested, from a nearby lounger. 'I'd put a tenner on it. Dollars that is.'

'Shall we run a sweep?' Lucy suggested. 'I'll make a list.' She reached into her basket for a notebook.

'OK, go on then, I'll go for Barbra Streisand,' Plum said.

'I'll have Elton John,' Mark decided.

'I wouldn't,' Luke quipped. 'Not for a million quid.'

'I bet you would,' Becky said. 'I would.'

'He wouldn't want *you*.'

'So who do you think it'll be then?' Shirley challenged him.

Luke thought for a moment. 'A sportsman, someone with picky food needs. Gotta be a rich one, so I'll go for Pete Sampras.'

'And put me down for Shirley Bassey,' Shirley said. 'Then I won't forget who I've picked.'

Two of the Steves argued over Madeleine Albright and settled it with the toss of a coin, the loser getting Leonardo DiCaprio. Cathy and Paul wasted twenty dollars putting themselves down for Lord Lucan and Elvis, the gold lady chose Luciano Pavarotti. Plum quietly opted for Julia Roberts on behalf of Simon, who seemed to have gone off for a wander. Thank goodness, she thought, as she handed over her twenty dollars to Lucy, they'd now all got something else to think about.

Eleven

There was an oppressive sense of waiting. The atmosphere in the hotel complex veered between apprehension and overexcitement, reminding Lucy of those dreadful weeks of pre-Christmas inertia when the whole of life seems to be on hold till the dreaded event is over. Hotel guests, in a pointless panic far too soon, cancelled excursions they'd planned, as if while they were out across the island, looking round a batik workshop or sugar plantation, or birdwatching in the rainforest, the hurricane would swoop down from nowhere and slam mercilessly into action, destroying everything in its path. As rooms were cleaned that morning, staff had left large black bin liners on everyone's pillows, along with instructions to seal their packed suitcases inside them to keep them waterproof during the storm. Guests picked the bags up, opened their doors and wandered into the corridors with them, looking for someone to share comment and speculation with. Some grumbled that the bags weren't big enough, others that they needed at least six. Plum said nothing, for she was privately amazed that fully grown humans could make such a fuss about a bit of black plastic, as if they'd never seen anything like it before.

'Do we get tidal waves then? Because if we do, it'll

be such a comfort to know that Theresa's frocks are bin-bag safe,' Mark said to Simon. Simon didn't trust Mark's sardonic amusement. He wanted to haul him into line, tell him he should take all this more seriously, but there wasn't much chance that Mark would listen to him. He would just shrug and grin, and wander off with his hands in his pockets to spread himself out on a sunlounger with his eyes closed. It was something Simon had noticed about him, that he was very much on the edge of them all, as if they could reasonably expect no more input than his mere presence. Simon hoped he would be more use during the storm. After all, who knew what might need to be done: it could be anything from bailing seawater out of rooms to keeping a game of cards going to distract the children (and here Simon's brain sneakily extended the phrase to women-and-children, as in *first*) through the worst of the wind. The way Mark was being just now, he'd probably just huddle in a corner under a damp towel, reading his Len Deighton as if things were no worse than a wet weekend in Torquay.

'We should get the Jeeps back to the town today,' Simon said to Lucy as soon as they'd finished breakfast, two days before the storm was due. 'After all, you never know.'

Lucy had planned to drive herself and Colette to the eastern, wilder side of the island to see the pelicans that Henry had told her lived on the high jagged rocks below which the fish were big and plentiful. She did not intend to have her day spoiled by Simon's overcaution. 'But we do know, don't we Simon? Meteorology isn't just a matter of hanging a bit of seaweed out of the window.' She led him to the noticeboard by the reception desk where the manager had placed a map of the surrounding islands with the course of the hurricane clearly marked by a blue line. Every few hours another cross would be added and the blue line extended as information was updated from the local radio news station.

'See? There's a hurricane report every fifteen minutes and it's still forty-eight hours away, and might even miss us if it goes a bit to the north. Unless you know better.'

She could see him flinch from her sarcasm, which made her feel bad. Simon was still too easy to tease. When she'd been small she'd been horrid enough to take advantage of his sheer niceness to her, secure as she was in her role as his cute and much-indulged little sister. It was as if she was practising bits of joky spite in case she needed the skill later. It was certainly useful for defence against the sniping girls at school who jibed at her for being driven to school each day in a series of her father's showroom cars, gleaming vehicles so upmarket that their parents disguised their envy with sneering remarks, which never failed to be passed on to her. With Simon, she'd specialized in blurting out statements guaranteed to embarrass him in front of his friends. She felt ashamed now to recall what a little monster she'd been at the age of eight, asking his gawky adolescent friends, in a tone of calculated faux innocence, if they had stinky feet like Simon's and sprayed Body Mist in their shoes every day like he did, and if they did, had they, like him, ever got it wrong and accidentally used oven cleaner? Their laughter and his blushes had been such a horribly satisfying reward.

She squeezed his tanned arm. 'Come out with us to see the pelicans, Simon. I'll drive, it'll be fun, just you and me and Colette.'

'No, no, you two go on your own,' he said, frowning

out at the benevolent sunlight beating down on the deceptively placid turquoise sea. Lucy couldn't help smiling. He looked so much as if he was puzzling out a way to get all this complicated weather back under control, make it do what it was supposed to do and be kind to his holiday. She could hardly blame him for his anxiety, whenever it happened the storm could be catastrophic. But, however much Simon fretted, it wasn't going to happen today.

Out by the pool, the timid tourists who'd decided to stay put for the duration drifted around aimlessly, already wondering if they'd been overcautious. They'd spend an hour on a lounger staring into the distance but not really focusing. They ordered mid-morning rum punches instead of their usual fruit ones (well, as they weren't going anywhere, what did it matter?), flicked through paperbacks, too twitchy to read properly, and then got up and stretched and went off to wander a hundred yards along the beach before scurrying back in case Armageddon should strike while they were out of sight of the beach bar. The Steves had taken to wearing their watches again, and to hell with the stripey tan, just so they could keep an eye on the progress of the hours. Perry told Shirley they looked as if they were doing a collective countdown for NASA.

'You'd think the Grim Reaper was waiting behind the big tamarind tree,' Henry commented as he and Lucy and Oliver banged nails into the boards that would protect the dive shop's door and windows.

'Too right. You should have seen them all after supper last night, drinking themselves into oblivion in the Sugar Mill bar as if they were about to be called up to fight World War Three. There was a wonderful gospel choir out on the verandah and some idiot with a sort of drunk-reverence voice said it was so much more appropriate than reggae.'

'Well that's kinda natural and pagan, don't you think? Having a crack at appeasing the gods.'

Lucy laughed. 'I think it would take more than a few hymns.'

'Yeah, and you know I never thought it was right, the way in churches having a good voice for singing meant like you were somehow closer to being holy. The time we lived in England, my dad used to take me to the local church and I always wondered what it was about the choirboys that made them saintly enough to dress up in angel frocks. I ended up scared that if you couldn't sing, you were gonna go straight to hell.'

'Yeah, well, don't forget I've heard you sing!' That first morning, with Henry up the tree, seemed months ago.

Oliver cut in, 'He can't even do happy birthday right!'

'I'll be able to see if you're right on Tuesday, Oliver. It's Becky's birthday. She'll be seventeen.'

'And I get to be there for the cake and the singing?' Henry asked. Lucy hesitated. Somehow Henry had become her friend, one she could now hardly imagine being without. Perhaps she'd gone too far, casually inviting him to join in with a family event. She bit her lip and bent to hammer a low nail so he couldn't see her face.

'You could come if you like, you and Oliver,' she said. 'Glenda too if she's around. It's just a cake and a quick drink before dinner.' She looked up and smiled at him. 'After all, it's not as if you don't know Becky.'

'Sure I do, the little rum punch girl with too much thirst and dangerous taste in men.' Henry grinned. 'OK, I'll be there, see if being one year older is making

187

her a year wiser about men and alcohol.'

Lucy laughed. 'At seventeen? I doubt it.' Or even at twenty-seven, or not far off thirty-seven, for some of us, she thought.

As she worked, Lucy could hear from the sea's edge the shrill, tense sound of Theresa taking care of her own children. Marisa had now negotiated for herself a good number of hours off to coincide with those of her smart nanny friend. Lucy had noticed that the two girls seemed to be getting a wicked thrill out of sprawling on loungers within sight of their employers, watching them making a hash of child-care, for the small children seemed gloriously inclined to play up far more to a parent than to a professional. The Norland girl's family consisted of a pair of serious-faced chartered accountants who tended their baby with meticulous over-concern. It seemed to require both of them to have hands-on (or fingers-on, for they handled this child and its accoutrements with nervous delicacy) input for even the simple task of changing a nappy. Marisa and her friend sat with sly smiles as they peeped over the tops of the hotel's old copies of the *National Enquirer* at these two struggling with tissues and lotions, wet-wipes and the wriggling, uncooperative child, and solemnly debating the tightness or otherwise of the nappy's fasteners.

Lucy, the boarding-up of the windows finished, sat on the sand next to Henry and sipped at a can of orange juice. She watched Theresa skipping about in the waves with her three giggling infants and wondered if Colette ever felt she'd missed out by being an only child. She'd always seemed to be such an independent girl, content to read or draw by herself rather than slop about being bored and pouty and whining for perpetual entertainment in the classic only-child manner.

In school holidays, she'd never complained about being hauled out of bed early in the morning to accompany Lucy to whichever house was being painted, often to spend the day in a draughty unheated room, huddled cosily beneath dust sheets with a pile of apples and a book. It crossed Lucy's mind, too, that Colette hardly ever watched television at home, partly because of the mountainous quantity of homework the school liked to set, but also because if the TV was off, it simply didn't occur to her to switch it on when she was absorbed in a book.

'Oliver, do you watch television a lot?' she asked him. He looked puzzled for a moment, as if she'd asked him something weird like did he spend time looking for aliens in the sky.

'Cartoons and stuff, sometimes, not much, movies I like. Oh and cricket when it's us.' He shrugged. 'Glenda thinks it's, what does she say Dad? Oh yeah, "a sorry waste of youth".' He exaggerated Glenda's English accent and he and Henry laughed.

'Just do it in the sea, Ella!' Theresa's voice cut through the laughter. Ella wailed something incomprehensible.

'No, just where you are, just sit in the sea, Ella sweetie. No, really, we don't need to go all the way back to the room.' An even louder wail from Ella told those on the sand that she didn't agree. The naked child, palely tanned all over now in spite of the Factor 25, splashed away from her mother to the edge of the sea. 'Sweetie, just sit down and do it there, do a wee-wee now, darling, it's all right, no-one will know.'

'Apart from the whole beach.' Oliver grinned at Lucy.

Denied her request for bathroom facilities, Ella, still

sobbing, finally squatted on the sand and sat for some moments concentrating hard while Theresa watched her and smiled gently, sure that she'd won the kind of battle Marisa never seemed to have to put up with. Lucy turned round and could see Marisa and the Norland girl smirking over their magazines at the little scene. There was a sudden appalled shriek from Theresa, who came dashing out of the sea. 'You should have said! Oh, you *dreadful* girl, why didn't you say you needed a *poo*?'

Ella's roar of protest, an infant's version of 'Well, you didn't ask' was almost drowned out by the delighted cackles from the two nannies. Theresa glared. Lucy tried to keep her face straight, glad it wasn't down to her either to clean up the sand or to warn Marisa that back in England, a cheap flight to Switzerland for the au pair might be Theresa's next Amex purchase.

Lucy wondered if it was her imagination that the air that afternoon seemed just that touch more sultry than before. The canvas roof of the Jeep was stowed behind the back seat, but the speeding wind that flicked Colette's hair across her face wasn't making her feel any cooler.

'It's sticking to my skin,' Colette complained, pushing snaky tendrils of it behind her ears.

'Tie it back then. Haven't you got a scrunchie with you?' Lucy was concentrating on avoiding ruts and potholes in the road.

'Yeah, somewhere.' Colette delved into Lucy's basket in front of her, rummaged around and pulled out a green baseball cap. 'There's only this.' She crammed it on her head, shoving her hair up inside it, then moved the rear-view mirror and pulling a face at her reflection. 'Whose is it? Did you buy it?'

'Oh that? No it's Oliver's, I think. I must have picked it up on the beach.'

Colette giggled. 'Good excuse to see Henry again then, to give it back.'

'We're seeing him tomorrow,' Lucy told her. They'd arrived at the east shore now and she pulled up beneath a clump of trees close to the sandy edge of the beach. The sea was much rougher here, crashing up the beach and ebbing back, leaving angrily bursting bubbles of foam burying themselves into soaking sand. She could hardly hear her own thoughts. She switched off the engine and turned to Colette. 'We've been invited to Henry's house, to have supper. Is that OK?'

Colette looked at her, puzzled. 'Well of course it is. Why wouldn't it be?'

Lucy climbed out of the car. 'No reason,' she said, 'I just thought you'd like to be consulted.'

'That's because it matters,' Colette muttered, jumping over the side of the Jeep. Then, louder, she said, 'You like him.'

Lucy waited for Colette to come round to her side of the car and then she put her arm round her. 'Of course I like him. Don't you?'

'You've liked men before.' Colette was looking worried, fearful.

'Well, this time we're only on holiday.'

'Yeah, shame.' She glanced up suddenly and grinned. 'Look! Out there by the rocks!'

About twenty pelicans sat in a row on a rocky promontory, just above the reach of the spray, like a gathering of ancient ragged witches. Their huge beaks preened now and then into their feathers and they stretched their great wings, flapping lazily but going nowhere.

'They look like they're waiting to pick over a dead man's bones,' Colette said.

Lucy laughed. 'If your gran heard you say that, she'd say you'd been over-imagining.'

Colette frowned. 'How can you *over*-imagine?'

'Don't ask me! It's a Gran thing. Though I do think it's possible to do too much imagining the worst.' They both laughed and then said together, 'Like Simon.'

They were the only people on the great wide beach. Lucy looked in the guidebook and read that tourist hotels weren't built on this side of the island because of the sea's roughness and the tides in early winter, which shifted the sands around and brought in great troughs of seaweed. Holidaymakers liked things reliably clean and calm and comfortable. This wasn't the kind of sea that you could trust with a pedalo or a jet ski and a group of teenagers overexcited by rum punch and too much sun. As she watched the pelicans swooping to the sea, scooping out fish, Lucy caught herself thinking that this would be such a perfect spot to come to at the end of a working day, just to sit and collect her thoughts before the evening. They had four days left of their holiday. She couldn't remember being in any other place where she'd felt so reluctant to go home.

'What do you miss most from home?' she asked Colette.

'Nothing.' Colette didn't even hesitate.

'No-one from school?'

'School? No!' Colette pulled a face. 'I haven't even sent anyone a postcard.'

'Not even Isabelle?'

'No.' Lucy waited but Colette went on staring out to the sea. She clearly wasn't going to say any more but Lucy could tell that this kind of silence was covering something that troubled her. Colette did this some-times, keeping her problems to herself as if she was making sure she didn't load them onto Lucy. Was it, Lucy wondered, something that lone-parent children, or even just lone children did? Or was it because Lucy tended to be pretty vocal when things in her own life went wrong, sharing her problems as if Colette was more of a best friend than a young daughter. Colette was probably protecting her from having to deal with a double set of unhappinesses, which was far more unselfish than *she'd* ever been. At least she hadn't told Colette how hard it was getting, trying to find them a new flat. She would make sure she kept that one under wraps. It wasn't fair to expect a girl of her age to have to think about anything more serious than problem-atical homework and finding the right kind of trainers in a size five.

A car pulled up under the trees, yards from where they were sitting. 'Never alone for long,' Lucy sighed. 'Even here.'

'It's OK, there's plenty of room,' Colette, ever grown-up and reasonable, told her.

There was the sound of laughter and a young couple ran from the car towards the sea. They hadn't seemed to notice that anyone else was there. The girl was young, blonde, slim and pretty. She wore a bizarre out-fit consisting of a bright pink bikini, a short and sassy bridal veil, long white gloves and white high-heeled shoes. Lucy and Colette watched as she kicked off the shoes into the sea and splashed in after them, giggling. Her new husband was wearing swimming shorts and a dark grey morning-suit jacket, nothing else. He was carrying a camera.

'Do you think they got married in just that?' Colette stared at them, grinning. 'I think that's just so cool.'

'Maybe. Or there might be a dress packed away back in its bag.'

'I'm going to think there isn't a dress. It's more fun.'

The couple strolled up and down the beach, paddling and splashing about in the shallow water, jumping the bigger of the foamy waves which pounded up the wet sand. The bridegroom took photos of his new wife as she posed sexily, hands crossed, Marilyn Monroe-style, across her tanned thighs, and then with her perky veil pulled half across her face. Lucy started to feel uncomfortable about their position as unseen watchers when the girl lay down on her front in the surf and posed with her chin resting on the white-gloved hands. She had put her shoes back on for the shot, and her crossed ankles waved up behind her head. There was something vaguely pornographic about the whole scene, Lucy thought, and it became even more so when she rolled over, arched her back and let the veil and her hands trail through the water. The bridegroom stood over the girl, one foot each side of her body, photographing her face as her body snaked beneath him.

'We'd better go,' Lucy said, pulling Colette up from the sand. 'We'll go into the town on the way back, see if we can get a *Telegraph* for your gran.' It felt important to keep talking, saying ordinary, even boring things. Colette, who could be just too perceptive, mustn't pick up any clue that about this couple on the beach, Lucy felt, deep inside, an absolutely crushing boulder of envy.

The Celebrity had arrived when no-one was looking, slipping in with no fuss and no recognition. Becky and Luke were furious – he or she must have sneaked in by a back gate. They, along with Tom, had hung around

194

the reception area since lunchtime, waiting for the exiles to arrive from the nearby island of Coranna. There, the New York-based owners of an astoundingly upmarket hotel, an internationally renowned last word in hedonistic luxury, had decided not to risk having their guests see the place at even one roof-tile short of perfection and had closed the place down till any hurricane damage was put right.

'It might not even hit Coranna. It's barely the size of a small field,' the gold lady had complained as the hotel staff dealt brusquely with their current guests' enquiries, which interrupted the intense concentration needed while the staff huddled together over computer print-outs and clipboards, allocating suitably luxurious rooms to the new arrivals. The gold lady had waited at the reception desk for twenty minutes, just to ask for an extra bin liner to put her suitcase into on the night of the storm. 'I've got a lot of baggage,' she'd explained, 'I need more bags.'

The deputy manager, a woman of usually textbook politeness, had frowned at her and dismissed her with a glare, snapping, 'We're busy right now. You can buy them at the store across the street.'

'Oh ho, the strain's beginning to tell,' Perry commented, overhearing.

The new arrivals came from the airport in small groups. 'Private planes,' Luke had a go at impressing Tom, 'they can only take a few at a time.' The three teenagers stood around in the lobby, pretending to check out the noticeboards and looking at the postcards. Shirley, reluctant to admit to an almost equal curiosity, found she was dropping into the hotel's gift shop more than once and spending a lot of time making up her mind between a hibiscus-flowered sarong and a pink straw hat, neither of which she would ever wear. A flurry of activity out by the reception desk had all of them peering round at a trio of American women, all well past sixty but clearly keeping up the glamour quotient.

'Jesus, what is she like?' Becky whispered to Shirley as they took in the sight of a blonde woman with a round chunky body and spindly bare legs, wearing turquoise shorts, high silver sandals and a tight translucent black top with the word 'Star' emblazoned across the front in silver rhinestones.

'Do you think that's her? The big celeb?' Tom said.

'It's no-one I've seen before,' Becky told him.

Shirley giggled. 'It certainly isn't Madeleine Albright,' she said.

'It's not even Elton John,' Luke spluttered.

Becky lost interest. 'Oh well, I'm not hanging about all day for some superstar to show up.'

It was only a couple of hours later that Becky, with Luke and Tom visiting Shirley's villa in the hope of getting all the Snickers bars out of her fridge, noticed a sleek silver Mercedes with black windows parked on the path where no cars had previously been seen.

'Bloody nerve.' Perry came out and stared at the offending vehicle. 'Rest of us humble peasants have to leave our hire cars up in the car park. You can't even say it's one law for the rich. I'm paying just as much through-the-nose cash for my top-of-the-range room as whoever this bloke is.'

'And the storm's going to make him just as wet and scared as us.' Shirley tried to pacify Perry. Perry ambled up to the car, hands in his pockets, giving it a professional look-over. 'Nice model this,' he commented to Luke, 'I've sold a good few of these to the Manchester football lads.' He put his hand out to stroke the car's bonnet but found his wrist suddenly clasped by a huge hand. Luke took a step back, terrified. The man looked exactly like a bouncer from a London club that he and his friends had wanted to go to but, having seen what was guarding the door, hadn't even tried to enter.

'Sorry, sir. The car is alarmed.'

'It isn't the only one.' Perry rubbed at his wrist and looked into the impenetrable mirror lenses of the man's sunglasses. 'So, whose is it then?' Perry went on.

'Sorry, sir. It's a real huge star, but who it is is privileged information.' The guard smiled, surprising Luke by showing ordinary white teeth and not an array of metal prongs like Jaws in James Bond films.

'Privileged my arse,' Perry growled. Luke laughed, delighted. 'Tell you what, lad,' Perry put his hand on Luke's shoulder and led him back into his villa's garden, 'if you want to know who we've got holed up in next door, you should pop round and ask if you can borrow a cup of sugar.'

'Perhaps it's not somebody famous,' Tom suggested. 'Perhaps it's a hostage. Some real rich person kidnapped.' Luke stared at him, trying to decide whether to tell him not to be so stupid or to admit to thinking that was quite a cool suggestion.

'Well, I expect we'll find out some day very soon,' Perry said, settling himself onto his cushioned steamer chair out on the villa's broad terrace. 'After all, everyone's equal under the stars when the roof's blown away and the rain's got in.'

On the drive into the town Lucy and Colette could see people busy shoring up their houses. There were no longer any tubs of flowers on porches, no toys lying around beneath the decking and even the dogs seemed to have disappeared. Some of the homes looked so flimsy, already patched together with corrugated iron and planks of painted wood that looked as if they might once have been floorboards, that Lucy could only cross her fingers for the occupants and offer prayers to all available gods for their survival. In the town itself, there was an overriding sound of the banging of nails into protective hoardings. With no cruise ships in, the marketplace was quiet and many of the stallholders had already packed up their stock and taken it into safe storage. Restaurants had notices outside offering half-price menus for the final night before the great shoring-up, and Lucy watched a woman unhooking coloured lamps from above her doorway and taking them inside her gift shop.

'It feels like the whole world's closing down,' Colette said. 'It's really sad.'

'It's only for a couple of days,' Lucy tried but didn't feel convincingly comforting. None of these buildings looked particularly substantial, though this wouldn't be the first hurricane they'd endured. She thought about the TV programmes she'd seen about extreme weather conditions, and for the first time felt mildly nervous. This storm might, remotely possibly, be something that none of them survived. But if they did . . . Lucy felt a surge of unusual immense determination that was almost like a tidal wave in itself. She wasn't, she decided, going to waste any more of her life or Colette's making do with dull compromise. It would be like being given a chance to have another go, get things right this time.

'How much do you miss the cat?' Lucy asked Colette as they stopped at a shop. It was an estate agent, and she slowed down to glance idly over the selection of places to rent.

'The cat?' Colette looked at her as if she was crazed.

'Hadn't you noticed? The cat's practically moved in with Sandy downstairs.' She looked at the apartment details in the one window left that hadn't yet been boarded up. 'I don't suppose she'd notice if we never went back.'

Lucy smiled and read the details of a flat with a small garden, just on the edge of the town. It was nice to dream, she thought, as she translated the price of the rent into quite an affordable amount of sterling, but the building might not be standing this time next week.

Twelve

It wasn't anything like the Devon holidays. Shirley could hardly believe she'd ever thought it would be, and that wasn't anything to do with the heat, or the distance from home, nothing as obvious as that. The past was like a used stamp; you couldn't go scraping it up and try to force it to stick to the here and now. There were too many people involved, for a start. It wasn't just Simon, Lucy and Theresa any more: they'd all grown these attachments – their children, their partners (though not Lucy, would it ever be Lucy?) and Shirley never saw all three of them without at least a few of the extras tacked on somewhere. It would have been nice, she thought, just for one evening maybe, to have been able to reassemble just the original family once again, see if they all slotted together in the same old way. They could have reminisced about all the things that the others wouldn't want to hear about, like long-gone relatives, Christmases and birthdays when they were little, old dogs and cats and that vicious ferret Simon had brought home from the boy at school. These were things she wouldn't mind going over a bit, just to reassure herself that it did all happen, that she didn't only spend what now felt like a mere ten minutes raising this family.

Sometimes, in quiet moments alone at home, she wondered if it had happened at all, if there'd been anything between being a teenager dancing with American GIs up at the air base and the *now*, just herself and Perry rattling around in the house that had grown much too big. She had to go to the old photo albums to reassure herself. Most of the earliest pictures were black and white, giving even more of a sense of unreality. Grey photos, grey skies, grey Devon sea. But her children had been full of colour and life and she needed to check that what she'd always felt were landmark moments in her life, were also – well, at least some of them – landmarks in her children's. It wouldn't work, though. They were busy making their own memories now with their own families, which was how it should be. And suppose she did persuade them to reassemble, just the five of them. What would they say to the others? Sorry, but you're only along for the ride so make yourselves scarce for a bit while we do a spot of recapturing the past?

Shirley watched Theresa carrying little Sebastian along the edge of the sea and wondered how someone who seemed to have everything going for her in life could look so troubled. With grown-up children you couldn't give them a prod and tell them they'd got a face like a wet Wigan Wednesday, nor could you get them on their own and ask them straight out what was wrong and then expect a full and honest answer. Whatever it was, and with Theresa it was certainly something, it wouldn't be put right with an extra secret ice cream.

Now that he'd got the painting back to the hotel and propped it up on the chest of drawers, Mark wasn't at all sure this was the right kind of present for Theresa.

Usually he was quite good at choosing. A little silver something from Tiffany always made her smile (and so it should) and, for a man, he was pretty good at underwear. The last success had been just before the holiday: lavender lace knickers and bra from La Perla. She'd probably never wear them for him now, assuming (rightly – that time it was the little Thai massage girl) that he'd only bought them out of guilt. She'd probably give them to Mrs Thing (OK, *Gwen*) to use for scrubbing awkward corners of the lavatory. Still, the painting was something for them both. When he'd seen it he'd had this idea of hanging it in the sitting room where its vibrant colours could remind them of . . . well, that was the big problem. It was by Frané Lessac, an original, not a print, so it would make a fair-sized dent in next month's Visa bill. It was a scene of an island market, complete with steel band, laughing children, stalls of mangos and bananas and fish and chickens and spices. It could only remind them of being *here*, which could be a problem. Reminding Theresa of being *here* would forever remind her of his cheap, shoddy bits of betrayal. All the same, the picture made him smile. (He adjusted the painting against the wall so that it was straight, and walked back across the room to get a good look at it. In spite of all the awfulness of this trip, the scene made him think of being warm and relaxed and reminded him that there were other worlds beyond bloody Surrey and the even bloodier 7.43 to Waterloo. If only Theresa could look at things the same way, maybe she'd work out that there was room for a bit more flexibility. He'd done a bad thing (three bad things) and he was sorry. He'd said so. He wouldn't do anything so stupid again, not ever. All Theresa had to do was believe him and trust him. If she couldn't do that, well, what was marriage all about?

*　　*　　*

After lunch the various tour reps rounded up their charges and told them to assemble on the terrace for another meeting. The new arrivals from the hotel on Coranna, who had no-one to herd and chivvy them, ignored the summons and lay back on their loungers to let the business of sorting the storm pass them by as if it was an inconvenient beach trader. Simon glared at them, feeling they were shirking from responsibility, and Perry quietly suggested to a man of about his age with a tan the colour of nicotine stains that it might be a good idea to put himself in the picture so he could at least tell the rest of them what was going on.

'This is the big one. The yes or no,' Simon said as they walked up the steps from the pool area.

'Heavens, Simon, don't sound so *portentous*,' Plum teased him, prodding him in the ribs, which hurt more than he hoped she'd meant it to. He felt mildly offended. No-one seemed to be taking things seriously enough. Ahead of him, he could hear the gold lady chatting away to the frightful barrel-shaped woman with 'Star' emblazoned across her jacked-up breasts about a selection of duty-free sapphires she'd seen down near the port. How were these two intending to while away the storm, he wondered. He could just picture them sharing a bottle of gin, a couple of hundred cigarettes and a game or six of contract whist while comparing the various merits of Bloomingdale's and Harvey Nichols. All around them, a few hundred years' worth of nature's precious trees and shrubs, along with possibly the entire housing stock of the island, could be wiped out while they nattered and chattered.

The manager looked even more serious than he had at the previous meeting. For the first time, Lucy realized that this storm wasn't something the island residents experienced annually and could feel blasé about. It was almost as much of a terrifying one-off event for them as for the tourists. This hurricane was going to happen, it was going to hit them hard, could rip the hotel and everything in it to splinters. She put her arm round Colette and the two of them went and sat near the back of the room with Becky and Luke. There was no flippancy this time, no-one trying to make light of anything.

'We now have a category-four hurricane,' the manager announced. 'I can confirm that it is on course to hit this island sometime tomorrow, probably during the early part of the evening.'

'Is category four worse?' Luke whispered to Lucy.

''Fraid so,' she told him. She squeezed his arm and smiled. He grinned back, confident that being fourteen and fit would guarantee his survival – it simply wasn't time for him to go yet. Lucy felt almost tearful. These kids had no real idea about weather. The only thing they understood to be really dangerous was standing under a tree when there was lightning about, anything worse just happened to other people on TV.

'The sea level is likely to rise by up to eight feet, so rooms on the ground floor may be in some danger of flooding or at least of having sand carried into them from the tide and the wind . . .'

'Shit, that's us,' Theresa whispered to Plum. 'That's all of us, except Mum and Dad.'

'. . . So we are going to reallocate those guests to sharing with others on the higher floor.'

'Do we take all our baggage too?' a rather frail-looking elderly lady asked.

'No. Leave it stowed high on the wardrobe shelves like it says on your instructions and we'll sort everything out after the storm.' He smiled suddenly. 'After all, chances are you'll be able to go back to your original rooms the very next morning. These are precautions we have to take, not a guarantee of mass destruction.' The laughter was polite but nervous. Further along the row of seats Lucy could see Cathy clutching Paul's hand tightly. She looked as if she might burst into a new set of tears. Paul put his arm round her and cuddled her into his shoulder.

'Hey, have I got this right?' The 'Star' woman's New Jersey drawl hollered out from the back of the room. 'Like we have to *double up with strangers*? I mean, like I paid for *de luxe*. Sharing ain't de luxe.'

'Depends who you get,' one of the Steves called out.

'Not you, honey, you're strictly budget class,' she flashed back.

There was a mocking chorus of 'ooooh!' from his companions and then the sound of sudden fierce rain pattering hard on the roof brought them all back to sober reality. The meeting dispersed slowly, with small groups lingering under shelter on the terrace to chat, trying surreptitiously to find out who would make good storm-companions if they all had to share room space. It would be a cramped way to spend a night, even though many of the rooms had a pair of king-size double beds. The hotel was almost full, thanks to the offloading of the hotel on Coranna, and some of the guests were feeling angry that the rush to evacuate those extra people had been a miscalculation: it now looked as if that island was likely to fare far better than St George. In addition, the mysterious celebrity, who had not yet been seen or identified, had an entourage of at least ten and no-one was taking bets that any of them would be asked to move from their rooms and spend a night holed up with strangers.

Simon was worried. He felt as if somehow he should be in control of things and there was nothing he could think of to do. He felt it was something to do with being A Man, and moreover A Man who was taking over from his father as Senior Family Member. The manager was by the reception desk, engulfed by guests who had each managed to think of just one more question. Simon approached and lingered at the back of the crush, hovering on the edge of the crowd with his hands in his pockets, gazing at the updated hurricane chart and waiting his turn as if it didn't really matter. Out of the corner of his eye he saw Carol walking down the corridor towards the main door. He felt himself beginning to blush and his hands went sweaty and when the manager asked him if there was a problem he was appalled to hear himself stammering.

'Er, er, th— th— there are a lot in our party,' he began. 'Is there any, er, sort of chance we could all be together for this, er storm thing?'

The manager frowned and studied his computer.

'Ah. Right. You have two over in Villa Hibiscus.' He lowered his voice. 'I think, between you and me, you should congregate over there for the duration,' he said. 'The reason being that the louvres in the villa's windows are wood, not glass as they are over here in the main block. You'll be safer there, especially as you have small children.'

The rain had stopped again and Simon returned to the beach, wondering if he felt reassured or not. On the whole he felt *not*. He was going to die. He would be sliced through the skull by a tumbling roof-tile. A flying louvre would skewer him to the wall. They were all going to die. He would never see his nice tall Wimbledon house, his patients, or his dog again and at the thought of this he was confused to find that his spirits felt very much lighter.

'Look what some sod's done,' were the words from Luke that greeted Simon as he reached the bottom of the beach steps and made for his lounger. Simon looked at the space next to them where guests had sat and sprawled comfortably before the meeting, but which now consisted of six empty loungers spread far out in a long and greedy row, guarded at each end by big men sweating in suits and ties and carrying what looked like mobile phones.

'It's the best spot on the beach. Whoever it is must be scared of sharing the air. People were asked to move,' Theresa complained.

'And did they?' Lucy, joining them, asked.

'Well, yes. They were told it was for a "special purpose" and thought there was going to be a barbecue set up for tonight, so off they went.'

'I wouldn't have moved,' Lucy said, wiping the raindrops off her own lounger and settling herself down with a book.

'No, well, you never did anything that didn't involve completely suiting yourself, did you?'

'Tessie . . .' Shirley warned.

Lucy said nothing, refusing to reward Theresa with so much as a scowl. It was childishly satisfying.

'Hello Theresa!' Cathy and Paul stood in front of her, holding out a carrier bag. Theresa shaded her eyes and squinted up at them. 'We got these! For your girls!'

'So the wedding's still on then?' Theresa asked.

'Of course it is!' Shirley cut in. 'You don't think they're going to let a bit of weather put them off?'

'If it did, no-one would ever get married in an English August,' Simon added.

'Don't know why anyone bothers any time.' Theresa was ungraciously grumpy.

'Yeah, but look at these dresses, come on Theresa, just look.' Lucy thought Cathy sounded as if she was trying to persuade a cross child out of a bad mood.

'All right, go on then.' Theresa folded her arms and waited to be appalled.

Cathy held up one of the little frocks. It was white, with a full gathered skirt and a deep frill round the hem, a high waist with an elasticated bodice and a pair of little white shoulder straps. The fabric was patterned with almost luminously pink leaves. The other dress was the same, but the leaves were a vivid shade of tangerine.

Theresa reached out and touched the soft cotton and smiled. 'Actually, they're rather sweet, wonderfully tropical. Yes, they'll look lovely.'

'And we thought flowers for their hair would be good but we'll pick those on the day and we got some ribbon as well. We were really lucky, all the shops were closing up.'

Lucy looked at the pattern and laughed before she could stop herself.

'What is it?' Theresa asked. 'What's so funny? They're lovely.'

'They are, they are,' Lucy admitted, her giggles increasing. 'It's just, the leaf shape . . .' Becky came and peered at them.

'Oh . . . yeah! That's cannabis. Yo, little cousins,' she called out to Ella and Amy digging in the sand. 'Cool!'

Given that the world might end for all of them about twenty-four hours from now, Lucy thought it quite ridiculous that she was going through a what-to-wear crisis. It wasn't as if she had that much choice. It was going to be either the black linen drawstring trousers or the grey ones, either of which would have to be teamed with the pale blue cotton top or the floppy white linen shirt. The blue top was stretchy jersey and clung around her breasts emphasizing every bit of the curve (not that there was much; looking at her naked reflection Lucy conceded that the family D-cup gene had been awarded to Theresa). Henry hadn't seemed to be much impressed by her attempt at sexy dressing the other night, so she might as well relax with her body slouched under the white shirt. She put the black trousers on.

'You've got paint on them,' Colette commented. Lucy looked down at the tiny yellowish flecks and recognized Farrow and Ball's Hound Lemon from a house in Richmond where the owner had insisted on 'authentic' eighteenth-century colours and then complained that it looked 'antiquated'. She hadn't worn these trousers to do the job, the paint must have found its way to them as she cleaned brushes in the kitchen sink at the flat. Too often, exhausted by early-morning starts and going on too long so as to finish at a satisfying point, she'd come home with paint-sodden brushes wrapped in clingfilm which she'd abandon next to the sink and rediscover late at night on her way to bed. Thoughts of the island colour schemes crossed her mind as she picked the paint flecks off the black fabric. Wherever she lived next she would find time for painting something that reminded her of this trip – hot pinks and brave turquoise, a mural of dancing figures perhaps, like the wall at the school along the beach . . .

'What time do we have to be there?' Colette was ready to go. She was wearing her favourite blue towelling skirt from a company that charged a whacking premium for its surf-cred label, and a plain white sleeveless hooded T-shirt. Lucy wasn't sure for a moment if it was a trick of the light, but her eye was caught by an unfamiliar shape to the fabric: it was a shock, though it shouldn't be. Her daughter was growing breasts.

'What are you looking at?' Colette met her gaze by way of the mirror.

'Oh, just you. You're growing up a bit faster than I'm ready for.'

'Yeah well, Mum, it's what we kids do. Didn't you realize?'

Mark was sitting on the pink sofa in the reception area reading a three-day-old *Daily Telegraph* as Lucy and Colette arrived to wait for Henry to collect them.

'Lucky you, an evening out.' He grinned at them.

'You could have taken Theresa somewhere. You don't have to stay in and suffer your in-laws.' Lucy sat down next to him while Colette dashed out through the entrance to look for Henry.

'I tried, actually. I rang round, but everything's closed up till this bloody hurricane passes. I'm not sure she'd want to go anyway.'

'Is she still angry with you?' It was just something to say, really. Of course Theresa would be angry; who wouldn't be? Though few women would be able to sustain an atmosphere of deep fury as well as, or for as long as, her sister could.

'Barely speaking. Just yes and no and who's-had-the-gin when she's peering into the mini-bar. I'm starting to wonder if she'll ever be normal with me again.' He looked helplessly miserable and Lucy almost, but not quite, pitied him. Theresa might well keep up the grievance for eternity. She might even be on the phone to divorce lawyers the minute the plane had touched down.

'Hmm. Well, I don't want to make you feel worse, but she can sulk for Britain. I should just hang around, be patient and try to be perfect then she won't have anything else to hate you for. You can't blame her for not trusting you.'

Mark sighed. 'I know, I know. But if we get back home and she's still like this, well . . .'

Lucy remembered when she was little and teenage Theresa had gone on a school geography field trip, leaving Simon in charge of her guinea pig, a scruffy-looking dirty white rosette-furred creature called Albert. Simon hadn't shut the cage door properly and Albert had got out and shuffled his way down their cul-de-sac on to the main road, where a car had run over him. It was Lucy, on her way to the sweet shop, who had discovered him. Flattened, he'd resembled a shag-pile carpet from a doll's house and she'd almost, but not quite, been fascinated enough to lift the matted fur to see if any of his organs were still there or if they'd been pressed flat into the road like petals between heavy books. Her father had scooped the poor animal up onto a garden spade and buried him under a Rambling Rector rose. Theresa hadn't spoken to Simon for almost three months, carefully keeping the thought of his mistake right at the front of her mind through mornings and mealtimes, his birthday (no present or card) and even the annual Easter egg hunt. Lucy didn't hold out much hope for Mark's chances.

'Henry's here!' Colette came running back in and grabbed Lucy.

'Sorry Mark, I've got to go. Just hang in.' Inadequate advice, but what else could he do, three thousand miles from home.

Henry's Jeep headed up above Teignmouth into the hills. Lucy watched the silhouettes of the tallest palms being buffeted by the wind. Already the air was full of extra movement, the trees bent and swayed against the blue night sky.

'Is this the storm beginning?' Colette asked from the back seat.

'Not yet sweetie. This is just like a warm-up match. This time tomorrow though, watch out!' Henry told her.

'You scared?' Oliver asked Colette.

'No. Well, a bit. Are you?'

Oliver laughed. 'Sure I'm scared! I'm scared I'll get hit by a coconut crashing through the roof!' He waved his arms around and thumped himself on the head. 'Like that!'

'You'll be fine.' Henry grinned at Lucy. 'All the kids here get excited because they get time off school. After tomorrow they might *have* no school.' He swung the car through a gateway. 'OK, we're here.'

Lucy felt strangely nervous about visiting Henry's home. For someone she'd never see again (probably) after three more days, it seemed to matter disproportionately that his taste didn't appal her. It had happened before with men who'd been a potential love interest (and of course Henry wasn't. He couldn't be. There was no time. He didn't even fancy her . . .). One of them, whom she'd met when he'd visited a house she was painting to check on the terms of a planning application, had confessed, as he drove her to his flat after a cinema visit, that he didn't much see the point of changing one's decor: if things like lamps and kitchen units were functioning, why bother to pretty them up or swop them for new ones? The words should have clanged out a warning so clear that she should have leapt out of the car there and then and gone looking for a cab: the man had no interest whatever in the delights of colour or design. The word 'serviceable' could have been invented for him, and for his bare light bulbs, clean but dull beige wallpaper, orange and green checked carpet, stained brown fake-leather sofa ('From my grandmother, last for ever!' He'd thumped it proudly) and no paintings, ornaments, nothing actually selected for its aesthetic appeal, no character. By contrast, Lucy now wondered if she'd only stayed with the treacherous Ross for so long because his apartment had resembled something out of *Elle Decoration* and she'd mistaken the taste bestowed by an anonymous interior designer for his own.

Henry's home gave her no immediate qualms. It was a low-built solid house with the usual broad verandah and a couple of dozing tabby cats by the door. Inside wasn't a riot of Caribbean colour, but a calmer version of the island's brightness. Immediately in from the main door, the sitting-room walls were a gentle buttery yellow, with the window frames and doors in a blue that reminded Lucy of love-in-a-mist. There were a couple of oversized navy-blue sofas, and a deep pink rug. On the biggest wall were three large paintings. They were portraits of island women working: one in a cotton field, one with fish and another bent over a box of spices. They were muted in colour as if the artist was catching the subjects at the twilight end of the day, but with confident broad bold brush strokes. Whoever had done these hadn't hesitated and dithered over the job.

'Glenda did those. What do you think?' Henry opened a bottle of cool white wine and handed her a glass.

213

'They're wonderful. The woman with the fish looks pretty angry.'

'She does?' Henry peered at her. 'You're right. Maybe the fish were off.' Lucy laughed and wandered to the window. Unlike most of the islanders, Henry didn't go in for lace curtains. Out across the trees on the hillside she could see the lights of the town below and the silvery glint of the sea beyond.

'This must be some view in daylight.'

'You could see it.' Henry was close beside her, looking out into the darkness. Lucy could feel her adrenalin level beginning to rise. 'Hardly,' she laughed, 'I think the hotel manager would like us all in before midnight. When I left I felt like a naughty teenager.'

'Well, not tomorrow, but before you go home. Come again.' The adrenalin lurched a little more but then abruptly, as if thinking better of being so close, he moved away from her. 'Hey, let's eat. Chicken's just about done.'

Lucy sat at Henry's kitchen table between Oliver and Colette, savouring the rich scents coming from the oven. The children were giggling together as Oliver described another Caribbean speciality called mountain chicken and Colette tried to guess what meat it actually involved.

'Tiger!' she yelled.

'No, not even close.'

'Kangaroo!'

'Have you *seen* kangaroos hopping about over here?' Henry asked, putting a hot casserole dish on the table.

'OK, monkey then.'

'No, give up?'

'Yeah. Tell me.'

'It's *frog*. A special type of big frog.'

Colette went quiet and eyed the steaming contents of

the dish. Henry and Lucy laughed. 'It's OK, honey, this is your regular chook-chook type bird in this pot. We don't get those frogs here, it's just Montserrat and a couple of other places.'

The food was delicious; besides the chicken there were spicy sweet potatoes, salad and bread. Afterwards, Lucy stayed with Henry in the kitchen, washing dishes and feeling comfortable. She'd drunk most of the wine, she realized, which was making her feel mellow and sleepy. She could hear the sound of Oliver and Colette arguing amicably over a computer game in Oliver's room across the hallway. It felt like home, she thought. The kind of home, with the kind of people, that she should have had. Appalled at herself, her eyes filled with tears. It was something to do with earlier in the evening, catching sight of Colette's budding chest. Time was passing too fast, too quickly for her to get life right. She sniffed and mopped her eyes with a corner of the tea towel.

'Hey, what is it?' Henry had his arms round her, pulling her tenderly against his shoulder. She drew back a little, embarrassed, praying he wouldn't think this was some kind of pathetic girly way of getting him close to her.

'I'm sorry. It's nothing. I . . . it's just today I realized I've spent the whole of Colette's childhood thinking things like *this time next year* everything will be OK, or *next time we move* or even *if I stick with this man*. Even Colette's school isn't right. It's like, oh I don't know, spending your entire life *camping*.' The blatant confusion on Henry's face made her giggle. 'You know, living in tents kind of thing.'

'Oh, right. That kind.' He smiled and pulled her close to him again.

'So stop doing it,' he whispered.

'If it was only that easy.'

'It's that easy. You like being here so stay here. I got space till you find your own. After this storm there'll be more of your kind of work than you can even begin to handle. Do it. Tell London to go screw itself. Tell England.'

Lucy laughed again, he made it sound so simple. Perhaps it was, oh apart from one thing. 'And who tells my family?'

'You do. You're a grown-up too – the choices are yours. Isn't that what you've just worked out?'

Thirteen

It was like being under house arrest. Each guest's possessions had been cleared from surfaces and drawers, packed away and shoved up on the highest shelves, leaving ghost-rooms that looked as if they'd never been occupied. Those who had a belt to spare had gone further and tethered their baggage to the hanging rail in their wardrobe, a tip suggested by a resourceful Italian guest and eagerly passed round, for no-one by now doubted that the wind could pick up and fling into the ocean the entire baggage allowance of even a first-class voyager.

No-one wanted to risk going out either ('We don't advise it' said the management when asked), in case the hurricane unexpectedly speeded up its progress and hit the island early. Not that there was anywhere to go; Teignmouth, it was reported, was as deserted as central Manchester on Cup Final day. Even the shops in the precinct across the main road from the hotel were now closed. The small supermarket was boarded up and the pizza café had its metal shutters down. The cab drivers who usually touted vociferously for trade outside the hotel had decamped, and even those who had baulked at the idea of handing back their hire cars had changed their minds for fear of ending up liable for new bodywork if a tree should happen to fall across the bonnet.

Eerily, there was no clue in the weather that this day would be different from any other: the sky was almost brazenly clear and blue and the only wind came in small sharp provocative bursts, rustling through the leaves and making everyone look up nervously as if they might need suddenly to leap off the sunloungers and race for cover.

Becky was bored and tetchy by mid-morning. If she sat still she felt sticky and hot, even in the shade, and was sure she was becoming a carefully selected target for bugs to bite. Simon offered to play tennis with her but just the thought of hurtling around the court made her feel her breath was running short. And if she felt like that, how much more of a risk was it for her father, whose blue linen shirt was patterned with abstract splodges of sweat? He could end up dead. She wandered along the beach to the furthest headland and thought about swimming out into the ocean beyond the point where she could hear voices wittering on about whether they were all destined to drown, be killed by falling trees or starve to death in the storm's aftermath. If they'd only all stop going *on*. It was only going to be for a few hours and then they could all get back to normal. She could hardly bloody wait. Glenda wouldn't let anyone take jet skis or sailing boats out either, because she'd got them all safely stowed away under the big awning next to the dive shop. Luke and Tom had been to see if they could sneak out a couple of pedalos, but Glenda had showed them how securely they were all tied down and told them quite sharply that if anyone was going to be allowed special dispensation, it certainly wouldn't be them, not with their track record.

'Bored, sweetie?' Ethan appeared very close to Becky, silently and unexpectedly as if beamed down from space. She moved away a bit and took a good cool look at him. His eyes were only just above the level of her own but his shoulders were broad enough to block out the sun. She still couldn't decide if he was really fanciable, though he was decidedly more fanciable than anyone else in the immediate vicinity. And there was nothing to do.

'You been to that beach round there?' He indicated the strip of land just beyond the hotel's boundaries. 'It's for nudists.' He grinned at her. 'All the Germans like it, and the Swedes and Danes. Never seen no Brits there though.'

It sounded like a challenge. Becky felt confused. Why would he want to see her with her clothes off *now*? He'd had a chance to see her body that other night. The night of the boring, stupid, tedious blow job. If he hadn't been in such a hurry, been so selfish and greedy, he could have had a good look at her all spread out on the sand in the moonlight. He could have flipped her over and back, played around with her, done almost anything he wanted. Perhaps he just wanted the chance to take his own clothes off and do some boastful displaying, especially in front of pasty, under-endowed Europeans.

'Yeah, all right then, let's go.' Even to her own ears, she sounded bored. She wondered vaguely how long it would take for the white bands of her body, where her bikini had guarded her skin, to catch up with the tanned bits, and if the contrast would look silly exposed to the sun.

He grinned even more broadly. '*OK!*' he shouted, punching the air as if he'd won something special.

'What's the big deal?' She was suspicious. Perhaps

he'd only asked her for some kind of bet, or a dare. She glanced round to see if he'd got a sniggering posse of mates hanging about in the background. She couldn't see anyone.

Ethan shimmied up close to her and nuzzled her neck. 'The big deal, baby, is that you're gorgeous.'

Becky shrugged him off and started to stroll towards the far beach.

'You mean you've got nothing else to do,' she told him. 'You should bring more of your stock with you. There's all these potential buyers hanging around who'd be desperate to part with their cash for your jewellery. You're wasting a great marketing opportunity.'

His eyes were glinting at her. 'I ain't wasting nothing, babe, don't you worry.'

Lucy quite liked the enforced inactivity. Although sure that she had a lot of major back-home decisions to consider (where to live, how to afford it, and then what to do about Colette's dull-girly school?) she did feel they could legitimately be postponed at least till after the storm. She and Plum sat side by side on loungers by the pool, reading. Lucy had found a selection of ancient Agatha Christie paperbacks on a shelf in the games room and was savouring the almost sinful indulgence of working her way through a snug country-house murder starring Miss Marple. Plum preferred Hercule Poirot and was deep into *Death on the Nile*.

'It's never really the butler who did it, is it?' Lucy commented.

'Certainly not. The lower orders knew their place!' Plum agreed. 'Though possibly the butler *might* have done it, if he was really the long-lost adopted son in disguise.'

It was an odd, antiquated notion, Lucy thought, 'knowing one's place'. It implied you really hadn't any choice about where it was. That could be comfortable, just as she was now, lazy on a cushioned lounger knowing she couldn't even leave the hotel area – so *this*, in the literal location sense, had to be her place. It also meant that you had few tricky choices to make in life, less chance to get things completely screwed up by pitching your aim too far outside your allotted circle. Henry had said she should trust her instincts more to choose what she wanted and believe it was for the best. 'Ask yourself,' he'd said as she mopped away her embarrassing tears the night before, 'who is this mythical Other Person you're trying to please?' She hadn't been aware there was anyone, but even as his words were out, she saw, in her mind, her family gathered in a group like a wedding photo, staring and smiling at her, persuading her to Be Like Them.

'I *do* please myself,' she'd told Henry. 'I get positively *accused* of it. I'm told I'm selfish quite often, so I assume I must be. Though,' she'd paused to think, 'I don't know what's so selfish about raising a child by yourself, or about not getting married to some safe but unlovely man just for the sake of a suburban townhouse, or about not giving up a job you like just so you can wear a smart on-the-knee skirt in an office and have your mother proudly tell her neighbours that you're some old sod's secretary.'

'You're right. We're the same, I don't want to wear a skirt either,' he'd agreed. That was just before he'd kissed her, which she certainly hadn't expected, not after the night of the unrequired condoms. And of course that had been exactly the moment she'd been reminded that there was more than herself to think about: you couldn't lose yourself in a moment of passion when your child is giggling with her friend in the next room.

'Trusting my instincts will have to wait,' she'd said, reluctantly pulling away from Henry.

'For now maybe, but there's time.'

'Not much of it.'

'Like I said, there's as much as you make.'

'Plum,' Lucy said now, 'have you ever thought your life might have been completely different from how it is? I mean if you'd made other choices?'

Plum looked at her. 'Doesn't everyone?'

'But do you think it might have been loads better?'

Plum frowned. 'If you're trying to get me to tell you I think Simon was one of life's consolation prizes then you're going to be disappointed. I rather like him, actually. And I like my job, which I rather think I should have stayed at home and got on with, not lazed about here. Anyway,' she yawned and stretched to emphasize her point, 'think of the sheer bloody upheaval of buggering off to start something else. It'd have to be severely worth it.'

'But suppose it was.'

Plum shrugged. 'It wouldn't be.'

Lucy closed her eyes. The brightness of the sun left the back of her eyelids shining brilliant pink for a moment. When she opened them again, Shirley was standing in front of her.

'I've just seen Becky wandering off with that beach trader,' she said to Plum. 'Don't you think you should go and see if she's all right?'

Plum smiled lazily. 'I don't suppose she'll come to any harm,' she said. 'After all, she can't go far.'

'It depends what you mean by far,' Shirley said dourly, parking herself on a lounger next to Lucy. 'Girls need watching.' She turned to Lucy. 'You wait till it's Colette.'

Lucy looked up at her and smiled. 'I will, thank you. I'll do just that. I'll wait.'

Becky didn't mind stripping off her bikini, or at least she wasn't going to let Ethan think it was any kind of big deal. They'd chosen a secluded spot high up the beach in a patch of sun between clumps of trees. There were quite a lot of people below them closer to the shore, though as they'd walked past she hadn't heard any English voices. Ethan didn't seem to be about to remove any clothes. Becky was surprised but didn't comment, determined not to express anything other than mild blasé boredom. She put on her sunglasses, spread out her sarong on the sand and sat on it, staring at the naked bodies down by the sea. It seemed strange how different they could look, simply by discarding a few square inches of swimwear. There were a few prune-fleshed elderly folk, but most of the beach's occupants looked as if they spent a lot of leisure time in the gym. There was a predominance of fair-haired men with extra-long limbs and torsos, giving the impression that their heads had stopped growing quite a long time before the rest of them. They reminded Becky of professional tennis players. Even the young women seemed to be built like Steffi Graf, all muscle and sinew. But then, she supposed, no-one would want to show off a mottled, dimpled backside, even if you did think a tan would improve things. A group of the more active people were playing volleyball which, she thought, involved a rather unnecessary amount of stretching and leaping and rolling about. Perhaps, for some people, being naked brought on an attack of true exhibitionism. As far as she was concerned they might

223

at least have the manners to keep their flesh still. She lay down on the sand and closed her eyes.

'You want me to rub on some lotion?' Ethan's shadow was blocking out the sun.

'If you want to. It's in the bag.'

She rolled over onto her front. Ethan knelt across her and started massaging the factor 10 into her shoulders. 'No-one can see us up here by the trees,' he said as he smoothed the lotion into her body. He was good at it. Becky felt as if her insides were melting away like a warmed choc ice. If he'd only done some of this the other night . . .

'Hello Becky. Didn't expect to see you here.' She hauled herself up instantly, throwing Ethan onto the sand. Mark was standing above them, carrying a bottle of Carib beer and still wearing shorts and a shirt, which, she felt, was definitely cheating. He was grinning down at her and she pulled the sarong across her body.

'What the fuck do you think you're doing?' she spat at him.

'Same as you. Enjoying the beach. Some nice views here, some not so.'

'You're overdressed,' she snapped. 'And where's Theresa?'

'Who knows or cares?' He started to remove his shirt. 'Can I join you?'

'No! Stop! Mark, this isn't . . . Just go away will you?' He was drunk.

'Yeah, man. We need, like, some privacy.' Ethan lit a spliff and Becky glared.

'Oh, great. Pass that round.' Mark sat down next to Becky. Ethan handed him the joint and he inhaled deeply. 'Haven't had any of this for a while. Should do it more.'

'No you shouldn't. You're old and you've got kids and stuff.' If he'd just go *away,* Becky thought. Go away and not tell anyone.

'Oh and that means I'm banned from all the fun?' His head wheeled round to face her. It moved, she thought, as if it wasn't really in control, as if it might loll off his neck. *That* drunk. That was good. It meant he wouldn't tell anyone he'd seen her, in case she told as well.

'So you're the guy who sells narcotics and necklaces. I've heard about you.'

Ethan grinned. 'You've heard good things?'

Mark thought for a moment and frowned. 'Depends which way you look at it. I've heard you collect women by nationalities.'

'Mark, what are you on about?' Becky interrupted.

'Yeah, you'll like this, Becks. He has . . .' Mark waved the joint in the direction of Ethan and then took another deep drag. 'This bloke, your *boyfriend* here, has like one English girl and then, say, a Dane, then another English girl and then maybe a German and so on. English girls in between because they're just so easy.'

'Perhaps there's just more of them,' Becky suggested. She could see where this was leading. From her father she expected lectures to keep her in line. From Theresa, even, she wouldn't be surprised at the odd criticism, but from Mark she expected only a stranger's detachment. What she got up to simply wasn't of any concern to him.

'I never had an Italian one,' Ethan cut in with a low laugh. 'Been wanting Italian, would make almost a full set.'

Mark chuckled. Becky scowled: how sordid were these two?

'So you see, Becky, you want to be careful.' Mark was back on the theme. 'Bloke puts it about like the supply of women's about to run short, well, you could catch something.'

'Not from me, man, I'm clean.'

Becky climbed back into her bikini, not looking at Mark in case he was looking at her. 'Haven't you ever heard of condoms, Mark? They're what careful people use. Makes everything safe.'

''S'like eating a sweet with the paper on,' he said, swigging the last of his beer. 'And they're not that safe. They break. Sometimes they break and then you're really in it, real live biological bug trouble.' He was almost slurring his words by now. Becky frowned at him. What was he saying, exactly? What had he caught? He was hinting at something, for sure. Perhaps it was one of those diseases that everyone thought had died out, like syphilis. Bits of him would fall off, he'd go mad (or mad*der* at any rate), he'd get pustules and die – they'd talked about it in history at school, even the back-row yobs had been fascinated.

'Mark,' she said, having worked herself up into a state that bordered on pity for him, 'Mark, come on, let's go back to the others.' With difficulty, for he was heavy and not particularly steady, she pulled him up from the sand and led him back towards the hotel. She waved to Ethan, who grinned back at her. However much she resisted it, she wasn't going to ignore completely what Mark had said. It had only been an illusion, the idea that she was more than just a notch on Ethan's shag-list, but Mark's words were clearly basic lousy truth, and, well, somehow Ethan didn't have the same appeal. How sad would she have to be to be *that* desperate?

*   *   *

The last-day-on-earth feeling continued through to the afternoon and increased when one of the tour reps let it slip that the airport was now closed and wouldn't reopen until the storm had passed. Six people who had been waiting forlornly with their luggage in the lobby for a taxi after lunch had been scheduled to fly back to Manchester early that evening but discovered that because of concern about possible storm damage, their plane hadn't even bothered to leave England. There was a general vagueness about arrangements for places for them on flights later in the week.

'There'll be a logjam at the airport. There'll be stranded folks all over the island,' Perry, the poolside philosopher, predicted grimly. 'It'll be chaos.'

'There'll be queues for miles,' Shirley agreed. Neither of them seemed too concerned, Lucy thought as she listened. If anything, the prospect gave them a certain amount of glee, being a chance to demonstrate that The Brits knew how to deal with mayhem and would show any panicking Johnny Foreigners that patience and the ability to wait your turn triumphed in the end.

Luke was bored. He and Tom and Colette couldn't think of anything to do and were starting to get tetchy. No-one was allowed in the swimming pool because the hotel staff were collecting all the chairs and tables from the beach bar and lowering them into the water to store them safely from the wind. The bar-football and table-tennis tables from the games room were also off limits, having been folded and fastened securely to a pillar in the centre of the room.

'Couldn't all this wait till later?' Plum complained on his behalf.

'I don't suppose many of the staff will *be* here later,' Lucy said. 'They'll all want to get home and be with their own families.'

'I suppose so,' Plum conceded with a sigh. 'I must say this is getting awfully tedious. First none of us can go out, then some people can't even go home, and now the facilities we *have* got are being gradually run down. Strange sort of holiday.'

'I think it's rather exciting,' Shirley said. 'It'll certainly give us something to tell them back home. Better than the usual "Yes thank you, we had a lovely time", with nothing else to report.'

Plum got up off her lounger and stretched her arms. 'Well, I think I'll go and get a bit of sleep. I don't suppose we'll get much tonight.' She walked off slowly in the direction of her room. Luke and Tom sat on the grass near the pool, watching the white ironwork of the gazebo to see if there were any lizards they could torment.

'There was a big one down by those rocks on the headland yesterday. It went into a hole so it might still be around,' Colette told them. 'We could go and look.'

The two boys considered, looking bored, then Tom decided, 'I suppose we could. And after that I want to get some supplies for tonight. Sweets and stuff, though Mum went off for a drink with some bloke after lunch and I don't know where she is and she's got all the cash.'

The three of them sauntered off along the sand towards the headland where the villas were. The dogs that lived on the shore had disappeared and the small black birds that scavenged beneath the trees seemed to have gone as well. Colette had the feeling that wildlife, better equipped with instincts than stupid humans, had gone into hiding till the storm was over. The sea was now quite definitely rougher than before and the surf was racing further up the beach.

'Is it high tide, or is this the start of the hurricane?'

Colette asked. She looked at her grandparents' villa, up on the promontory, and wondered if it *was* going to be far enough out of the water when everything got really rough. She felt a tingle of something that wasn't quite fear, but wasn't comfortable enough to be just excitement.

'The sea's crashing on the rocks quite a lot too. It's spraying right up to the wall,' Tom said. 'I wouldn't want to spend the night up there.'

'Thanks, Tom. Just a great thing to say,' Luke hissed at him. Colette's eyes were looking alarmingly round and afraid. And nothing had even happened yet.

'Yeah, well, it'll be even worse in the dark, won't it, 'cos you'll only be able to *hear* it, won't you.' Tom was enjoying being persistent with the gloom.

'Tom, just *shut up* will you.' Luke pushed him to emphasize his point and Tom slid over in the sand.

'Hey, thanks! Well if you're going to be like that I'll just go off and find my mum for some cash. You can stuff your fucking old lizard.' Tom turned and strode off angrily, hands in his pockets and his head down.

'Now you've hurt his feelings,' Colette said.

'Don't you start . . . Oh sorry, hey I'll apologize to him later, OK?'

Colette giggled. 'If we live that long.'

'Look, we'll be OK.'

'I know.' Colette laughed again. 'After all, Gran keeps saying "It's only a bit of wind."'

'Yeah, like it's some giant fart in the sky or something.'

The two of them were still laughing as they climbed up the rocks to find where Colette had seen the big lizard. The sea was pounding hard against the rocks, sending jets of spray high in the air. Colette moved along so that more of the water splashed onto her. 'It's

229

lovely, like a warm shower,' she told Luke.

'So where's this huge iguana thing?' he asked, peering into rock crevices.

'It wasn't an iguana, but nearly as big as that,' she said. 'And it was kind of blueish.'

'Can't see anything. Let's go down to the other side.' He moved a bit closer to her and lowered his voice. 'And we might see the Great Celeb, sunbathing out on his or her terrace.'

'They've probably put special screens up.'

There were voices, though, and someone doing some low giggling. Instinctively, Luke and Colette started creeping slowly and carefully along the rocks in the direction of the murmurs.

'They sound . . . naughty, like they're up to something,' Colette whispered.

Luke agreed, though the word he'd have used was 'sexy', which was probably because he was a couple of years older. He was desperate to see what was going on, but also wondered if Colette perhaps shouldn't. Then suddenly there was no choice. Across the next rock, immediately below them, was the vision of a couple celebrating their not-so-hidden liaison with a bottle of champagne. The woman's bikini top was on the rock behind her and the man, as they watched, poured the bubbling liquid down her neck and leaned to lick at it as it trickled onto her breasts. Her head went back as he made his way up towards her throat, and some movement from the two teenagers caught her eye.

'Run!' Luke hissed at Colette and she scuttled backwards behind the rocks.

'Spying little bastards!' The woman's voice rang out after them. There was a crash of glass breaking and the man swore loudly. Colette and Luke, barely able to move from laughter, managed to hurl themselves across the promontory wall and into Shirley and Perry's villa garden, where they collapsed on the spiky grass, gasping for breath. 'The gold lady!'

'And one of the Steves! Oh yuk!' Colette pulled an appalled face.

'Double, triple yuk! I mean she's someone's *mum*!'

Abruptly Colette's laughter stopped. She stared out over the wall towards the sea.

'I suppose she is. So's my mum,' she said.

'What do you mean?' Luke was puzzled. Of course Lucy was Colette's mum, what did that have to do with anything? His mum was a mum too.

'Oh. I get it,' he said. 'You mean that she might . . . like that . . .'

'Well, she probably does.' Then Colette added quickly, 'But not with just anyone.'

Another snort of laughter escaped from Luke. 'And not in public!'

'No, not in public.' And the giggling started again.

'It's like being summoned for nursery tea,' Mark grumbled as he and Simon walked up the steps to the terrace restaurant. It wasn't even six o'clock yet and Mark was beginning a dry-mouthed hangover that could do with a bit of sleeping off, but the staff were eager to get the hotel guests fed early and despatched to their rooms to wait for the storm to hit. The latest forecast was that it was due sometime between nine and ten, but it was anyone's guess how long it was likely to go on after that. As guests wandered in from the beach and the poolside, staff collected the sun-loungers and piled them up, roping them in heaps together and tying them to the big tamarind tree beside the pool or to the turpentine tree beside the beach bar.

'They'll reek of oil after this,' Perry commented as he watched. 'You don't want to put anything too close to that tree, the whiff lingers.'

Lucy smiled at him. 'I quite like the smell, it reminds me of paint,' she said.

Mark grunted gloomily. 'Well, I'm glad you don't get trees that smell of my job, I can tell you. I wouldn't want to go on holiday and get smelly reminders of the bank.'

'Wait till your three are teenagers,' Plum teased. 'They think there *are* trees that resemble banks. They think money grows on them.'

The dining area had been transformed. Many of the tables had already been removed and stacked close to the wall to keep them safe. Those that were left had been laid out in long lines ('like school dinners', Colette said to Lucy), covered with bright pink cloths and arranged with free bottles of wine from which cheery silver balloons on green ribbons floated in the breeze. Out on the open section of the terrace a barbecue was blazing and reggae was belting out over the PA in the lobby. Everyone was to eat at the same time and all together, children and babies as well. Marisa, determined to have a good time too, handed over her three charges to Theresa and went to the far end of the table where she could sit with her new friend. The atmosphere was of determined party jollity, with people making jokes about being swept away and meeting up again on the Venezuelan coast. The Manchester group who'd missed out on their flights home had recovered quickly from their disappointment and were now crowing about getting more than a free lunch, and even Cathy was happily inviting everyone to her wedding the day after: 'If the place is still standing, and even if it's not,' she declared.

'Hey, boys, it's party time!' the 'Star' lady called out to the Steves. 'Come sit by me and open a bottle!'

'She's cheered up,' Perry said to Lucy.

'Happy Hour started at four, that's why. But they've closed the bar for the night now, which was sensible,' Simon told him. He was frowning. He'd got used to the idea that this hurricane was a serious event. Now the atmosphere felt like the last decadent party on a sinking ship. Drunk people could be a liability – they might do stupid things like come out of their rooms and run about in the wind. Those who were sober would have to rescue them and risk their own lives.

'Lighten up, Simon. We'll be OK.' Lucy prodded him gently. 'Have a glass of wine, relax.'

'I'm not sure relaxing is such a good idea. Suppose we need to be alert?'

'Then we will be. No-one's going to overdo it, they're all too scared.'

It was almost at the end of the meal, when the brief Caribbean dusk had passed and it was now dark, that the wind suddenly stepped up its force. The edges of the tablecloths started to flick and flap upwards, reminding Lucy of whippy updraughts at underground stations that send skirts swirling. Napkins blew off the tables, then leaves began to appear among the food, blown in from the outside terrace. Rain started pounding on the roof just as everyone was finishing the fruit and ice cream, and there was an all-round breath-intake as the lights flickered in a particularly sharp gust.

'This is it,' Shirley said.

'No it isn't.' A passing waiter grinned at her. 'This is nothing yet.'

Lucy's thoughts turned to Henry. She imagined him snugly blockaded into his home with Oliver and Glenda and Glenda's friend Abby who shared her studio home. She wondered if they were making a party of it too, fending off the potential disaster with good food and wine and jokes. She wished she was with them, curled up with Henry on the big blue sofa along with Oliver and Colette, just like a real family. She imagined the preparations they would have made, the bath filled with water in case supplies were cut off, the candles and lamps ready for when the electricity failed, the cupboards full of emergency food because the roads into town could be strewn with fallen trees. Henry had said there'd been panic buying at the stores in town, with everyone stocking up for a long period of upheaval. All Lucy had with her by way of emergency supplies was a bag containing her toothbrush, her passport, knickers for the next day and the Agatha Christie book she'd started that morning. It was hardly the stuff of survival.

'I haven't got enough cigarettes, I'm sure of it.' The gold lady, looking nervy, appeared next to Lucy as they went down the steps on their way to their allocated rooms. There was an outbreak of loud giggling behind them and the two women turned round to find Colette and Luke in fits of uncontrollable laughter.

'What's the matter with them?' the gold lady asked.

'No idea. Some private joke I imagine.'

The gold lady frowned and rubbed at her neck nervously, which sent them off into spasms of hilarity again. Her tan deepened into a blush and she jabbed a painted fingernail towards them. 'Yes, well, you two, just remember that some jokes need to stay more private than others.'

Fourteen

'Oh good. Simon's going to be Safety Officer. That'll make him happy.' Theresa sipped at a glass of white wine as she watched her brother carefully lining up all the wooden louvres on the villa's windows and doors so that they lay down flat and wouldn't give any provocative resistance to the wind. It was important (it had said in the instructions) that the air should be able to flow freely across the rooms and out the other side where possible. Otherwise the excess pressure had nothing to do but try to lift the roof off. Simon had no doubt that if he didn't make all efforts to stop it, it would succeed. 'Well, someone's got to do it,' he said. 'Unless you want one of these wooden planks hurtling across the room. They're solid teak. It would be like being whacked with a cricket bat.'

'I'm not ungrateful, Simon, really,' she smiled at him, 'I'm just amazed you can be bothered to be so meticulous.'

'It's his job to be meticulous,' Plum defended him. 'If he can line up a thumb-sucking twelve-year-old's overbite, he shouldn't have any trouble with a couple of dozen slats of wood.'

Simon had a vague feeling that in spite of this superficial support, Plum had joined Theresa in taking the piss. Why was he bothering to try to make them safe? Why didn't he just lock them all out on the terrace and let them die? No-one had any imagination; they couldn't seem to connect this storm with the donations they occasionally credit-carded over to world disaster funds. They could be reduced to a miserable set of statistics by the morning, mentioned in sombre tones on the international news as being among The Rising Death Toll. They were behaving, he decided, like small children at a birthday sleepover, preparing to giggle the night away wrapped in blankets while they guzzled their way through Shirley's laid-in supplies of drinks and crisps and ice cream. Or at least ice cream till the electricity gave out and the fridge gave up the ghost. That was the only kind of disaster bloody Theresa understood: running out of ice for the gin. Only Lucy was being quiet and refusing to get overexcited. He put that down to understandable apprehension. At least she'd got a brain, he thought, at least she was sensitive enough to work out that this could be their last night on the planet.

Lucy was out on the terrace with Colette watching the sea and the sky for signs of change. In spite of Simon's assumptions, she was not praying away her last hours but thinking how beautiful the night looked. The sky seemed as if it were divided into two, with the area directly above them an almost clear rich deep shade of navy, lit by occasional stars and scattered with a few puffy grey-black clouds. Further away was a thick matt blackness, as if the earth had travelled too close to the edge of the universe and was about to fall off into this infinite hole. Lucy assumed it was the leading edge of the storm, though it looked only slightly different from any other night-time rain cloud. It was certainly coming nearer.

'It's quite windy now, but nothing special. How will we know when it really starts?' Luke asked as they perched together on the sea wall.

'Don't be stupid,' Becky sneered. 'I mean what are you going to do, say "Oh is this a hurricane, or do people usually get smacked in the mouth by a flying table?"'

'Well, the wind's already stronger than it was during supper, so I guess it just gets worse until you feel it's time to go inside and make sure the doors are locked,' Lucy told them.

'The sea's *definitely* rougher,' Luke decided, having stared at the dark water till he could barely focus.

'And it's splashing up much higher,' Colette agreed. Each foaming wave was speeding way up the beach now. The Caribbean tides were normally barely noticeable, but now the sand was covered as far as the first row of thatched beach umbrellas.

'Don't suppose those'll be standing in the morning,' Mark said, then he leaned over to Becky and whispered, 'Any sight or sound of our illustrious neighbour?'

Becky squirmed away from him and dashed back into the villa without responding.

'Something I said?' he asked Lucy.

'Probably. She is sixteen after all,' she laughed. 'And to answer your question, there's silence from the Great Celebrity next door.'

'Probably hiding under the bed.' Mark grinned. 'Which must mean he's a leader of one of the world's major powers.'

Just then a powerful blast of wind howled across the terrace. It was as if the weather gods had stepped on some kind of celestial accelerator.

'Time to go in,' Lucy declared, leading Colette back through the doors.

'Yes, and time for another drinkie.' Theresa made for the fridge but Mark got there first. There was a small tussle over a bottle of wine, interrupted by Marisa. 'You come say goodnight,' she ordered, 'so the children will sleep now.' Lucy watched the Swiss girl shoving herself expertly between Theresa and the fridge. Perhaps she had to do a lot of that at home too. Theresa, unbalanced, staggered a bit. Lucy reached out and steadied her.

'It's OK, Lucy, I'm not about to fall over. I'm off to kiss my babies.' She was smiling in a vague way.

'We'll both go,' Mark said, taking Theresa's wrist and leading her through to one of the villa's two bedrooms where all three of the children had been put into the king-size four-poster bed.

'If you're this pissed now . . .' Lucy heard Mark begin as the door was firmly shut.

'Oh this is really jolly. All the family together, just how it should be.' Shirley settled herself comfortably onto the sofa and looked around her. Everyone she cared about was right here, either in the room, or, in the case of Theresa and the little ones, just the other side of that door. The teenagers and Marisa were sprawled about on the floor, blankets at the ready in case they felt like dozing off. Shirley felt there was an air of excited expectation, though, unlike Simon, she didn't antici-pate danger. By Luke's age she'd done danger in wartime Manchester, seen a whole street bombed out, leaving shattered walls standing, with flowered wall-paper tattered in the wind. Below, the collapsed rooms were nothing but heaped-up rubble, poignantly strewn with shoes and broken crockery and the newspapers the dead inhabitants had been reading that day. Once you'd done a war, she reasoned, you'd done your stint

238

of the Worst that Could Happen. What people did to each other was the worst on earth – weather couldn't come close.

'It's just like Christmas,' she laughed.

Lucy grimaced. 'I was thinking that too, locked in with your family and no escape. Still, at least with this you don't have to go through it all again a year later.'

'Your mother meant it was *nice* like Christmas.' Perry was frowning, warning.

'Yes I know she did. I was joking, though actually I don't see why I'm not allowed to disagree.'

'Then why say anything at all? Don't *spoil* things, Lucy.'

Oh, that word again. At one time they used it on Simon, way back. Then Theresa took it over. Why did it always *spoil* things if she expressed her thoughts? And she *had* only been joking – well, almost.

'I quite like Christmas,' Luke commented. 'Can I have another Coke please Gran?'

'Yes of course you can. Anyone else fancy a drink? I think we could treat ourselves to a little something.'

'Mark and Theresa have got a bottle on the go up there by the sink,' Plum said, rising from her chair to go and get some wine. She picked up the empty bottle. 'Oh. Well, they *had*, it all seems to have gone. Funny, I thought Mark was off booze.'

'Theresa must have had it,' Becky suggested.

There was a small, awkward silence in the room while everyone avoided commenting on Theresa's booze capacity. The murmuring voices beyond the bedroom door were getting louder and nobody wanted to hear.

'Wind's picking up now,' Perry said, going to the window and peering through the louvres.

'Just as well, if those two are going to have a blazing

row,' Lucy murmured to Colette. Colette laughed.

'What's funny Colette? Come on, share the joke.' Shirley was looking hard at her. Colette went silent. 'Nothing, it was just . . .'

'Just something I said, private joke, that's all.' Lucy smiled at her mother. There was a tumult of rain battering on the roof. Fat drops of it splashed in through the louvres close to the main door and collected in a rapidly spreading puddle on the tiled floor. The wind, that had at first whispered through the windows on the side away from the sea, now picked up sound and speed, whooping and gusting viciously. Marisa crept behind the sofa and wrapped her blanket round her tightly. Colette went to sit with her and the two of them huddled together between the sofa and the wall.

The noise of the wind no longer seemed real, Lucy thought. It was beginning to sound mad, crazily wailing and roaring as if it was trapped inside something, hurling itself at the edges to escape. The only time she'd heard anything like it was on TV cartoons when the characters were struggling along, bent horizontal against the exaggerated pretend-elements. Simon's preparations had been all too effective, for the storm now seemed to be using the villa as a conduit. As the wind made its way across the room, it sent Shirley's magazines skittering to the floor. Suntan-lotion bottles on a ledge tumbled into the sink. Plum got busy, collecting up all dangerously loose items and stuffing them at random into drawers.

'Are you sure you got it right, Simon?' Lucy asked. 'Wouldn't all the shutters be better firmly closed? Rain's coming in horizontally.' It was true. Shirley went into the bathroom and came out with a towel to place under the window by the main door. As she bent, there was a fierce metallic clatter and the mosquito screen behind the louvres fell to the floor, just missing her head.

'God, if it's like this now . . .' Plum muttered.

'Are you coming out or are you going to stay in here all night?' Theresa was pacing the bedroom but keeping her eyes on Mark, who had snuggled down on the edge of the bed close to Ella. The children had drifted off to sleep, unaware and uncaring that beyond the window the elements were waging a war. The mosquito net covering them fluttered up and down in the breeze that was sneaking in through unseen gaps.

Mark opened one eye. 'What's to come out for?'

'To be with the others, of course. We should at least try to look as if we're, you know, together. I'll make an effort if you will.'

Mark sat up and rubbed his eyes. He'd been drinking hard all day, making up for the days of antibiotic-enforced sobriety. He was tired and if he didn't get the light out soon he felt his delicate brain would be burned away through his eyeballs.

'I don't *need* to show anyone we're "together" as you so coyly put it. And anyway what sort of "together" do you mean? As a so-called happy couple or as people who can just about walk a straight line with their eyes shut?'

Theresa paced harder. 'You're so fucking exasperating Mark.' Sebastian rolled over and grunted so she lowered her voice again. 'I just don't want everyone else knowing our sordid bloody business. Or even suspecting it.'

Mark smiled lazily at her. 'Ah. So we're not "together" but we've got to look "together" just for the sake of dear Mumsy and Dadsy. I get it. What's it worth?'

'*Worth?*'

'Yes, *worth*. You want me to do something for you so what will you do for me?' He gave her a louche grin and lay back with his hands behind his head.

'You're disgusting,' she hissed. 'There won't be any of that for . . . well, ever.'

He shrugged. 'Then why should I be nice to you? Come on Tess, lighten up. I made mistakes, got caught and now you're going to make sure the punishment's worse than the crime. How fair is that? If you loved me . . .'

'If *you'd* loved *me* you wouldn't have . . .' She was shouting now.

'I do but I did. Can't we put it behind us? Move on? Because if you won't, there's no point pretending any more. I might just as well go right in there and give your precious sodding parents a divorce announcement. That should make their bloody night for them.'

A gust of wind blew one of the louvre slats to the floor. Mark stood up, alarmed. All three children stirred in their sleep but didn't wake. Theresa looked at the gap in the window and shuddered. 'Do we put it back? Will they all fall out?'

'The rain'll pour in if I leave it out.' Mark pushed the piece of wood back into place, not holding out much hope that it would stay there. It seemed to be bent. The noise outside, he now noticed, was horrendous. Through the gap in the shutter he could just about make out trees wildly waving. 'Jesus, it's like something out of a horror movie,' he said.

'I'm scared.' Theresa was next to him. He put his arm round her and she didn't pull away.

'Come on, let's join the others for a bit,' she said. 'But if it gets any worse we'll come back in here with the kids. If we're all going to die, we'll all go together.'

'So I don't tell them we're getting divorced?'

'No. Anyway we're not. I've put twenty years into this marriage, I'm not giving up on it now.' She sounded almost as fierce as before, which confused Mark.

'You make it sound like a life sentence.' He risked a grin.

'You've just defined marriage,' she said, opening the door.

'We could play a game,' Plum suggested.

'What about Botticelli?' Colette suggested.

'Boring. Anyone got any cards? We could play poker, for cash,' Luke said.

'No cards,' Shirley decreed. 'In fact, before we do anything else, this might be a good moment now we're all together . . .'

'Yes. We've got something to tell you.' Perry sat on the sofa next to her.

'I knew it.' Simon got up and started pacing the room. 'How long have you known?' he accused Perry.

'A couple of months. We've been waiting for the right moment.'

Simon was biting his knuckles. Lucy looked at her brother and gestured to him to sit down. It must be sad to assume that all unexpected news could only be bad – neither Shirley nor Perry was looking as if it was.

'We've decided it's time to offload some assets,' Perry began.

'And to make a move. It'll be our last one,' Shirley added.

'Last one? So you *are* ill? You've got something serious?' Simon chipped in.

Shirley laughed. 'Well at our age we've all got something serious – it's called old age and it's terminal. No,

243

Simon, apart from the odd angina twinge, and I've got something for that from the doctor, we're both fine. No, it's just that we decided recently that it's time we saw more of our family, while we're still mobile and most of our brain cells are still functioning.'

'Well you're certainly seeing them now,' Plum commented. Simon glared at her.

'So we've sold the house in Wilmslow and we're coming south. To be nearer all of you.'

'Why didn't you say anything before? Why the big secret?' Lucy asked.

'Well there was always that risk you'd try to talk us out of it,' Shirley told her. 'You'd come up with all the usual: "You don't want to move far at your time of life", "What about all your friends", "The price of property in the south". We'd thought of all that, we're not babies.'

'I wouldn't have said any of that. You're more than old enough to make your own decisions,' Lucy said, then added as a reminder, 'we all are.'

The sound of the wind filled the silence that followed. The noise was now constant and high-pitched, no longer in gusts, and reminded Lucy of the almost shocking explosiveness of an express train blasting through a quiet country station, only this seemed to be a train with an endless number of carriages.

'Where will you live, exactly?' Mark's question hid plenty of others: were his in-laws proposing the conversion of his Surrey double garage into a granny flat? Would they (oh please God) require a paying stake in their grandchildren's education? Plum wondered (with dread), would they require a slap-up traditional roast *every* Sunday? And, worst of all, would Simon now run to his mother with every glitch in their family life? Would every teenage fault, that would not escape

Shirley's eagle eye, be down to Bad Mothering?

'I think it's very brave of you,' Lucy said at last. 'Not many people have the guts to uproot themselves from a lifetime in one area and settle somewhere new.' She thought about Henry telling her 'So don't go home', as if it was that simple. And here were her parents preparing to move on at nearly eighty. It made her, at less than half their age, feel pretty cowardly.

'Of course we won't be descending on you lot for ever. Well, only for a month or two till the flat in Hove is ready. We fancied being by the sea,' Shirley told them. She didn't, Mark noticed, specify exactly on whom they would be descending. 'A month or two' was a long time when it came to live-in in-laws.

Perry smiled. 'Even above the howling wind I can almost hear the sighs of relief.' There was a lot of bright, denying laughter. 'And of course the other thing is,' he went on, 'with the house sold, we'll be able to pass on some of the cash. Then if we make it past the next seven years, there's less death duties to pay. Don't want the Government taking a chunk of our hard-earned money.' He tapped the side of his nose. 'I'll tell you how much you get if we make it to the morning. No point getting your hopes up if Shirley and me are going to snuff it in this wind like a pair of burnt-out candles.'

There was a spooky silence when the wind abruptly ceased. Perry was dismissive, saying, 'Is that all we get? I've been out on worse Sunday afternoons on the Matlock hills.'

The new stillness was eerily oppressive and Lucy felt as if she could hardly dare breathe, as if the wind had swept all the oxygen away leaving a dangerous vacuum in its place.

'That's the start of the eye,' Simon told them, as if they hadn't all heard the manager's lecture. 'This is the dangerous bit. Nobody must go outside; part two could start up any second.'

It was too late, Luke and Becky had already unbolted the double terrace doors and were breathing in the stifling, immobile air. Lucy went to look too, to see what was different. The sky was clear again, as if nothing had happened, but below on the beach the skeletons of the once-thatched beach umbrellas looked tatty and forlorn. Against the sky she could see the silhouette of a ragged palm tree, its few remaining leaves shredded and broken. She couldn't see the rest of the hotel grounds without opening the villa's main door, but that would push Simon's patience too far.

'Mum, come back in. I'm scared.' Colette stood in the doorway, shivering, though the night was even warmer than it had been at dusk. Lucy shepherded Becky and Luke back inside, shut the doors again and let Simon do his bit with the locking and the careful readjusting of the louvres.

'Goodness, it must be hot out there. You've let all the humid air come in now.' Shirley was fanning herself with a guidebook. 'Lucky we've got the fan.'

'Lucky the electricity hasn't given out too,' Theresa commented. She felt drowsy, which she put down to the wine, and arranged herself under the ceiling fan where it wafted welcome draughts into her hair.

'There's still the second half of the storm to come,' Simon warned.

'Oh, the harbinger of doom,' Theresa mocked. 'We're all right so far, it's not that bad, Simon, give it a rest.'

'Let's all have a cup of tea,' Plum suggested brightly. She was feeling claustrophobic and thought that sitting about waiting for disaster was a waste of time and energy. It was well past midnight now. They could all just stop anticipating the worst, surely, and spread themselves out for some sleep. Why on earth didn't Shirley and Perry just go and get some sleep in the other bedroom? Theresa and Mark could go in with their three and the rest of them could curl up on the sofas and the floor with their blankets. There was no need to sit up like this as if it was a jolly and wonderful party that no-one wanted to leave. She filled the kettle and opened the cupboard to look for tea bags and cups. Perhaps she could sneak a shot of the mini-bar gin into each of them, get them thinking about sleep.

The storm's return shocked them all. It began with a bizarre, violent hammering at the terrace doors, as if something monstrous was demanding to get in.

'Jesus, it's like that bit in *Jaws* when the shark comes back to the boat . . .' Lucy said.

'It's coming from the other direction this time. Hurricanes do that.' Simon's voice was now shaky and scared: being well-informed was obviously no longer a comfort. However bad the wind had seemed an hour ago, this was far worse. Lucy thought he sounded as if he wanted, suddenly, to abandon his role as troop leader and crawl under a table. Perhaps they all should. The banging continued, alternatively heaving and crashing at the doors till the wood began to splinter and split.

'Shit, it's giving way! So much for your system, Simon.' Mark hurled himself at the double doors to try to force them back into place but the thick dense wood was already buckling outwards under the wind's power. The noise was dreadful now: a constant long low whooing sound exactly like the moment before a speeding underground train emerges from the tunnel at a station. Except this noise was relentless, terrifying. Becky and Colette had their hands clasped over their ears. Marisa was whimpering softly, crouched behind the sofa again with the blanket over her head.

'We'll have to leave it!' Simon said. 'We'll just have to let it go.'

'But we'll be sucked out over the wall and into the sea!'

Lucy felt a dragging pain of terror. She could hear, somewhere among the howls and roars of the wind, water lashing against the outside walls. It could be the rain, she prayed for it to be the rain, but it wasn't constant, it was intermittent like huge handfuls of sharp pebbles being hurled at windows. It probably *was* pebbles, which meant it had to be sea spray, lashing over the wall. She looked at the villa's main door. From there to the main part of the hotel was a run of at least two hundred perilous yards. Stuff would be flying about everywhere and wind this powerful was far too strong to fight. Already she could hear crashes and thumpings from close by outside, presumably roof-tiles were hurtling about like frisbees. What was it Henry had said? 'Don't go out: more people are killed by flying debris and coconuts . . .' She sent up a quick prayer for his and Oliver's safety, just as rain started to pour in through the roof.

'Turn the fan off! The water's coming down the wire!' Plum shrieked, pointing upwards. Simon raced to the light switches and tried a few at random.

'Simon, don't . . . !' It was too late. As his hand flicked at the correct switch he was flung backwards by a bolt of electricity.

'Aaagh!' he yelled, clutching his hand.

'That was a daft thing to do,' Perry pronounced. 'You should have used a bit of wood.'

248

'I know that *now*.' Simon sat on the soaking sofa clutching his hand and breathing heavily.

'You OK, Simon?' Lucy sat next to him and handed him a glass of water.

'Yeah. Stupid thing to do, Dad's right.' He looked gloomy. Lucy guessed he felt mildly mortified.

'Let's get out of this room, it's all soggy now anyway,' she suggested. 'We'll hole up in the bedrooms till this passes.'

'All together, though.' Shirley looked nervous. 'I don't want us splitting up. We'll go in with the little ones.'

Lucy collected up all the blankets then went into the second bathroom and brought out the pile of thick snowy towels to take with them. The buckled door was just about holding but water was trickling in through the roof. She was thankful she was wearing thick-soled trainers (the gold lady's query about what to wear hadn't been entirely fatuous), for the centre of the sitting-room floor was now inch-deep in water and the electricity was still functioning, which was convenient though potentially lethal.

The wind was blasting through the villa but inside the bedroom Mark forced the door shut and he and Simon sat on the floor, leaning against it. The windows in here were smaller and less vulnerable but it was still like trying to keep demons out – they tugged and rattled at the shutters and forced fierce whistling draughts through every hairline gap. This room, though, with a flat concrete roof and no tiles to lose, was at least dry.

'Well it won't get any worse,' Luke announced from the bathroom doorway. Behind him, having claimed for herself the large shower area, Becky had curled up under a couple of towels, trying to sleep.

'Won't it?' Plum asked. 'It feels like it's going to be like this for ever.'

'No, course not.' Luke was scornful. 'See, if the middle of it's the worst bit, like close to the hole where the eye of the storm was, well now we've had nearly an hour of that, well, it's got to be moving on towards an outside edge. Like the doughnut. Get it? So it'll get better, in the end.'

'Makes sense.' Shirley could only just make herself heard above wind which didn't seem to be letting up all that much. 'So, Luke,' she congratulated him, 'you really do manage the occasional bit of thinking beneath that dreadful floppy hair! I'd assumed that there was no room for anything inside your head but bits of tunes from that Walkman-thing you keep clamped to your ears.'

'He does OK at school, we've told you that.' Plum defended her son.

'Oh I know, but seeing him a bit more often, seeing all of you, we'll be able to see for ourselves, won't we?' Shirley beamed at her.

'I think it is stopping, a bit.' Colette was listening hard, as if when her concentration wandered the wind would get in and snatch them all out and into the sea.

There were gaps now between the wind's rampaging attacks and these seemed to be gradually losing their power. Becky, too uncomfortable to sleep, had now sat up and leaned against the shower screen picking at her mosquito bites.

'Does that mean we're not going to die tonight?' she asked.

'I think you're safe enough,' Perry told her. 'Though it's still a good while till morning.'

'Time to talk about what happens when we get home then,' Theresa suggested. 'Who do you and Mum plan

250

to stay with till your flat's ready? Me or Simon?'

'Well, as it's for a while, if you don't mind, we thought both in turn. A few weeks with you first, maybe, and then off to Simon's.'

Plum seethed quietly. So it was a foregone thing, was it? And who would do the extra cooking and the general looking-after? Simon would plead pressure of work, which, of course, in his parents' generation's view was such an acceptable *man's* excuse. She too had a job, one she should be at home doing right this minute rather than sitting feeling sweaty on a hard floor waiting for the weather either to let her out or kill her. Simon would say she was ungrateful. After all, they'd paid for this holiday. But just a word or two, a bit of being consulted, that's all it would have taken. Who needed all this silly secrecy?

'What about Lucy? Doesn't she get a visit too?' Theresa smiled sweetly at her sister.

'Don't be silly, Tess,' Shirley scolded. 'Where would Lucy put us? She doesn't have room in that little flat. Though with a bit more money she'll be able to do something about that. It's high time she was properly sorted. You could smarten yourself up a bit Lucy, with the extra cash, get a proper car instead of that old van.'

Lucy smiled and closed her eyes; the thought of being 'sorted' was a depressing prospect. 'It would only get messed up with paint,' she said.

'Yes, well, in time . . . Anyway Theresa, are you try-ing to pass us on down the line?'

'Oh I'll be happy to have you, don't get me wrong, it'll be lovely. I just thought Lucy wouldn't want to miss out.'

'Well I won't, will I? They can come for supper or lunch or whatever any time.'

'If you're there.' Theresa's voice was heavy with concealed meaning.

'Why wouldn't I be?'

'Well you've got your new boyfriend here, haven't you? Aren't you tempted to shack up here in paradise with him?'

Lucy looked hard at her. 'Yes I am, actually, Tess, how clever of you to guess.' It hadn't seriously crossed her mind. How childish they could all still become when pushed.

'Now, Theresa, you made her say that. Stop getting at her.' Shirley tried some gentle refereeing. 'And Lucy, don't rise to it. You know you'll be on that plane.'

'Oh it's OK, I know Lucy.' Theresa's face was contorted with spite. 'They're always Mr Right for a fortnight or so. I'm surprised she hasn't got at least twenty children.'

'Now Tess . . .' Perry started.

'Theresa, why are you being so nasty to me? I can't believe this, you sound as if you almost *envy* me!'

Theresa glared. 'Oh well, you've got all the choices, haven't you? You've always had it easy, having Colette just when you felt like it, and then *not* having more because you didn't. All that casual fertility was wasted on you. I should have had it. You don't know how hard it was for me, all those years of not being able to have them. And . . .' Theresa was getting seriously steamed up now, 'and you could never do anything wrong. Always Daddy's little favourite. He's always worrying about whether you've got enough money, he's even paying your kid's school fees.'

'That's all I do pay. She won't take any more,' Perry interrupted.

'Oh God, Tess, have you really grudged me having Colette all these years? She's about the only thing I *have* got. I know it was hard for you but you've got your children *now*. And that whopping great house. And Mark.'

'Oh well, *Mark* . . .'

'You're being horrible. And Henry's really nice,' Colette told Theresa.

'He is, dear,' Shirley agreed. 'But he's only a holiday romance.'

'Actually he's not even that.' No-one took any notice of Lucy.

Shirley went on, 'Holiday romances are nice to have, but Henry's from a different culture. They don't mix.'

'His parents were from different cultures, too, one black, one white; one from here, one from England. They mixed,' Colette pointed out.

'Yes but . . .'

'Yes but . . . not in our family? Is that what you mean?' Lucy said quietly.

'No, I don't mean that, of course I don't,' Shirley insisted, smiling to lighten the mood. 'Actually, it's just me being purely selfish. We're looking forward to seeing a lot more of you, help you get your life sorted a bit. It's not the colour thing, of course it's not.'

'Funny that,' Lucy said. 'But when people say that it's like when they're saying "It's not the money, it's the principle." You can tell immediately it's the money.'

'Listen. The wind's dropped right down,' Mark interrupted. Perversely, the small children at last started to stir and wake.

'You're right, it's almost gone,' Simon said. 'And we've survived.'

'Have we, Simon?' Lucy said. 'I'm glad you think so.'

Fifteen

Lucy was awake again as soon the night sky faded to a sulky grey. The rain was still falling, but more gently now, as if the sky was exhausted, and the wind had calmed to a brisk warm breeze no worse than on any English beach in July. Her body was aching and stiff from lying on the hard stone floor and there seemed no point in trying to get any more rest. If her own room had survived the storm, perhaps later she could catch up on sleep.

In the bathroom, the loo flushed successfully but she couldn't hear the tank filling. She turned on the basin taps, but only a sad trickle emerged. She was reluctant to open the villa doors, afraid she would find that most of the hotel was lying flat beneath sand and rubble and fallen trees. There might be bodies out there, people caught running from tumbling buildings and then struck down by falling trees. She smiled, recognizing in herself a streak of Simon's doom predictions, and padded back into the drenched sitting room. The towels that had once been so plump and white were lying crumpled on the floor, filthy and soaked with mopped-up rain. The room was steamy and hot now that the fan couldn't work, and mournful drops of rain were still plopping from the ceiling onto the table. One of the sofas, for which they hadn't been able to find a large enough section of dry roof, was sodden and stained with reddish-grey patches from where the rain had soaked through the remaining roof tiles.

'Have you looked outside yet?' Simon unrolled himself from the dry sofa.

'No. Too scared. I had this awful half-dream that this is the only building still standing and that we're the only people left alive.'

'Oh it can't be that bad, surely. We'd definitely have heard if the other villas had collapsed into the sea. Come on, let's look together.'

Simon unlocked the front door and they took their first look across the bay towards the rest of the hotel.

'Oh those poor trees,' was Lucy's first reaction. Not one of the magnificent palm trees had its leaves intact. All that was left on each was a pitiful stubby plume of tattered, broken stems. The remaining leaves hung miserably, as if they were clinging desperately to the trunk. The grass and the beach beneath were carpeted with shattered foliage, coconuts and shards of twisted fronds.

'The hotel looks as if it's still standing, or at least it does from here.' Simon peered across the bay to the hotel's three main blocks. The big stone sugar mill bar was still in its place on the far headland, where it must have faced a good couple of centuries of storms. It had probably seen far worse than this in its time.

'We can't see much from here. What I *can* see though,' Lucy pointed to the grass a few yards away, 'is our water tank. It must have been wrenched off the roof.'

The ground beneath was sodden with lakes of rain that had nowhere to drain to, and mud had swept down from the hillside behind the beach, depositing an oozy slick across the ground, but the sea had retreated, leaving a new covering of fresh wet sand across the first ten yards of grass at the top of the beach. Huge boulders and pebbles now lay scattered on the foreshore where only smooth silvery sand had been the day before.

'Happy birthday to me, happy birthday to me!' Becky sang, joining Simon and Lucy at the doorway. 'Where are my presents then?'

'Happy birthday Becks.' Lucy kissed her. 'I have got you one actually. It's in my emergency bag.' Lucy went back into the bedroom to find her basket and returned with a small package. 'It'll remind you of being here – though you might not think that's a good thing.'

Becky ripped the paper off and scattered it on the floor, pulling out wind chimes made of blue ceramic fish. 'Oh, it's so pretty!' she said, 'I love it, thanks! I'll hang it at my bedroom window and think about last night's ultimate wind.'

'Henry's mother made it. She's a painter really, but she does these too.'

'An all-round talented family!' Becky gave her a suggestive nudge and Simon frowned. 'Becky, no smut please . . .'

'Hey, I'm seventeen, I know about these things.'

'I sincerely hope you don't.' Becky and Lucy looked at each other and laughed.

'I'm *seventeen*, Dad.' Becky hugged Simon. 'Now isn't seventeen a very significant age? Isn't there something you're supposed to be able to do at *seventeen*? And I'm not talking "smut" as you put it.' Simon extricated himself and grinned at her. 'Wait till your mother wakes up. I'm saying nothing about your present till she's here, so don't ask me.'

Only the small children had slept properly. The

others woke after too little sleep and grumbled about aching backs and necks and feeling like wrecks. Perry reminded them that they could be feeling a lot worse.

'I'm starving. Shall we get breakfast?' Luke suggested as soon as he was awake.

'If there is any.' Mark felt as if he had a hangover but couldn't remember whether this was likely to be true. A part of his barely functioning brain told him that if he really couldn't remember, then the hangover was a probability.

Lucy and Colette set off with Simon ahead of the others, making a detour, at Lucy's request, to check on the damage to the dive shop. The shop itself seemed to be intact, with only a small piece of the boarding ripped away from the door. 'Probably one of the bits you did, Mum,' Colette teased. The pedalos and jet skis had fared less well: the tarpaulin that had covered them had ripped away, taking with it a couple of canoes and one of the jet skis, which lay on its side nearby pinned down by a fallen almond tree. Lucy could see a bright pink pedalo floating upside down on the churning sea about fifty yards from the shore.

As they walked along the path above the beach the extent of the hotel's damage became clearer.

'Look at the games room!' Colette yelled as she got close to it. Sand had been washed up the beach and in through its open sides, far enough to half-bury the football table. Next to it, the beach bar's semicircular roof had completely disappeared. 'Jesus,' Simon said, 'what kind of strength did it take to blow it clean away? There's no sign of it.'

'It's probably in the middle of the ocean by now,' Lucy told him. The sea had swept through, easily pushing aside the carefully laid sandbags that had proved so inadequate a barrier. A dead fish lay by the bar, a sad, poignant casualty. 'Red mullet, I'd say,' Simon said, looking at it.

'You don't *really* know,' Colette teased him. 'You just think you should pretend you do because you're a man.'

Simon sighed and gave her a woeful smile. 'You're too young to be such a cynic,' he told her. 'Though, OK, I don't know for sure, but it does *look* like a red mullet.'

Closer to the central building, Lucy tried to work out what was missing, what had changed. The whole land-scape seemed different in ways that were confusing. At first it was hard to tell whether there was a huge gap in the view or whether the pool terrace had always been so open. She had to think, to refamiliarize. Then she realized: the huge tamarind tree that had stood beside the pool had gone. Most of the tree, they could now see, was upended in the pool, which was muddied and full of leaves and sand. Flagstones on the terrace had been ripped out and cracked apart as the tree's massive roots, which were now almost obscenely exposed to the air, had been hauled out of the earth. The white gazebo was another casualty, crushed to useless sad scrap beneath a slab of corrugated iron that must have flown from a roof nearby. The small speedboat that was used for water-skiing and which had been tethered to the turpentine tree was upside down, the branch it had been tied to stabbed through its windscreen.

Other guests wandered in the drizzle, staring about them, dazed like people in shock who'd stepped unscathed from a dreadful car accident. No-one spoke: there was too much damage to take in, as well as grow-ing amazement at their own survival. The more Lucy looked around her, the more awe-stricken she felt at the power of the elements. She gazed up at the terrace. Most of the dining-area roof was still there, though there were a few gaps and holes. Staff were already up ladders, fixing palm fronds back into place and improvising with thick polythene to keep the worst of the rain out.

'We should check our rooms,' Simon murmured to her. Lucy nodded.

The worst of the damage to their block was visible from just past the terrace. Lucy stopped and gasped at the scale of it: that mere moving air could do so much. The whole end section of their two-storey building was missing, leaving the corner rooms, upstairs and down, open to the air. The lower one was Simon and Plum's room, wrecked as if by a bomb. Chunks of plasterboard were strewn across the floor. The chest of drawers was on its side and the minibar had been flung into the middle of the soaking wet bed. Light fittings dangled from the walls. The manager had been right about the louvres in the windows: there was glass everywhere and the balcony from the room above had fallen through the overhanging terrace shelter which was now crushed beneath concrete. A slice of the tiled roof had landed in the centre of the room above and Lucy could only pray that there was no-one beneath it. Simon went as close as he dared, feeling acutely distressed about the little green finch's nest which could only have been destroyed. There was no sign of the birds, and the creeper where the intricate nest had been was flattened to the ground. Absurdly, he somehow felt it was all his fault. If only he hadn't lured the lovely Tula in . . .

'The wardrobe doors are still on.' Simon's voice was shaky. 'Our stuff should be OK.'

'It's being on the corner, this bit must have taken the

worst. I expect it's the same the other end, from when the wind changed direction.'

There were several holes in the building's roof, from where pieces of tree had crashed through. A branch, with a gouged pale rip along the edge where it had been torn from the tree's trunk, was lodged through one of the upstairs windows as if someone had picked it up like a javelin and hurled it. The floor in Lucy and Colette's room was rain-soaked, with broken glass everywhere and sand and leaves blown in, but otherwise the room seemed to have got off lightly. She checked the beds and tested them for dampness. They seemed more or less all right. Perhaps at least Colette could sleep for a while. It looked like the rest of them would be involved in major clearing up.

'I can't believe the staff have managed to organize food like this,' Shirley said, astounded that tables had been set out, with fresh cloths, in rows like the night before. Smiling staff, relieved as the rest of them to be alive, came round to the weary guests with comforting pots of coffee and tea.

'Did any of you get any sleep?' Perry asked Tula.

'No, sir,' she smiled at him, 'it was too exciting!'

'Not the sort of exciting I'd want to do again in a hurry,' he told her. 'Still, as long as everyone's OK.'

They were. Miraculously, no-one had been hurt except one of the Steves who had cut his hand in a drunken fall through his door, landing on broken glass.

Lucy went to get food from the buffet. She felt as if she wasn't real. It was partly lack of sleep and partly amazement that everyone in the hotel had escaped a messy death in spite of the massive damage. When the gold lady tapped her on the arm and said, 'You OK?'

Lucy was horrified to find herself in tears. The gold lady hugged her and said, 'It's OK, it's not just you. Everyone's feeling like this.' Only Shirley, Perry and the other older guests seemed unaffected.

'At our age, it's on to the next day and be glad you're there to see it. You don't dwell on things,' Perry told Lucy as she returned to the table with her toast.

Plum ambled in for breakfast after the others and was pounced on by Becky. 'OK, now you can tell me about my present,' she demanded.

'It isn't just you older ones who move on fast,' Lucy said to Perry.

'Well? Let me guess . . .' Becky was eager. 'Is it something that there's more than one of and you need a provisional licence to do it?'

'Well, you've been hinting long enough . . . so here you are.' Plum grinned and handed over an envelope. Becky ripped it open.

'Oh, great! A driving-school voucher! For a *serious* amount of money!' She frowned. 'Don't you expect me to pass, then?'

'We just want you to be competent. Not rush at it,' Simon said.

'Very sensible,' Shirley approved. 'You've always been thoughtful that way, Simon.' He looked at her, puzzled.

'You were always the one with a puncture-repair kit in your bike saddlebag. Don't you remember?' Lucy reminded him. 'I bet you've got a cast-iron pension scheme too.'

'Well of course,' he told her. 'Haven't you?'

Lucy laughed 'Oh, Simon, you haven't a clue, have you?'

*　　*　　*

Theresa wanted quite desperately to have a bath and unpack something else to wear. She felt as if she'd worn the same blue linen dress for weeks, though in reality it was only on its second day. It had been the one she'd worn during the evening of the drunken swim (both seawater and alcohol drenched away in the shower) and, what with that and the horrendous storm, she now decided that it was a bad-luck garment and would have to go. Perhaps Lucy would like it. Theresa bit her lip and felt herself tingling with guilt. She'd been horrid to Lucy, really awful. The dress would hardly start to make up for it. And, too, would she be passing on the bad luck with it?

As soon as the children had finished breakfast, she intended investigating whether her room was habitable, dragging all her clothes out of the bloody wardrobe and soaking away all the night-time fear and sweat and mud in a deep and scented bath. In a big block building like that, surely there wouldn't have been any damage to the water supply. And if there was, perhaps the high-paying guests in the villas would be priority to have their accommodation repaired, so she could use Shirley's bathroom, once the muddy water had been swept out.

What she didn't intend to do, she thought as she sipped her coffee on the dining terrace, was wander about aimlessly in the rain gawping at the damage like so many of the other guests were doing, clad in enormous white plastic bags with holes cut out for arms and legs, that the management had provided. It was rather late, she thought, those would have been handy the night before to protect the sofas and beds. One or two people seemed to find it amusing to attempt some kind of design statement with the bags, fashioning hoods, belting them and showing off childishly to others too exhausted to tell them to go away. At least Marisa was on the kind of form they were paying her to be on this morning. She was being wonderful with the children, cheerful and chatty and almost delirious with the joy of being alive. In contrast, Theresa could see Cathy and Paul slumped in a corner, arms around each other and Cathy clearly sobbing inconsolably. Paul caught her eye and she felt she had no option but to go and talk to them.

'Cathy, what's wrong? You didn't get hurt or anything did you?'

Cathy blew her nose loudly and Theresa stepped back a little.

'My wedding! How can I have my wedding?'

'Why can't you?' Theresa was puzzled.

'It's all ruined! The white thingy's all broken and the tree's in the pool and everything's *spoiled,*' she wailed. Theresa looked round, feeling embarrassed and at a loss. Lucy was across the room and Theresa beckoned to her.

'What's the matter?' she asked. She looked at Theresa nervously, as if expecting a new set of long-held grudges to be unleashed.

'Cathy says she can't get married because the marrying place by the pool is all ruined. What do you think?'

Lucy thought for a moment. 'Well, first of all, is your dress still OK? And how's your room?'

'The dress is fine, the room's not too bad, it just needs sweeping out and stuff,' Paul said.

'Couldn't you get married on the beach? With everyone from the hotel? We could all do with some celebration. And the one thing hotels don't run short of is booze.'

Cathy sniffed heavily but the sobbing had stopped at last. 'It was supposed to be this morning.'

Theresa took hold of her hand, which surprised Lucy. Theresa had never been the tactile sort, never comfortable with people who hugged at random and pulling herself in when trapped next to anyone who tended to emphasize conversational points with nudges and touches.

'So, OK, today's not really on. But if you go ahead tomorrow,' she told Cathy, 'just think about it: you'll have one hell of a story to tell. "My hurricane wedding nightmare". It's almost sellable.'

Paul's expression perked up enormously 'Perhaps it *is* sellable. We could get some great pictures . . .'

'There you are then. So much better than some ordinary dull old wedding.' Theresa smiled. Lucy was suspicious. Theresa sounded mildly patronizing and manipulative, as if she was successfully getting her own way with a grizzly child. She couldn't work out what she was up to. As they headed back to join the others she pulled Theresa out into the lobby where no-one could hear them. She had to ask.

'Theresa, why do you care so much whether they get married or not? I didn't think you even really wanted the girls to be bridesmaids.'

'I don't much care, to tell you the truth. Though Cathy and Paul are really rather sweet,' she conceded. 'I just think it will do Mark good. I intend to make him come along to watch. He needs a bloody good reminder about what those vows were.'

'Ah. A wasp in paradise,' Lucy said.

'What the hell do you mean?' Theresa rounded on her. 'Has he said something to you?'

Lucy hesitated but quickly made her choice. 'No, nothing at all,' she said. 'But talking of things being said, what was all that last night? Now I've had time to think about it, you were making out I was some kind of serial man-killer, working my way through the population of south-west London. I don't do that. Actually, you were a complete bitch. I want to know why.'

Theresa sighed. 'I don't know. Maybe you were right, perhaps I am a bit envious of you. You've got Colette *and* you've got your freedom. You might not have someone to curl up with on a cold night, but then you haven't got someone to hurt you either.'

'No? Well, after last night I reckon I've got you for that.'

Theresa covered her face with her hands and began to cry. 'Lucy, I'm so sorry.' Lucy put her arms round her, which felt very strange. She couldn't recall the last time she'd hugged her sister – probably in the hospital after the birth of Sebastian, though even then Theresa had backed off with a brief bit of two-sided air-kissing.

'It's just that you've got away with it all your life,' Theresa wept. 'I do all the things I'm supposed to and Mum and Dad think Mark's so bloody perfect and that I'm so *lucky* to have him!' She was dripping tears on Lucy's shoulder. 'Why do they never say he's lucky to have *me*?'

Lucy laughed. 'If I knew the answer to that one . . .' she began. 'Theresa, you surely can't have missed the way Mum's forever on at me to find a nice man and be transformed into the perfect woman, just like you. I've had more digs than Alan Titchmarsh's garden.'

Theresa raised her tear-streaked face 'Hell, she's got no idea, has she?'

'No,' Lucy agreed. 'But we're grown-ups. Let it pass.'

The morning turned into a mammoth session of clearing up. Simon and the Steves found their natural levels as team leaders, organizing groups of guests into the clearing of branches, the sweeping of glass and rainwater from rooms and the refilling of 100 cisterns with sea water. There were a lot of remarks about the gritty British and why weren't the Americans joining in.

The manager called a meeting for all the guests after a scratch lunch of grilled chicken and last night's fried-up potatoes, and before anything else was said, the Star woman raised her hand and demanded, 'Who do I sue?'

From the assembled guests there was a chorus of jeers and groans. 'Bloody typical American,' was muttered by almost every Briton.

'What do you want to sue for? Have all the safety measures deprived you of a nasty death?' Mark called across the room. There was a round of applause and one of the Steves called to her, 'I expect we could still arrange something for you . . .'

Still in shock at the hurricane's effects on his buildings and business, the manager announced that the hotel was too badly damaged to continue functioning properly and would be closed as soon as possible. Guests who were due to stay longer than two more days would be transferred to Antigua, to continue their holiday at another hotel.

'If we can get the accommodation,' the manager said, 'and when the airport is opened again. Just now the damage there is being attended to as a matter of priority. But right now, most roads are blocked by fallen trees, wrecked vehicles and fallen power cables.'

Lucy felt a wave of sadness for the island's losses. Farm animals had died in their fields, killed by flood water or hit by trees and debris. Homes had been devastated, one hamlet north of Teignmouth had been completely flattened and the occupants had spent the night sheltering in terror in a banana plantation.

'We got off lightly, really,' she said to Shirley as they returned to clearing-up duties.

'It'll soon get back to normal,' Shirley said. 'Things do. They did in the war, they do in weather.'

'And what about us?' Lucy asked.

'Us? Well tomorrow evening we catch the plane home and then *we* get back to normal. What else is there?'

Late in the afternoon there were still no telephones working. Lucy was mildly worried about Henry: she knew that if he possibly could he'd want to come down to the beach to check on the damage to the dive shop. She wished there was some way she could contact him, tell him it wasn't so bad. The fact that he hadn't arrived by four o'clock had to mean that he simply couldn't get there. She sent in a request to all the immortal powers for the reason to be merely road damage, not home-and-family damage. She pictured him in his sea-green kitchen, laughing with Oliver as they cooked up rice and prawns together, and she hoped that the roof, which had looked sturdy enough, hadn't let in rain to destroy the colours, to dull them and spoil their brilliance. She thought of Glenda's paintings and tried hard not to let her imagination picture them smashed among broken glass, in a room swamped with leaf-stained rain water.

Gradually, as the rain drifted away and the hot sun shone down on the soft fresh new sand, the hotel's guests gravitated back to the beach.

'It's amazing,' Simon commented, 'how little it really takes to keep a Brit happy on holiday.' Sunloungers had been trawled out of the devastated swimming pool and regrouped to dry out on the sand. The sad skeletal frames of the bald beach umbrellas were draped with wet towels to provide shade, and those whose books had survived on the drier side of sodden were settling themselves once more to laze away the rest of their bizarre holiday. The mysterious Celebrity did not send any minders out to plunder the best spaces on the beach but kept to him or herself in whatever was left of their own villa. As Theresa had predicted, the water there had been swiftly reconnected and, with Perry and Lucy wielding brooms, their own rooms were reasonably habitable again. Plum and Shirley and the gold lady walked along the sand, picking up fallen leaves and bits of branch and strange tangles of twine washed up from the sea and stuffed it into bin bags. 'They look like council litter-pickers,' Perry said to Lucy, but he was smiling at the time and she could detect a certain amount of pride in his voice.

Amazingly, the hotel's chef had managed to come up with a birthday cake for Becky. It was a wonderfully gaudy one, with white icing topped with swirls of turquoise and orange. The family assembled on the terrace above the pool and Plum hugged the chef in amazed and close to tearful gratitude that he could have remembered to make this cake when he was up against the sheer logistics of feeding a hotel's-worth of people three times a day with food stocks running low and half the kitchen flooded out.

'It was no problem,' he told her, 'I made it yesterday and kept it in the cold oven overnight for safety! You can't disappoint a girl on her birthday.'

The gold lady and Tom joined them for tea and cake, along with two of the Steves, Cathy and Paul, the hotel's severely stressed manager (fraught from a day of dealing with difficult guests, each one convinced *they* were the ones entitled to priority when it came to any available flight out) and several of the staff. Lucy took a last look around for Henry. There was no sign of him. She shouldn't even have hoped for him to turn up. He must have a million more important things to do.

'*Happy birthday to you . . .*' they all started to sing. Lucy gave up hoping to see Henry and joined in. Becky blew out all her candles in one and a voice behind Lucy shouted, 'Be careful what you wish for.'

Henry was right there. Just as she turned she felt his hand on hers.

'Are you all OK?' he asked.

'We're all OK. Are you and Oliver and Glenda OK?'

'They are. So that's all of us. Hey! We're OK!' He put his arms round her and crushed her against him. Over his shoulder she caught sight of her mother. Shirley was smiling across at them, looking, surely not . . . looking happy. Approving, even. Could one night really make such a difference?

Sixteen

It was the last day of the holiday. There still wasn't any news about whether the airport was functioning, and Simon was fretting because he couldn't plan the timings for leaving the hotel later that afternoon. It was important, he felt, to be able to give each of them a different time for congregating in the lobby, cases packed, passports and tickets at the ready, according to their accustomed reputations for tardiness. For Becky and Luke, who would go wandering off somewhere unless closely watched and constantly reminded, he would allow an extra half-hour, possibly a whole hour to be on the safe side. For Theresa he'd have to allow the same, not because her punctuality was suspect but because she had the complication of small children who would all need to go to the loo at the last minute. His parents would be there on the dot of whatever time he gave them with no fuss but as for Lucy, well, Lucy didn't show any signs of going anywhere at the moment.

'What do you think?' he'd asked her after breakfast. 'Do you think we'll get away today? There'll probably be a delay of course, but if we get to the airport good and early . . .'

'Oh Simon, who cares?' she'd interrupted, grinning

in a peculiarly vague and absent way, almost as if she'd, well, as if she'd *taken* something. She wouldn't do that, he was pretty sure. There must be something odd going on inside her head.

'Why worry about everything, Simon?' Plum said as they went to have a final hour or two of toasting themselves on the beach before the crazy wedding that seemed to be going ahead just before lunch. 'We'll hear soon enough about the airport. There'll be a notice up. But anyway, even if it isn't open, how much can it matter whether we're a day or two late home or not?'

'You sound like Lucy,' he grumbled, 'all laid-back and don't-care. It's all right for her, I've got patients booked in and a reputation to think of.'

'I think she's got work to go back to as well, actually. You don't have the monopoly on professional integrity. And I've got classes to run and students to deal with too.'

Plum's words sounded like a thorough telling-off. Simon felt rather comforted by this. At least she still cared enough to put him back in his place now and then. He wouldn't say it reminded him (fondly) of his mother, because he didn't want to have to consider the psychological ramifications of that, but the evidence of continuing nurture from his wife made him feel that at least, as a couple, they hadn't yet sunk into mutual apathy. Sharp words could go too far though, he also thought, as with Mark and Theresa. He couldn't actually recall, during the entire fortnight, a single moment when those two had looked or sounded like a properly devoted couple. There was a tense undercurrent there. Nothing he could put his finger on, but when Theresa called Mark 'darling' the teeth-gritting insincerity chilled the blood. If he was a betting man he'd put odds on those two separating within six months. It made him quite sad. It had been so hard for them to get those lovely children. He wouldn't point that out if and when the time came. He'd leave it to his mother – it would come so much better from her, and come it surely would.

Becky didn't expect to see Ethan again. Nor did she want to. In spite of the mild humiliation of having to return home still as virginal as when she'd left Gatwick (and at *seventeen* now, too, double horror) she'd rather not have to look into his leery eyes again. She assumed that after the storm he'd have clearing up of his own to do, wherever it was he lived. He surely wouldn't think the hotel's guests would be interested in purchasing souvenir knick-knacks on the beach as if there was nothing in the world to think about but making sure they'd bought enough presents for those back home.

Becky lay flat out on her sunlounger, switched on her Walkman and closed her eyes. Just as she could feel herself drifting off into a blissful sun-sodden doze, a shadow fell across her face. She opened her eyes, expecting to have to shout abuse at Luke. 'Ganja to take home?' Ethan shoved impolitely at her bare tummy so that she had to move over and then he plonked himself down beside her without even asking. She could feel her thigh squashed against his and didn't like it one bit. She sighed. It was such a shame. Only a few short days ago such contact would have had her panting like a corgi in a hot car. Now it made her cringe.

'Do you think I'm completely stupid?' she said. 'Do you really think I'm going to risk going to gaol carrying a titchy bag of grass through the British customs? I can get all that stuff down the local pub.'

'But this is cheaper, better! And it's no problem man, you girls got places you can hide stuff.' His hand snaked up her leg and she grabbed it at upper-thigh level before it could reach its goal.

'Ugh! Sod off!' Becky pushed him away. It was all Mark's fault. If he hadn't said all that about Ethan's girl-rota she'd have . . . well, on balance she was glad now that she hadn't.

'OK man, no worries.' He leaned forward so that his breath tickled her face. 'But you know I'll give you all the stuff you want, for free, if you just come and . . .'

'No. I don't want to, thank you for asking. Now please go away.' Becky turned up the volume of her Walkman and closed her eyes again. Ethan drifted away and was replaced by the cheeky small black birds dipping for crumbs and insects in the sand beneath her lounger. She could sense their flapping and squabbling. 'Is there no bloody peace?' she said to herself. She ripped the headphones off, stalked down to the sea and splashed out into the waves. The sea was a peculiar colour, with the sand beneath still churned up from the storm. It was as if a brilliant translucent sheen of turquoise had been spread over a caramel base. Becky lay on her back staring at the sky. There was no sign up there that the hurricane had ever happened. Someone had said that it had moved on towards the east coast of America. She imagined the frantic population of Florida boarding up their homes or moving further inland away from the damage, a long traffic jam of cars heading out of the state. With millions of square miles of America to drive off to in search of shelter, she wondered how any of them could understand how it felt to be trapped like they'd been on a tiny little island.

'You know you don't have to go. You can stay with us,' Henry told Lucy for the fourteenth time that morning.

They were sitting on the sand outside the dive shop. The boarding had all been removed, leaving ugly nail-holes in the wood. Lucy itched to fill them in and repaint.

'I know.' She didn't list any excuses or reasons why she absolutely had to leave. There weren't any. If she didn't want to go, then she didn't have to. What was difficult was trusting any decision she came up with. She couldn't stay just because of Henry. But then she couldn't leave just because of Colette's school. She couldn't stay just because the weather was better and she liked the particular shade of blue the sky happened to be over this island. And she couldn't go home just because Aline Charter-Todd was desperate for a kitchen in the Paint Library's Bittermint.

'Are you going because of your job? Because you can work here. Especially now.' Henry was still persuading.

'I like my job,' Lucy told him. 'But there are aspects of it I don't like. Money's one.'

'Money's always one!' Henry agreed.

'The problem with being the painter is that you're the last one down the chain. The client has already been stuffed by the plumbers, the carpenter, the electrician and the kitchen-fitters, so the pockets are empty. The other thing is that as a woman you have all the other craftsmen looking at you in that *doubtful* way, like you might be all right for a spot of gentle rag-rolling but will you need them to carry your ladders for you, all that.'

'Same everywhere. At least here you get the sun.'

Lucy laughed. 'You don't give up, do you, Henry?'

He leaned across and kissed the tender skin at the back of her neck. 'Not when there's something I really, really want.'

* * *

Theresa and Marisa had finally got the girls dressed in their bridesmaids' frocks. They'd wriggled and jiggled and complained while they were washed in a few inches of tepid bathwater (the guests had been asked to economize with it – supplies were still a long way from back to normal), but now Amy and Ella had their long fair hair up in high bunches tied with big clumps of orange and bright pink ribbon. They did look awfully cute, though Theresa wasn't sure that dresses decorated with cannabis leaves would go down too well in a Surrey summer. Though, she thought with a smile, who among the velvet-headband brigade would dare admit to knowing enough about marijuana to comment? Perhaps it would be rather fun, next spring, to send the girls to snotty Lizzie Twilley's daughter's birthday party dressed like this. She could imagine the arched eyebrows, the hesitation and then the 'Oh! Oh, how *sweet*!' After about half an hour of sidelong glances and half-begun sentences, Lizzie, on the outside of a couple of spritzers, would finally ask, 'Exactly what *sort* of leaves are they supposed to be?' The pre-Caribbean Theresa would have bluffed and lied that they were maple. The post-storm version, glad to be alive and ready to face the demons with Mark, would tell the truth and not care.

'Are we ready?' Cathy's face appeared round the door. 'Oh, your room's hardly damaged at all, is it? And you've still got your telly. Ours got full of rain and had to go.'

'Cathy, you look stunning.' Theresa pulled Cathy further into the room for a better look. She was wearing a sleek and simple spaghetti-strapped bias-cut white silk dress. Her blonde hair was loosely piled up and held in place with a slide covered in pale blue plumbago flowers.

'It's gorgeous,' Theresa admired her dress, 'just like a 1930s nightie.'

Cathy did a twirl in front of the mirror, frowning. 'Ugh, do you think so?' Then she giggled, 'Well, I'll just have to keep it on for bedtime, won't I?'

'Have you got something borrowed?'

'Only the money to get here, courtesy of NatWest Bank.'

'Here you are, wear these.' Theresa opened her bag and pulled out a tiny velvet pouch which contained her diamond stud earrings. 'Mark gave them to me when Sebastian was born.'

Cathy gave her a quick hug. 'Thanks, Tess. If Paul and me can be like you and Mark, well, we'll be OK, won't we?'

Theresa bent to adjust the ribbons on Ella's hair. 'You'll be a lot better than that, I'm sure.'

It wasn't goodbye yet. Henry was only just along the beach, sorting the jet skis out and checking out the damage to the pedalos. As she walked back towards her room to sort her luggage Lucy noticed that outside the villa next to her parents, the mysterious Celebrity's black-windowed Mercedes had reappeared, along with its ever-present besuited driver with his wraparound mirrored sunglasses. She smiled to herself. Who on earth would want to go to the trouble of keeping so many staff on hold and then never come out? It was like having people to do all your living for you. Hotel staff, possibly sworn to eternal (and surely pointless) secrecy, had been seen entering the building with mops and buckets and screwdrivers and spanners, so presumably the villa was more or less back to its former luxurious habitable condition. Perhaps he or she was allergic to sunlight. Lucy certainly wasn't. She thought about the dismal prospect of the short grey days of winter, those miserable late November afternoons that her mother always loved for their closed-curtain cosiness.

'We'll just shut the world out,' she used to say, pulling the heavy green velvet drapes across the window. Lucy had hated that, feeling as if she was being denied access to that world, imprisoned by the cold and dark that pressed against the far side of the walls. She remembered after-school toasted crumpets when she was little, mugs of hot chocolate, oxtail soup. You needed so much comforting against the damp-nosed chill of late autumn. With the extended time-scale of children, winter had seemed to go on for ever till she'd imagined with a terrified dread that they were stuck for ever and ever in this one gloomy season. Her mother had pointed out the daffodil spikes pushing through the earth, the hyacinths blooming, to reassure her. But the days were still chilled and night came too early so she hadn't trusted these flowers as signs of spring, more as evidence that the cold and dark really were for always and that people, like the plants, were all going to have to adjust to it. Now, when they got back to England, people would be starting to mention Christmas and making plans to get everything done *really early* this year. Lucy always felt that was like wishing half the year away, the best, the warm and sunny half, as if they'd raced too carelessly through the precious long hot days of summer and that the bleak cold was something like getting back to normal.

'Your mother's worried about you.' Perry appeared by her side. Lucy wondered if he'd been following her, waiting to choose his moment.

'When did she ever *not* worry about me?' She grinned at him.

'No, but seriously, Lucy love, about this money. I want to give the three of you twenty thousand apiece. Your mother's worried you won't take it. She thinks perhaps you could put a deposit on a little place for you and Colette. Get settled at least with somewhere to live, seeing as you don't seem to be settling with some-*one*.'

'OK. Thanks,' Lucy said simply. She hugged him.

'OK? You mean you'll take it?' Perry looked astounded.

'Hey, there's always a first time! There's just one condition though.'

'Oh. I thought there might be. What is it?' he asked warily. She took his arm and led him to sit with her on the low wall beside the children's playground. The swingboat was still standing, but the climbing frame was buckled and broken and the roundabout that looked like a little train was crushed by a fallen section of palm tree.

'There's to be no conditions,' she told him, 'that's the condition. It's really kind of you and I will use it for somewhere to live, I promise, but not necessarily to buy, not just yet. I'll see how things go.'

Perry frowned. 'You've spent the past thirteen years seeing how things go. They're not though, are they?'

'What do you mean,"they're not"? They might not be on your terms but I'm taking good care of Colette, aren't I? I run my own business, I'm good at my job.'

'Painting. If you can piss you can paint. Doesn't take a genius. You had a good brain, A levels, you could have done anything.'

'But I do what I enjoy doing. I like working with colour and texture, I love getting a scruffy knocked-about room to look clean and new and fresh. What's wrong with that?' Lucy was sick of being defensive about her job. This would be the last time. No-one ever said to Simon, 'Oh, how horrid. How can you spend your working life staring into open mouths and wiring up adolescents' grotty teeth?' If anyone else in the family wanted to have a go at her she'd just grin at them inanely, she decided, let them think the paint fumes had gone to her head.

Perry shrugged. 'Nothing's wrong with it, I suppose. As long as you're good at it, as long as it makes you happy and brings you in enough to live on. Things like that hurricane, well, perhaps they make you realize you only get one go.'

'Heavens, Dad, you'll be proclaiming "Peace and Love" next!'

'Anyway,' he went on, 'about the money. All right, no conditions.' He wagged a finger at her, playing at being serious. 'Just don't fritter it.'

'I don't fritter.' Lucy giggled. 'I'd be no good at it, I haven't had any practice.'

'And what about this young man, this Henry? Does he fit in anywhere?'

Lucy hesitated. 'Henry's just a friend, Dad.'

'"Just a friend" she says. With a relationship there's nothing more important. Don't knock it.'

'I'm not. There is one thing though, he's different from all my others, and I don't just mean he's a different colour.'

'He's different all right, he's three thousand miles away from home. I expect you'll get over him. Plenty more in the sea and all that, though I don't suppose you want to hear that . . .'

'Not really, Dad. No, what I mean is that there's something he knows he can't have from me, something

279

all the others expected to have and didn't like not getting.'

'Do I want to know?' Perry pulled a face at her. She laughed. 'Not *that*. I told you, he's just a friend. No, the thing is that he doesn't expect to get priority with me, he would never expect me to put him first. Colette is the most important person in my life. Oliver is the most important in his. Whoever either of us end up with has to understand that. I think that for both of us nobody else has understood that so far.'

'Hmm.' Perry considered. 'Looks like you've been doing some serious thinking about this.'

Lucy shrugged. 'I have. Though whether there was any point or not I'll probably never know.'

'Thinking's never wasted, pet. It'll always come in handy sometime.'

Paul and Cathy had taken Theresa completely literally. With a view to selling their story to one (or perhaps more) of the less glossy but highly popular women's magazines, they had gone out of their way to select the most disaster-hit background for photos. The preacher who was to conduct the wedding ceremony was astounded to be led to the devastated pool area instead of to a beautiful stretch of beach.

'Right here. This is perfect,' Cathy ordered, arranging herself and Paul beside the wrenched-out roots of the tamarind tree. They were surrounded by the worst effects the hurricane had had on the hotel. Chunks of corrugated roof from the central block of rooms were still scattered across the terrace. The pool water had turned a turgid dark brown and there were unidentifiable slabs of wood and plasterboard and glass lying everywhere. Most of the hotel guests, the manager and many of the staff had congregated to watch the wedding, and there was a lot of surprised murmuring about the choice of venue.

'The Sugar Mill's still standing, they could have gone up there. With the sea in the background it would have been so pretty,' the gold lady said.

'What are their families going to think? And how can you display your photos on the sideboard when you look like you're standing in a demolition site?' Shirley whispered to Plum.

'If they wanted urban blight, they could have stayed at home and popped up to Moss Side,' Perry commented to Theresa.

'It reminds me', Mark said, 'of those fashion shoots *Vogue* used to have in the late Sixties, all industrial wasteland and thousand-pound ball-gowns.'

'But don't the girls look lovely?' Shirley admired her granddaughters, who stood solemnly beside Cathy and Paul, clutching their bunches of bougainvillea that Tula had picked for them out at the front of the hotel and tied up with trailing green vines from the lobby.

Theresa, watching the simple exchange of vows, found the ceremony more moving than she'd expected. Tears, she thought, were becoming rather a habit, one she wasn't very keen on. She looked forward to going home and regaining her usual composure. It wouldn't do to be an emotional wreck, she'd end up weeping over the cook-chill cabinet in Waitrose. It wouldn't do to let Mark think he'd turned her into a pathetic pushover either. That way he'd feel he'd won, that he'd got away with his appalling behaviour. He might even think he could sneak off and do it all over again. One way or another, she would have to make sure he didn't want to. Before that, though, what had to be faced was the ordeal of The Clinic for the clearing up of any disgusting bugs he'd passed on to her.

As she smiled encouragement at Cathy while she and Paul exchanged rings (rather broad gold bands, she noticed, as if they were a bolder statement about marital intent than the slender little narrow ones she and Mark had), her thoughts were on the delights of the medical examination to come. She'd have to go somewhere miles from home, somewhere anonymous in central London, probably. She'd have to give a false name, and even then what if there was, after all her care about secrecy, someone there that she knew? Suppose there was someone she used to work with? Or another shamed Surrey mum that she'd have to face at the school gate? That would be such typical bad luck. And what could you say? What kind of appalling conversation could you have in the waiting room? At that type of clinic there wasn't any doubt about what you were there for. You couldn't speculate about whether each of you had a touch of flu or needed a course of malaria pills for a holiday. No, it was a case of what are you in for? Chlamydia or clap? Trichomoniasis, herpes or what was that pretty-sounding one she'd read about . . . gardnerella? What she did know was that she wasn't having any patronizing little just-out-of-training doctor thinking she'd been up to anything herself, catching sordid diseases and handing them round like a bag of sweets. She'd make damn sure they knew where the blame-finger was to point, that was for sure.

Lucy caught up with the hotel manager as he was about to return from the wedding to his office.

'The airport is open now,' he said, anticipating her questions. 'And the road to it has been cleared. The runway lights don't work though, so they say any planes leaving have to be out by sundown. I was just going to put up a notice.'

Lucy felt enormously disappointed. Somehow she'd assumed there would be such a backlog of people ready to go that they'd be told to hang on, wait just another few days. The manager wanted them all out. He needed all these people off the premises so he could close and get on with serious repairs.

'So you'll be back to work with no delays!' He sounded as if he was jollying her along, trying to cheer her up.

'It looks as if you could use my services better here,' she commented. 'I'm a painter and decorator, a good one. I could give you a hand.'

He grinned at her. 'Hey, every few months we get one or two who can't bear to leave. We're never surprised, St George is the most beautiful place in the world!'

'So you won't have any trouble finding enough workers to get this place back to normal again then?' she said.

'Ah, well, I didn't say that,' he conceded. 'The island doesn't have *that* many skilled workmen. There'll be a lot of angling for the best pay. Could take ages, but that's island life.'

'So take me on. I don't do angling,' Lucy told him.

The queue at the airport made the check-in line at Gatwick that had so dismayed Theresa look like a Sunday afternoon bus queue in the depths of the country.

'There must be about five thousand people here,' Shirley said as they all climbed out of the hotel's minibus.

'They must be all the people who couldn't get away the last few days,' Plum said.

'But we're actually booked on this flight, they have to let us go.' Simon craned his head to try to see if there was another point of access to the terminal building. If there was, it would be down to him to find it, usher them to the departure lounge where seats and sanity could be found for his parents. Surely the old and frail, and the very young like Theresa's brood shouldn't have to stand around on a blazing hot pavement, shuffling along slowly with all their luggage and nowhere to shelter from the sun? The gold lady was twenty yards ahead of them and a little way back in the queue Lucy could see two of the Steves swigging beer.

'So many people, think of the state of the loos,' Theresa muttered, pulling her children towards her as if to protect them from the inevitable scattered tissues and soaked floors.

'Listen, give me all your tickets and I'll wander up and have a look-see.' To Simon's annoyance, everyone handed over their documents and Mark sauntered off before he could protest, taking over as troop leader without any consultation.

'You're very lucky there, Tess.' Shirley prodded her arm. 'He's a lovely chap. I've always said so.'

'Yes Mum.' Theresa looked at Lucy and they both giggled.

'Now what have I said?' Shirley demanded.

'Nothing, just what you always say!' Theresa told her. 'But that's OK. Sometimes you like what you're used to.'

'Well, of course you do. Unless you're Lucy of course,' Shirley said.

'Now Shirley, don't start . . .' Perry warned with a grin.

'Yeah Mum,' Lucy laughed, then she and Theresa chorused, 'Don't spoil things!'

'OK, we can go up the front.' Mark returned still brandishing the tickets. 'I've managed to swing a couple more upgrades. They were so grateful for the extra tickets. So come on . . . let's go home!'

It was almost too abrupt, as if they were being too quickly snatched away from her. Lucy's determination, at the last minute, was close to wavering. She and Colette did the rounds of hugging and promising. Yes we'll phone, yes we'll come back for Christmas (Lucy already wouldn't call England 'home'), and yes, Lucy said, she'd sort out the flat and her possessions with the long-suffering Sandy-in-the-basement. Everyone said the usual parting words, mostly on a theme about the world not being as big as it once was, about them only being nine hours away. Perry's voice was shaky as he hugged Colette. 'Don't forget, you can always come back.'

'We know. But we want to try this,' Colette told him. She made it sound so simple. He could only hope that it was.

Lucy stayed till they went through to the departure lounge. Her mother lingered behind the others, reluctant to let go.

'I won't be able to keep an eye on you when you're this far away,' Shirley said as she hugged Lucy for the last time.

'I know, Mum,' Lucy said. It would have been horribly unkind to mention that that was rather the point.

Lucy and Colette moved their possessions into the Villa Hibiscus. Henry's offer had been tempting but it was too soon. They could wait, there was time, so much of it now, to see how things worked out. Lucy and two of the hotel's maintenance staff were to start work on all the villas the next day, as, with their roofs already mended, water reconnected and all the damaged furniture taken away, they were ready for some cosmetic renovation. The walls had been badly stained by salt-laden rainwater but would be ready to paint after a thorough wash-down and some repairs to chipped plasterwork. After the villas were finished, with any luck the builders would have the rest of the hotel well on its way to being ready for her skills, though, as the manager had shrugged and told her, with island life you could never tell. 'It's a different pace. Well, you'll see,' he'd warned her.

It was close to sunset. Henry and Lucy sat together on the beach in front of the dive shop.

In the water in front of them Oliver and Colette splashed about, diving and swimming, leaping around and having fun. Close to them was only one other figure, a large man with a beard. He reminded Lucy of a pirate.

'Sing us something,' Colette demanded.

'Yeah,' Oliver joined in, 'sing us something from the Three Sopranos.'

Lucy groaned. 'Sopranos!' she murmured to Henry. 'Aren't kids priceless? It's a pity the gold lady's gone. She'll never know she won our sweepstake.'

'First you sing something to me,' the man said.

'OK.' Colette thought for a moment and conferred hastily with Oliver, then the two of them sang the first verse of 'Morning Has Broken'.

'Now it's your turn,' she said, and Luciano Pavarotti, standing waist-deep in the Caribbean sea, sang 'Nessun Dorma' to an audience of four.

Against the darkening blue of the sky and the first few stars of the night Lucy could make out the lights of a plane leaving the island. 'That's probably them,' she said quietly.

'But no worries?' Henry asked.

'No,' she told him. 'No worries.'

THE END

A SELECTED LIST OF FINE WRITING
AVAILABLE FROM BLACK SWAN

99830 3	SINGLE WHITE E-MAIL	Jessica Adams	£6.99
99821 4	HOMING INSTINCT	Diana Appleyard	£6.99
99564 9	JUST FOR THE SUMMER	Judy Astley	£6.99
99565 7	PLEASANT VICES	Judy Astley	£6.99
99629 7	SEVEN FOR A SECRET	Judy Astley	£6.99
99630 0	MUDDY WATERS	Judy Astley	£6.99
99766 8	EVERY GOOD GIRL	Judy Astley	£6.99
99768 4	THE RIGHT THING	Judy Astley	£6.99
99619 7	HUMAN CROQUET	Kate Atkinson	£6.99
99853 2	LOVE IS A FOUR LETTER WORD	Claire Calman	£6.99
99687 4	THE PURVEYOR OF ENCHANTMENT	Marika Cobbold	£6.99
99756 0	A BAREFOOT WEDDING	Elizabeth Falconer	£6.99
99770 6	TELLING LIDDY	Anne Fine	£6.99
99795 1	LIAR BIRDS	Lucy Fitzgerald	£5.99
99760 9	THE DRESS CIRCLE	Laurie Graham	£6.99
99774 9	THE CUCKOO'S PARTING CRY	Anthea Halliwell	£5.99
99848 6	CHOCOLAT	Joanne Harris	£6.99
99779 X	BRIDGE OF SHADOWS	Karen Hayes	£6.99
99736 6	KISS AND KIN	Angela Lambert	£6.99
99771 4	MALLINGFORD	Alison Love	£6.99
99812 5	THE PHILOSOPHER'S HOUSE	Joan Marysmith	£6.99
99696 3	THE VISITATION	Sue Reidy	£5.99
99764 1	ALL THAT GLISTERS	Mary Selby	£6.99
99788 9	OTHER PEOPLE'S CHILDREN	Joanna Trollope	£6.99
99723 4	PART OF THE FURNITURE	Mary Wesley	£6.99
99769 2	THE WEDDING GIRL	Madeleine Wickham	£6.99